SOLITUDE

A NOVEL

MICHAEL PENNING

SOLITUDE

First edition. Mar. 2023
ISBN: 978-1-7388551-0-0 (paperback)
ISBN: 978-1-7388551-1-7 (hardcover)

www.michaelpenning.com

For Jon,
who shows me how to be a good friend.

Chapter 1

Megan Danforth had to see the bones for herself. Her knuckles were white on the wheel as her 4x4 pickup rumbled over the deep ruts of the dirt road. Years of brutal backcountry abuse had killed the Ford's suspension. Megan rocked and bounced in her seat. Her head came close to hitting the cab's ceiling, but she didn't ease off the gas.

Towering pines flew by on either side and whipped against the side mirrors, showering the windshield with needles. Fallen leaves carpeted the muddy road with red and gold. The gray day had threatened rain since the morning, and the sky was now a steel wire threading through the treetops.

On the stereo, Marshall Tucker bemoaned what his woman was doing to him. Megan had thrown the CD on that morning; the Bluetooth on the battered, state-issued Department of Conservation truck never seemed to work right. The music had been welcome company on her pre-dawn drive to the trailhead, and she had hummed the tune for most of her patrol to Wilkins Pond.

Now, after the news she had just received, her thoughts

were a howling riot, and she found the song's twanging guitars just added to the din in her head. She hit the button and killed the music. The squeaks and groans of the seat springs filled the cab as she roared from the forest access road and hit the smooth blacktop of NY Route 30.

The text had come through just after four. Megan had just regained cell reception after spending the afternoon deep in the Adirondack wilderness. She'd arrived at her truck at the trailhead when she plucked the phone from her pocket and saw the terse message from Sam Hayden, Balsam Lake's chief of police:

Come ASAP. Bones found in the lake. Human.

Megan's heart leapt into her throat, her phone nearly tumbling from her nerveless hand. Her backpack slipped from her shoulder and her knees drained of strength beneath her. The tall pines encompassing the trailhead danced before her eyes.

They've found him. After thirteen years…

The single-lane route hugged the winding contour of the long lake as it snaked northward toward town. Before long, the first hints of the outskirts of the village of Balsam Lake popped up along the wooded side of the road—the rustic Timber Lodge, followed by the shabby Red Roof Inn where all the thrifty hikers stayed.

Megan kept left at the fork that splintered off toward Pilot Point, sped across the short causeway over the finger islands and the scenic pull-off with its sweeping view of the Seward Mountain Range to the east, and shot past the Trail's End Pub on the edge of town.

It was early-November, the quiet season between when the

tourists stopped coming for the autumn leaves and when the snow started attracting them back to the High Peaks region for winter sports. The city people wouldn't be returning to their lakeside cottages until the weekend. Late on a Thursday afternoon, locals were the only ones coming and going from the shops on Main St. Megan would have blown right through the town's only traffic light if it wasn't for a pedestrian waiting at a crosswalk.

She sped by High Peaks Pizza and the Dragonfly Cafe, turned right at the town square, where fall decorations still festooned the white-washed gazebo, and slammed the truck into park in front of the quaint building that housed the town's station house. A stiff breeze swirled fallen leaves and sent them scratching against the building's stone foundation.

Megan recognized Chief Hayden's SUV in the parking lot as she approached the entrance. She marched up the steps and glimpsed her reflection in the glass door: five-seven and fit from hundreds of miles of forest patrols. Mud from the day's hike still spattered the legs of her forest-green DEC uniform. She kept her dirty-blonde hair cropped short just below her ears, framing her heart-shaped face and focusing attention on enigmatic eyes that appeared hazel or green depending on how the light fell. She moved with a purposeful stride, the Glock 21 handgun she was required to carry as a New York State environmental conservation officer bumping against her hip.

Megan whipped open the door. The interior of the small station comprised one high-ceilinged room. Large windows on either side let natural light into the tiny police bullpen.

Deputy Joanna Ward was working at the reception desk.

She was in her late-thirties, with light eyes and auburn hair that no one had ever seen in anything but a ponytail. She was diminutive, but carried herself with a calm assurance and a devilish sense of humor that earned her the respect of the locals. No one gave her a hard time when she busted them for speeding or escorted them from the Trail's End after a few too many pints.

Today, Joanna's expression was drawn and perplexed. Her fingers were a flurry of movement as she punched details into a report on her laptop.

She jumped to her feet as Megan barged in. "Megan…"

"Where's Sam?" Megan breezed by Joanna's desk without stopping.

"Take it easy, Megan," Joanna cautioned.

The town's other deputy, Noah McCrae, was tied-up in an animated phone conversation at one of the two administrative desks behind Joanna. He was a chisel-chinned twenty-six-year-old, the same age as Megan. They had dated for a few weeks as seniors in high school. She had been an edgy loner and Noah had assumed she'd put out in gratitude for his attention. It had come as a shock to him when she was the one to break it off.

He was tall and stocky and had been on-track to a full-ride hockey scholarship to Notre Dame before deciding he wanted to be a cop instead. Megan had always suspected he settled on the career because he was reluctant to leave their small town. It was a failing that had prompted her to end their relationship.

Noah gave Megan a sideways look as she marched past him, unable to break away from whoever was on the other end of his call. She headed toward the back of the spacious room, where a wall of windows separated Hayden's private office from the open area of the bullpen. The blinds were pulled, but the door stood open.

Chief Sam Hayden appeared in the doorframe before Megan got there. He was in his late-thirties, young for a police chief—a distinction many of the locals never failed to remind him of. He had a full head of close-cropped hair that was just starting to go gray, and a rugged layer of matching stubble on his solid chin. Despite a routine diet of steak and potatoes, he still kept himself in good shape. He was an average height, and his uniform fit well in his lean frame. His eyes were penetrating and dark like black coffee. If he ever got married and had children, his smooth voice would make for enjoyable bedtime stories—not that it was ever likely to happen.

"Is it him, Sam?" Megan demanded.

Sam gave a grim frown. "We don't know. All we've got at this point is a partial skeleton. It could be anybody."

"Bullshit," Megan snapped. "You wouldn't have sent me that text if you believed that."

Sam hesitated and cast a glance at the two deputies, who were doing a poor job of pretending they weren't eavesdropping while they worked. He ushered Megan in through the door.

Sam's snug office was organized and tidy. A large desk sat in the center, its neat blotter illuminated by the waning daylight streaming through a large window. Sam's obligatory credentials hung in frames on the walls. There was also a collection of rare daguerreotype photos of Balsam Lake's earliest days as a timber village that Sam had rescued from the station's basement. A trophy largemouth bass mounted over the door had been there since before Sam's time as chief, and he'd never removed it. There were no hints of Sam's personal life to be seen—no hunting trophies, or photos from the solo trip he had taken to Ireland a few years back, the only time he'd ever flown overseas.

Megan's job as an officer with the DEC had brought her to this office dozens of times, and she always found it as impersonal as a hotel room. She got the impression that while Sam had taken over as chief almost three years ago, he'd never felt comfortable enough to make the place his own.

Sam lowered his voice as he stepped in after Megan and shut the office door behind them. "I need you to pull some strings to see if you can get a dive team up here."

Megan raised an eyebrow. "A conservation team? We're talking about human remains. Why not just get the state police to assist?"

Sam shook his head. "We bring in the state boys now and it'll be the end of this station. Wade Ramsay and the village board have just been waiting for an excuse to shut us down and outsource the policing of the village to the county troop. I can't let that happen. We gotta handle this one ourselves." He swallowed. "Besides, we don't even know if we have a crime yet."

Megan gave him a cagey look. "You sure you're not keeping this quiet because of your dad?"

Something dark and angry flashed in Sam's eyes. His tone grew chilly. "I've called in a favor from an old hunting buddy who's a retired forensic tech. He'll be here the day after tomorrow to give us his two cents, and we'll take it from there. We'll likely need access to dental records to make an I.D."

Megan nodded. "Where are the bones?"

Sam nodded over his shoulder. "We've got 'em in the evidence locker."

"I want to see them."

"Not gonna happen."

Megan's eyes hardened. "You want a dive team up here? You're gonna show me that skeleton."

Sam looked Megan in the face and saw inflexible granite staring back at him. "C'mon," he sighed, and swung the office door open.

Sam led the way, ignoring the curious glances from Joanna and Noah as he crossed the bullpen. He headed toward the narrow corridor that led first to the station's interrogation room, then the holding cell, and finally, to the evidence locker.

Megan waited as Sam unlocked the last door in the corridor and flicked on the fluorescents. Their low hum filled the silence, and the harsh overhead lights cast the cramped and dingy evidence room in a sickly green hue.

Megan's limbs tightened as she entered the claustrophobic space. The door clicked shut behind her, and she had the sudden urge to throw it open again to let some air in. Despite her overwhelming desire to see the bones, she now wanted to get it over with so she could exit this room and its humming lights as quickly as possible. God, she hated these damned fluorescents.

With her skin tingling, Megan stared at the array of

evidence bags laid across a table at the centre of the room. Each contained a yellowed fragment of skeleton. From what she could discern, there was a skull, many vertebrae, an entire rib cage, and a couple of long arm and leg bones. Sam and his deputies had dutifully sealed and labelled all of them.

Megan drew a breath and moved to the table to examine the assortment of human remains. "Who found them?"

"Tad Eames," Sam replied. "He was out fishing before dawn and snagged his lure. Hauled hard on the line and nearly snapped it until these started bobbing up. His hook must've pried them loose from the lakebed."

"Where?"

"A little inlet at the northern tip of Grindstone Bay."

Megan tried to picture the spot in her mind. She frowned. "That's on the other side of the lake from where—"

"I know," Sam said.

Megan turned her attention to the skull. A jagged gash nearly split the cranium in two. She glanced up. "Whoever this is had their skull cracked open. You seriously think there's no crime here?"

Sam stared back at her, but remained silent.

Megan stood back and chewed her cheek, unable to tear her gaze away from the catastrophic damage inflicted on the skull. "Do you think it's him, Sam? Is this my father?"

Sam gave a grim shrug. "Could be. Then again, I don't need to tell you your dad's not the only one who's gone missing out there over the years."

Megan nodded distractedly. Her mind was still working to put together pieces of information. "There's nothing around Grindstone Bay but forest for miles in all directions. The only way to get there is by boat."

Sam nodded and completed her train of thought. "Which means this body was dumped there."

Megan inspected the bones again. She had been required to take an introductory class on forensics as part of her degree in Environmental Science at the University of Massachusetts at Amherst. Six years had passed, but some lessons still lingered in her memory.

"These bones are old," she observed, noting the telltale traces of algae stuck in the cracks and crevices. "They've been in the water a long time."

Sam stepped forward and placed his palms on the table. "Give it a couple of days, Megan. Let's wait and see what the expert says. In the meantime, go home and make some calls."

Megan exhaled and frowned. "Getting a dive team up here won't be easy."

"Tell them whatever you have to," Sam insisted. "Just get them here quick. These bones hold a dark secret, and I'm betting there are more waiting for us at the bottom of that lake."

Chapter 2

Russ Thompson was pricing styrofoam containers of night-crawlers when the door to the Balsam Lake Beer 'n Bait swung open. Megan was approaching the counter with a large manilla envelope.

"Evening…" Russ grinned.

Megan tossed the envelope on the counter. "Got tired of looking at it."

Russ's grin faded to a grimace of chagrin. He opened the envelope and pulled out a stack of fishing permits. "Shit. I'm sorry, Megan. I was going to swing by to get 'em, I swear."

Megan shot him a doubting glance from the corner of her eye and kept walking to the shelves of liquor.

Russ was about her own age; tall and sturdy, but not overweight. Grins came easily to his face, and the twinkle in his light eyes made him seem more handsome than he actually was. He wore a short beard he trimmed maybe once every couple of weeks. Tufts of thick brown hair stuck out from beneath a frayed trucker's cap that seemed permanently stapled to his head. His wardrobe consisted of jeans and a rotating assortment of flannel shirts.

Maybe it was because of his laid-back free spirit, or because he was relatively new in town and knew nothing about her past, but Megan had a soft spot for Russ when she shunned the company of others.

"Sure you were," she grumbled. She turned her attention back to the rows of bottles, selected her usual bourbon, and brought it back to the cash. "You took over the shop a year ago, Russ. Time you got your shit together."

"Whoah, what kinda language is that?" Russ exclaimed with mock indignation.

"File a complaint. See if you can find another government employee who'll go out of her way to do your job for you."

"Point taken. Don't bite the hand that feeds."

Megan glanced around at the clutter. The Balsam Lake Beer 'n Bait was a favorite hangout for locals, and it saw a fair amount of traffic, given the Adirondacks' rich network of lakes and rivers. Racks of fishing rods and lures lined the wood-paneled walls. Decades-old advertisements for brands that had long since disappeared plastered the empty spaces. A pair of commercial refrigerators kept the bait and beer cold.

"You really should get out of this place sometime," Megan said. "You've got an entire state park at your doorstep."

Russ shrugged. "People need bait, and fish don't know what time it is." He lowered his voice. "Hey, you hear about the body they found in the lake this morning?"

Megan's chest clenched and her eyes narrowed. "How do you know about that?"

"Small town. Word travels fast." Russ's languid gaze drifted to a large bulletin board mounted on a wall near the door.

Instead of the usual *FOR SALE* and *HELP WANTED* ads, the cork surface was overflowing with a jumbled assortment of notices for lost and stolen items.

HAVE YOU SEEN MY PORTABLE BBQ?

STOLEN: BRAND NEW TOOLS. REWARD OFFERED.

PLEASE RETURN MY CANOE, NO QUESTIONS ASKED.

There were well over a hundred notes, some going back decades. The oldest were yellowed and faded, the writing barely visible beneath the newer ones tacked above. The chaotic arrangement had taken on the look of a modern art installation.

In the centre of it all, someone had posted a note scrawled in big black marker. It read: WHO IS SPOOKY? Below the note, people had tacked photos of their proposed candidates: the infamous photo of Bigfoot; a cartoon alien smoking a joint; Christopher Walken.

"You think *he* had something to do with it?" Russ asked. "Spooky?"

Megan rolled her eyes. "Nobody around here actually calls him that."

"Guy's been breaking into houses around here for almost thirty years. What else would you call him?"

"How do you know it's a guy?" Megan remarked.

Russ continued, undeterred. "Hundreds of burglaries. Never a witness, never any clues, never as much as a wrinkled blanket or pillow. Sometimes people don't even realize they've been robbed until weeks or months later. He slips in and out like a ghost. *Spooky...*"

Megan shook her head and shifted her attention to the

bulletin board. On the way, her gaze avoided the racks of fishing poles. The sight of them still brought back memories she had fought hard to lock away.

"That damn thing's looking like some kinda shrine." Russ was still admiring the cluttered cork-board. "I'd take it all down, but I can't bring myself to do it. That's thirty years' worth of local history right there. From what I gather from the folks that come in here, Spooky's become as much a part of this town as fishin' and fuckin'."

Megan gave him an amused smirk. "Spooky's nothing but a local myth, Russ."

"Some myth." Russ snorted as he rang up her whiskey. The bottle had been a weekly routine for as long as Russ had known Megan. He couldn't help noticing it was the cheap stuff, the kind that was only good for getting drunk.

"Dougie told me that as a kid, he thought Spooky was the goddamn boogeyman. Almost pissed himself one night 'cause he thought Spooky'd broken into the house." Russ propped his forearms on the counter and leaned closer. "Gotta be a local, huh? Not that I blame him. Considering the size of some of the lake houses they're putting up around here these days, I'd say he's doing the city folk a favor to be unburdening them of such excessive material dependencies."

"Or maybe there is no Spooky," Megan argued. "Just a bunch of people breaking into their neighbors' houses and stealing shit under the cover of a decades-old urban legend."

Russ gave an unconvinced frown and changed the subject.

"Hey, you didn't hear it from me, but Wade Ramsay was out on the lake this morning. Word is, he busted his daily quota of brookies. I wouldn't normally be telling you, but

Wade's a racist prick and I don't like him. Where I come from, rich dicks like him don't deserve to be hauling a bigger catch than the rest of us."

"What an asshole," Megan muttered. "Brook trout season ended last month." She turned for the door with her bottle concealed in its paper bag. "Thanks for the tip."

"Sure thing," Russ said as he watched her go.

The sun had set, and the leaden sky had given way to the blue hour of twilight when Megan stopped for a takeout deli sandwich and fries at Brenda's Diner at the far end of Main. The discovery of the bones and what revelations they might stir up had tied in knots in her stomach, but she figured her appetite might open up once she knocked back a few drinks.

Unwanted images of the fractured skull locked in Sam's evidence room kept flashing in Megan's mind. If she was going to sleep tonight, she would need the whiskey. The need for alcohol had been scratching at her ever since Sam's text had popped up on her screen. There was a constant tension in her muscles, an extra beat in her heart-rate that wouldn't relax. The urge for a drink was never very far from her mind. It was an uncomfortable sense of missing something, like an item on a to-do list that needed to be checked before she could relax.

As she drove, Megan's eyes kept straying to the bottle cradled in its paper bag on the passenger's seat. It seemed to exude a magnetic force over her. Her heart quickened with that familiar longing just thinking about her first soothing gulp. She veered the pickup off the darkened road onto a hidden driveway surrounded by black forest. Her headlights cut through the gathering gloom and illuminated her secluded timber cabin sitting deep in woods on the edge of the lake.

Gravel crunched under the truck's heavy rubber treads as Megan came to a stop and killed the engine. With her bag of takeout in hand and her bottle of whiskey in the other, she mounted the cabin's porch, unlocked the door, and pushed it open. She entered and flicked the lights on.

Her home was tidy and nondescript. Wood panelling covered the living room on three sides. A wall of windows looked across the back porch and the open expanse of the lake. Tall shelves of books stood against the opposite wall. Megan's collection of old *National Geographic* magazines filled an entire unit. A flagstone fireplace occupied the far end of the room. The carpet leading to it was thin and worn. Megan's old couch sat in the center of the space. A couple of woolen throw blanket lay rumpled across the arm and back cushion for when Megan didn't make it upstairs to her bedroom. In front of the couch was a battered coffee table. She didn't own a TV.

Megan plunked her takeout on the table before liberating the whiskey from its bag. She uncapped the bottle and tipped two-fingers into a tumbler still sitting on the table from the night before. The glass left another faded ring on the wood when Megan raised it to her lips and took a long sip, relishing the burn as it coursed down her throat. She inhaled a deep, relieved breath, and felt the tension in her chest finally relax. This wouldn't solve anything, but it was better than the alternative—sitting alone with her thoughts, replaying images of those old bones over and over again in her head. She would have to face the reality of the situation eventually, but for now, she was content to lose herself in the oblivion of alcohol.

Setting the empty glass next to the bottle and her bag of food, Megan headed upstairs to the bathroom. She stripped off her mud-spattered uniform and tossed it into the hamper before slipping behind the curtain into the shower. Her muscles ached, and there was a chill in her bones that had nothing to do with the autumn air.

She cranked the hot water until steam swirled around the small room. The spray hit the back of Megan's neck and sluiced down the black and gray tattoos that covered her arms from her shoulders to her elbows. Most of her skin art expressed her connection to nature. A large compass adorned her inner arm and there were numerous depictions of birds, mountains, trees, and a variety of leaves. The most recent addition—a wolf's head rendered with incredibly lifelike detail—was only a few weeks old and had only recently shed the last of its scab.

Megan's thoughts were far away as she remained there beneath the stream, leaning on one bent elbow propped against the shower tiles. The whiskey was already muting her mind enough for her to realize Sam was right: those bones at the bottom of the lake could belong to anyone. Thousands of people ventured into the rugged Adirondack backcountry every year. Some were hikers, others hunters and anglers. Unfortunately, some never made it back out.

But only one of them had been Megan's father.

The sight of those yellow bones all neatly bagged at the station had done something to Megan. It was as if they had folded time between her and her thirteen-year-old self. She was suddenly dragged back to the day her father had disappeared and all the old fear and trauma that went with it.

Megan spent long minutes lost in thought until she snapped back into the moment. She soaped herself and shampooed her short hair before rinsing and snapping the faucet off. She wrapped herself in her towel and went across the hall to her bedroom, where she pulled on a pair of sweats and shrugged into a hooded UMass sweater.

Downstairs in the living room, the threadbare couch crumpled beneath Megan's weight as she sat and unwrapped her food. She nibbled a few cold fries and took a couple bites of the sandwich, chewing with no enthusiasm. After a moment, she dropped the sandwich back onto its red and white checkered wrapper and shoved it aside. Instead, she reached for the whiskey and helped herself to another pour before crossing the room to spark a fire.

A brass trophy of a small pair of boxing gloves sat on the heavy oak mantle above the fireplace. The engraving on the brass plaque read: *Golden Gloves Tournament of Champions.* Megan sipped her drink and gazed at the trophy while she waited for the kindling to catch. She had taken the top prize in the prestigious amateur boxing tournament in her senior year at UMass. It had been her last fight before hanging up her gloves for good.

Once the flames had leapt up on the grate, Megan left the room with her glass in hand. A small backroom served as her home office. She snapped on the desk lamp and revealed more bookshelves against the length of an entire wall. The only other decoration was a framed diploma hanging at a slightly crooked angle: *University of Massachusetts School of*

Earth & Sustainability. The glass of the cheap and flimsy frame was opaque with dust.

An acoustic guitar stood on a stand in the room's corner. Megan gulped from the tumbler as she crossed the room for it. She had started playing when she was fifteen, shortly after moving in with her aunt. The neck on the acoustic was slightly too wide for Megan's fingers, but she'd rather endure a few bum chords than admit she needed to trade-in her full-size Dreadnaught for something smaller.

Megan stopped halfway to the guitar, her eyes drawn to a framed photo tucked among the books on the shelves. The picture was old, and the colors weren't quite right. A handsome young man with piercing eyes sat in the back of a canoe on a pristine mountain lake. He wasn't posing or looking at the camera. His gaze was off to the side and far away, admiring the view from the water as he paddled.

Megan had no other mementos of her father. She only kept this photo because her mother had been behind the camera in the canoe with him. Megan stared at the picture a moment longer before grabbing the guitar by its neck and snapping off the light.

It was full dark when Megan stepped onto the porch and closed the screen door behind her. With the acoustic in one hand and her bottle in the other, she sat on a rocking chair and rested the bottle on the upturned apple crate she used as a side-table. She lit a Coleman lamp and its warm glow filled the porch.

The smell of woodsmoke from the chimney drifted through the darkness. It was a chilly evening, far too cold for crickets. But the tree frogs still hadn't gone into hibernation yet. Their song rose from the shadows as Megan took a drink from the bottle. Then another. For a long moment, she stared into the black void of the lake. The guitar lay forgotten in her lap. Her thoughts were someplace else—somewhere long ago…

* * *

In her memories, Megan is thirteen. It's night, and she's in the garage with her father. The door is open and rain comes down in heavy sheets outside. The glare of the overhead fluorescent light sends a sickly green glow out into the downpour.

Megan is punching a heavy bag strung from the rafters. She's dressed in boxing gear: green shorts and a white tank top. Her hair is sweaty and pulled back in a ponytail. Her gloved fists strike fast and hard.

BAM! BAM! BAM!

Her father is behind the bag, holding it in place. Graham Danforth is tall and slim. His cheeks are shadowed with three-day-old stubble and there are ugly dark rings around his cold eyes. He looks nothing like the man in the photo Megan would keep on her office shelf years later.

He looks haunted.

"C'mon! Harder!" Graham shouts.

BAM! BAM! BAM!

Megan tries her best to make him happy, but she has no more strength left to give. The garage is a cluttered mess around her. Her father's tools are scattered haphazardly across his workbench at the far end. The walls are crammed with useless car parts, busted fishing gear, and mildewed boxes of

Christmas decorations that haven't left the garage since Megan's mother was killed. A plastic snowman leers at Megan's efforts. Dust and grime coats its scuffed surface. Much of the red dye has worn off the plastic of its molded earmuffs.

Graham steps back and laughs at Megan. He reaches for an open can of beer and takes a big swig. "You're useless," he sneers.

Megan's trembling shoulders sag in defeat.

"Take 'em off," Graham orders.

Megan looks at him, confused and suddenly fearful.

"The gloves. Take 'em off."

She recognizes the menace in his voice and does as she's told.

Graham puts the beer down. Steps forward. Raises his hands to expose his lean mid-section. His stomach is concave beneath his bony ribs. "Now hit me."

"Dad…"

"Do it!"

Megan gives in and punches her dad in the gut with her bare fist.

He snickers contemptuously at her effort. "See? You got nothing, ya little pussy."

Megan slugs him again. And again. And again. Graham goes on taunting and chortling at her desperate blows until—

WHAM!

He clubs her across the head with a hard right hook.

Megan's left ear bursts into flames and a blinding supernova goes off in her head. Streaks of exploding stars scream across her vision as she reels and staggers across the garage. She hits the ground in a daze, the grit on the floor grinding into her bare palms when they shoot out at the last second. The room whirls in and out of focus like she's watching an out-take from a movie scene. The hum of the fluorescents fills her ears, and that damned snowman is cackling at her through its jeering smirk.

Her father has hit her dozens of times before, but never like this. Never with a fist. Megan is dreadfully aware this escalation is just the beginning of something new. They have crossed a line into a new realm of violence. The thought makes her go cold with dread.

Graham swoops into view. He looms over Megan, leering down at her as he lights a cigarette. A veil of blue smoke shrouds his scowling face. "That's how ya do it," he chuckles.

* * *

A booming roll of distant thunder jolted Megan back from her memories. Her head snapped up, and she glanced around the empty porch, as if fearful someone might be there to witness her sudden jerk.

Far across the lake to the west, a purple flash lit the night sky. A few seconds later, the low rumble of thunder rolled across the water. A storm was brewing over the vast wilderness of the Adirondack Park. Megan could feel it in the air, heavy and electric. The wind was picking up, and the trees around the cabin swayed and creaked ominously in the darkness.

Megan shivered with a chill colder than the breeze coming off the water. She took another swig of whiskey to chase away her memories and strummed the guitar. Music had always been her solace, and as her fingers plucked the strings, her song flowed through her like a river, each note a droplet in the current. The melody was slow and haunting as the rumbling storm crawled over the mountains toward her.

Chapter 3

Piper Flynn awoke to a booming crack of thunder. The tent was absolutely black around her. She could hear her parents breathing in the darkness as they slumbered in their sleeping bags on either side of her, but she couldn't see them. She couldn't even see her own hand in front of her face.

A flash of lightning went off outside the tent, followed by another angry growl of thunder. The storm Piper's parents had been talking about all day was getting closer.

Piper's dad had wanted to get another mile in before they made camp. But the looming threat of a downpour had forced a change of plans. Instead, they had pitched the tent about ten yards from Calamity Brook, a swift stream cutting through the bedrock of the mountain.

"Mom…" Piper whispered in the dark.

"Mmmm…"

Mom's sleepy groan drifted like a disembodied voice in the night. Piper strained to hear her over the constant sound of the stream's rushing water.

"I need to pee."

"Okay," Mom murmured. "Stay close."

"I need paper."

"In my pack."

There was a rustling, and Piper knew Mom had rolled over in her sleeping bag.

Piper's instinct was to reach for the flashlight on her phone. Then she remembered Mom had made her leave it in the car at the trailhead. It was now about four hours and who knows how many miles away. Not that Piper minded. She could catch up on her friends' posts in a couple of days. She would never admit it to the other ten-year-old girls at school, but she secretly enjoyed these getaways with her parents in the woods.

Oh, she could do without the bugs and the mud, but Piper loved the way these excursions deep into the wilderness brought them together as a family. Her parents were different out here, more relaxed. They didn't complain about work or the price of gas or groceries. They didn't seem as tired or impatient with her—or with each other. The forest and mountains brought them comfort, and Piper knew it.

The lightweight sleeping pad crumpled beneath her as Piper shimmied out of her sleeping bag. It was new and warm, a gift from Dad on Piper's birthday in July. She probed the darkness with her hand until she found the door. The noise should have been cringeworthy as she zipped it open, but the steady rushing of the nearby stream drowned out the sound.

Piper found her boots inside the tent's small vestibule and fumbled around in her mom's backpack for the roll of toilet paper. She unzipped the outer tent door and was hit with a blast of chilly night air that almost sent her scurrying back into the warmth of her sleeping bag.

The pressure on her bladder was only growing more urgent. Piper had drank too much water before crawling into the tent, and now it was catching up to her. Sleeping sandwiched between her parents with only a couple inches of inflatable pad between her and the forest floor was uncomfortable enough. She'd never get back to sleep while she still needed to pee. She'd just lay there awake for hours, staring into the darkness while her discomfort grew even worse. And with the storm rolling in, she wouldn't get another chance to relieve herself without getting soaked.

Piper darted back into the vestibule and thrust her hand into the tent for the thick fleece sweater she'd left at the foot of the sleeping pad. Mom and Dad were both sound asleep and didn't even stir. Piper shrugged the sweater on and ventured back out into the cold.

The forest was just as black as the tent. There was no moon or stars tonight. Even if there was, the impenetrable canopy of the forest would have obscured their light. Campfires were forbidden in the backcountry for fear of forest fires, so there were no glowing embers to illuminate the campsite. There was just endless darkness unfurling in all directions.

Piper took a few steps away from the tent. She was about to squat when a sudden thought made her a pause. The constant rush of the stream seemed loud enough to cover any noise, but what if her parents woke up and heard her while she peed? Worse yet, what if Piper misjudged how close to the tent she was and they awoke in the morning to find her pee-stained wad of paper lying in the dirt just outside the door?

It was all too embarrassing to think about. Piper moved further away.

She turned and headed in the opposite direction from the stream. The last thing she needed was to stumble into the frigid water while she fumbled around in the dark.

When she was sure she was out of earshot, she squatted in the underbrush. Something prickly poked her bare backside, and she scooted around to shift position, only now realizing she could easily have waded blindly into a patch of poison ivy. God, how uncomfortable would *that* be? Would the itch be gone by the time she went back to school on Monday? There was no way she'd spend the day squirming in her seat next to Jackson Mathers, trying to not scratch her crotch and butt.

Piper's hand groped the dark for a branch or something sturdy enough to hold on to, but she found nothing. She'd just have to take her chances she wouldn't lose her balance and pee all over her panties and sweats while they were down around her ankles. When she was finished, she wiped and hiked up her pants.

And realized she didn't know the way back.

Somehow, Piper had gotten disoriented in the impenetrable dark. Now, she felt the same as when they'd blindfolded her and spun her around before handing her the piñata stick at Mia Cooper's birthday party. She had no idea which direction to go.

Piper forced herself to calm down and think. The tent couldn't be that far away. All she had to do was turn around and head back toward the stream.

Piper started out, her steps slow and uncertain, putting one foot in front of the other as she pushed through the underbrush. The gnarled tangles were thicker than she remembered coming through, and a slow dread gnawed at her insides as she realized she was walking way too far. Still, she was certain she'd come across the tent any minute.

Except she didn't.

Instead, she reached the bank of the stream.

An icy tingle of fear rippled down Piper's spine. Which way was the tent? She looked to the left and right, straining to see. There was nothing but darkness in either direction. It occurred to her then that she could have been walking *away* from the tent, not toward it.

"Mom?" Piper called. She wrapped her arms around herself as she waited, trying to ward off the chill that was seeping into her bones.

There was no response.

"Mom!"

Still nothing.

Thunder crackled and a gust of chilly wind swept through the forest. Dead leaves swirled around the ankles of Piper's boots.

"Mom! Dad!"

A lump formed in Piper's throat and her heart thudded in her chest. Where were they? And why weren't they answering? They couldn't be that far away. Were they sleeping that heavily? Or was the sound of the water rushing down the mountainside drowning Piper's voice?

A blast of lightning made Piper cringe. In the blinding flash, she saw no sign of the tent. She was shivering now, her fear mounting into panic. Was she actually lost? No, that was impossible. She hadn't wandered off *that* far. Just a few yards, ten at the most. Maybe twenty. People didn't get lost this way. They got lost by making mistakes; by misreading maps, or not *having* maps; or not knowing how to use a compass; or taking unexplored "shortcuts"; or relying on cellphone service for directions. Nobody got lost like this, not this close to their own tent. It had to be around here somewhere.

Piper scanned the darkness in both directions again, but still couldn't discern a thing. She sniffled and wiped her eyes, trying to stay strong. She recalled what she knew about being lost in the woods. The important thing was to not wander aimlessly. Just stay in one place and let help find you. That's what she would do. She would just remain right here next to the stream and wait for her parents to realize she was gone. Sooner or later, they'd come looking for her.

But how long would that take? What time was it, anyway? How many hours until the sun came up? Piper couldn't wait here all night. Her teeth were already chattering from the cold and the impending storm was going to unleash something wicked any minute. She'd freeze to death if she waited out here too long.

There was only one option Piper could think of. She decided she'd follow the stream in one direction for a few minutes. That wasn't wandering aimlessly, not if she stuck to the water's edge. If she didn't stumble across the tent, she would try again in the other direction. She'd find it eventually. She had to.

Another blast of lightning crackled through the forest, and Piper glimpsed something that made her blood run cold.

There was a figure silhouetted in the brilliant flash.

Piper could no longer see it in the darkness that rushed

back when the lightning subsided, but she was sure she had seen someone lurking among the trees not twenty yards away. She opened her mouth to call out, but some primal instinct told her to keep silent. Whatever was out there wasn't one of her parents.

Something else was out there with her in the dark.

Terror shot through Piper like an icy gust. Whatever she had seen stalking through the forest had been still and silent, but that didn't mean it didn't know where she was. That dark figure could be creeping through the darkness toward her even now. Piper could almost feel it drawing nearer, nearer…

All thoughts of finding her parents drained away and Piper was gripped by an irresistible compulsion to run, to flee the terrible black shape she had seen illuminated in the hellish light. She couldn't stay here, not with whatever was out there. Thunder roared through the night as she spun and dashed headlong into the unending blackness.

Chapter 4

Hank Morrison had his fingers crossed for a Yankee comeback in game six of the American League finals when his phone lit up with a notification. He glanced at the screen, bolted upright in his recliner, and sloshed beer across the trailer's threadbare carpet.

A few weeks ago, the old caretaker's nephew had convinced him to install motion-activated trail cameras around the summer camp. There had been countless break-ins at Camp Whippoorwill over the years, and while they all happened during the winter months when Hank vacated his summer caretaker trailer, he would be damned if he let it happen again. Not this year.

Hank was on the back end of his sixties and had little use for technology. Sure, his phone was a necessity these days, but he had no interest in the social media crap that went with it. And he certainly had no taste for this "streaming" thing everyone seemed to push on him. Hank enjoyed his Yankees on the transistor radio and his Jackson Browne on the good ol' turntable, thank you very much.

Still, his nephew made a convincing point. The cameras might not prevent another break-in over the winter, but if they could capture some footage of the thief, that good-for-nothing police chief, Sam Hayden, might finally identify and catch the bastard.

Hank had mounted four cameras around the camp. They were small and camouflaged and intended to capture high-quality images of wildlife remotely. They could detect movement up to ninety feet away. When triggered, they sent photos and videos directly to an app on Hank's phone for inspection. Hank had installed one camera at the end of the long dirt road that accessed the camp, another way out back where the cabins spread out along the shoreline, a third inside the camp's cavernous mess hall, and the last facing the edge of the forest behind the big lodge itself. The cameras hadn't been cheap, but Hank figured it was the camp's money, not his.

Judging by what he now saw on his phone, they were worth every penny.

Something had triggered the camera along the tree-line behind the lodge. It happened often enough, deer or foxes or pine martens, mostly. The videos were a nuisance, and Hank always deleted the footage without much thought.

This time, a hooded figure blew across the screen.

The hulking figure was painted greenish-grey by the camera's infrared night-vision as it threaded through the dense forest, bouncing between bushes and trees and dodging puddles of foot-sucking mud. It had a fast and confident stride, as if it knew every obstacle in the woods. Each step fell on a root or rock to avoid leaving footprints on the soft forest floor. The figure wore a bulky, worn-out jacket, and carried an empty duffel bag slung over one shoulder.

Hank's grip on the phone tightened as he watched the figure approach the edge of the forest and pause. Its hooded head tilted side-to-side as it surveyed the deserted camp. Then it pushed through the brush and scurried to the rear door of the lodge.

The figure got smaller as it moved further from the camera. Hank squinted his gray eyes and brought the screen up to his face to get a closer look. His nephew had been right: the image quality on these cameras was damn good. Even at this distance, Hank had a clear view of the figure searching his jacket pocket for something as it crouched next to the back door.

A brilliant blast of lightning blanked out the screen. When the image came back, the figure was fumbling at the door's lock. Hank peered closer. What was this guy doing? Were those keys? Yes, they were! Hank *knew* the bastard must've somehow gotten his hands on a set. He was now trying them on the lock, one after another.

"Not this time, asshole," Hank muttered. After last winter's burglary, he'd changed the locks in the spring. A satisfied grin came to his face as he watched the intruder give up and drop the key ring back into its pocket.

Instead of retreating to the forest, the figure skulked over to a window.

Hank's smile drained away as the intruder produced some kind of tool from his duffel bag. Good Lord, was that a small wood planer? What the hell was he going to do with that?

Hanks watched with growing disbelief as the intruder shaved a groove in the window frame. Four brisk cuts. Curled ribbons of wood fell to the figure's booted feet. The man plucked a pocket-knife from his jacket and inserted the blade into the gap he had made in the frame. With a flick of the wrist, he spun the clasp. An instant later, he had pushed the window open and hoisted himself through.

Hank ran a hand over his grizzled chin. Another video popped up on his app, this one triggered from the camera hidden inside the mess hall. The hooded intruder breezed across the screen, creeping through the deserted dining room toward the kitchen. The figure was at the very edge of the video frame now, partially obscured by the kitchen door. Hank could see enough through the kitchen's service window to know the intruder was rummaging through the pantry. He wouldn't find much; the camp had been closed up since Labor Day. Still, whatever was left got stuffed into the duffel bag. Some cheap chips, a few boxes of cookies, cans of beans, bags of marshmallows and boxes of graham crackers left over from s'mores.

A booming peal of thunder shook Hank's trailer and jolted him. He realized he'd been holding his breath the whole time he'd been watching the intruder. About thirty seconds later, the same thunder rolled from the video. There was a delay in the transmission to Hank's phone, but the hooded figure still seemed to be in the kitchen.

Hank's caretaker trailer was about fifty yards away from the lodge. The cold weather would chase him from his summer accommodations in another few weeks, but Hank liked to hang on as long as possible to save a month's rent in town. There wasn't time to call Chief Hayden, but if he moved quickly, Hank could corner the intruder himself.

He got up and went to the closet in the back of the trailer to get his shotgun.

Lightning forked through the night and wind buffeted Hank's flannel shirt as he crept across the distance toward the lodge. The squat bulk of the timber building stood cloaked in darkness ahead. Hank had stashed his phone in the pocket of his jeans for fear the glow of the screen would give him away as he approached, but the hooded intruder was still looting the kitchen when Hank had last checked before leaving the trailer.

Still, there was that delay in the video transmission. Where was the intruder now? Still inside or already gone?

A nervous flutter swept through Hank's gut. The weight of the reliable Remington 870 was reassuring in his hands as he drew near the window the intruder had left open. Only now did it occur to him he didn't have a plan. What was he actually going to do? Go in there after the intruder? Or wait here in ambush?

A deafening crack of thunder made Hank flinch. It was the loudest one yet. The storm was right on top of him now and was about to let loose any minute. Hank shivered, his nerves getting the best of him. He'd always been afraid of storms, and the thought of going after this mysterious figure during a raging one filled him with dread.

Another disconcerting thought crossed Hank's mind as he wavered by the window: what if the intruder was dangerous? If this was the same guy who'd been raiding places around the lake for over thirty years, what would he do once he was finally cornered? Hank knew the intruder carried a pen knife, but was there something more deadly concealed in that bulky jacket? Something like a handgun?

Hank's blood drummed in his ears. He listened carefully for sounds inside the mess hall, but there was only unnerving silence. Maybe he was too late. Maybe the intruder was already gone.

He glanced around at the darkness of the surrounding forest. Gusts of wind rocked the tree boughs. The rustling of leaves and creaking of branches filled Hank's ears, and he swore he could feel eyes staring back at him.

What the hell was he doing out here? He wasn't a cop; he unclogged toilets and shoveled ashes from fire pits. Isn't this what they paid Hayden for? When it came down to it, Hank didn't know if he had it in him to shoot anyone. Deer and ducks were one thing, but to kill a man? Hank's stomach churned at the thought, and sweat sprang to the palms of his hands.

Without warning, the bulky duffel bag came tumbling out the window. The hooded figure hurdled out after it. The ground thudded under the intruder's heavy boots. He reached for the sack.

Hank let out a startled yelp and swung the Remington up. "Don't you make a goddamn move!"

The intruder froze with his back to Hank. There was a slight twitch of his hooded head, just enough to recognize the barrel of Hank's shotgun.

Hank glowered at the intruder from the other end of the gun. From the look of the man's filthy jacket and the sour reek coming off him, he had to be homeless.

"Get your ass down on the ground or I swear to Christ I'll fill your face with buckshot!" Hank shouted.

The figure hesitated, and Hank had the sinking sense the man knew he was bluffing. Jesus, this guy was big. Much taller than Hank was. Was the intruder weighing his options? The edge of the forest was right there. All he had to do was dash for it. The old caretaker was bluffing. He wouldn't shoot…

CHK-CHK! Hank loaded the pump-action, hoping the sound might be more convincing than his empty threats.

Oh God, please don't let this guy turn around…

Hank's heart thundered in his bony chest. He'd never been more frightened in his life.

Just don't turn around. Don't make me shoot you…

The intruder moved.

Hank flinched and almost blew the man's head off when he realized the intruder was dropping down to the dewy grass. He lay flat on his stomach and put two gnarled hands behind his hooded head.

The air whooshed from Hank's lungs as he found he could breathe again. He kept the shotgun trained on the intruder with one hand while he pulled his phone from his pocket with the other.

* * *

It was nearly midnight, and Balsam Lake's station house was deserted. The doors were locked, and the lights were dimmed. Lightning flickered beyond the windows and thunder rattled the glass panes as Sam stood at the large bulletin board in the bullpen, surveying the missing person notices posted there.

The Adirondack State Park was enormous, roughly the size

of Lake Erie. People went missing all the time in a wilderness that large. Most were found alive, usually within twenty-four hours, though fatalities from drowning, hypothermia, falls, and natural causes like heart attacks were common enough. Since the Department of Environmental Conservation began keeping official records of disappearances in 1971, only nine people had never been found, either alive or dead.

Seven of them had been in the vicinity of Balsam Lake.

The disturbing implications of that aberration kept Sam up at night. What was it about his isolated neck of the woods? Was there actually someone out there preying on people? The same person who'd been plaguing the town with break-ins for the better part of thirty years? It didn't seem possible. A serial killer here? In the sleepy village of Balsam Lake? The thought of one of Sam's neighbors murdering unsuspecting victims was just too hard to fathom.

Still, seven people had vanished from the woods without a trace. No clues. No bodies.

Until now.

Sam's gaze wandered over the missing person notices tacked to the bulletin board, and he wondered if the remains of one of them were locked away in the evidence room down the hall. Was this the break he'd been waiting for? The beginning of the end of the town mystery?

Sam turned from the bulletin board, his gaze traveling involuntarily toward the darkened hallway. Framed portrait photos of Balsam Lake's previous police chiefs lined the wall on one side. The earliest went back nearly a century. The gloom at the far end of the row obscured Sam's own photo. There was a conspicuous blank space immediately preceding it. Wade Ramsay and the village board had voted to have that particular portrait removed eight years ago.

Sam now kept his father's photo buried in his desk drawer.

A phone rang and yanked Sam from his contemplation.

He could no longer afford to have officers on duty twenty-four hours a day, not since the village voted to slash his budget. Outside of regular business hours, all calls to the station were now routed to the state police dispatch in Ray Brook, over a half hour away. Sam was so distracted it took him a second to recognize the ring of his own phone. Who would call him at this late hour? He left the bullpen for his office and plucked it from his desk.

"Chief Hayden." Sam listened, his expression turning to one of disbelief. "Keep him there, Hank! Don't let him out of your sight! I'll be there in twenty!"

Sam made it out of town and down Route 30 to Camp Whippoorwill in a little over fifteen. His SUV roared into the windswept summer camp. The headlights knifed through the darkness, illuminating Hank Morrison near the lodge. He stood with a wide stance, his shotgun aimed downward. A motionless figure lay facedown in the leaves at his feet. Hank glanced over his shoulder, squinting into the blinding glare of Sam's lights.

The wind howled. Streaks of lightning filled the sky. The storm was about to let loose.

Sam slammed the truck door and rushed toward them, pulling his pistol and cuffs from his belt along the way. Excitement surged through his veins. Was this really happening? After all this time? Part of him didn't believe it was possible. He'd been pursuing this mystery for so long, he felt like he was chasing some mythical being. Maybe this was just some copycat. Not all break-ins involved the local boogeyman.

Hank lifted his shotgun and backed off as Sam pressed his knee into the small of the hooded man's back and cuffed his wrists. The man didn't struggle or resist.

Sam yanked the hood off, revealing the face of a middle-aged man. His grey-streaked hair was long and wild. An enormous grisly beard obscured much of his features, but he wore a pair of thick, scratched glasses.

The man's disheveled appearance threw Sam a curveball. He wasn't aware of any homeless in the rural village of a couple thousand people. Was this lanky vagrant really the legendary figure known as *Spooky*? The man who had tormented Sam's community for decades? Who had committed over a thousand burglaries and evaded capture since the days when Sam's own father had been the chief of police?

"What's your name?" Sam demanded.

The man remained silent.

Sam patted him down and searched the pockets of his dirty jeans and jacket. Though both garments were filthy, they were relatively new, the jacket an expensive one filled with down from Canada geese. Sam realized the man had likely stolen the clothes from one of the lakeside homes. There was a battered paperback book stuffed into one of the deep pockets of the man's bulky coat, but nothing else.

"No wallet," Sam said when he'd finished frisking the man. "Tell me your name. Now!"

Still no response.

"I am arresting you for criminal trespass and burglary. You have the right to remain silent. Anything you say can and will be used against you in a court of law. You have a right to an attorney. If you cannot afford an attorney, one will be appointed for you. Do you understand?"

The man stayed mute.

"Do you want to call a lawyer?"

Nothing.

"Do you understand your rights?"

A booming clap of thunder cracked the night.

"Answer me! Do you hear what I'm saying to you?"

The wild-looking man refused to make eye contact. His light blue eyes remained fixed longingly on the forest.

Sam recognized something mournful in the man's stare. He'd seen it before in a hospital room, in the eyes of a man looking on as the doctor unplugged his wife from a respirator following a catastrophic car accident.

It was the heartbroken look of someone saying goodbye to a loved one.

Lightning crackled and slashed across the sky. The rain came down in fat drops, pitter-pattering hard on the lodge's wooden roof.

Sam hauled the man to his feet, marched him to the SUV, and tossed him into the back. He turned and shouted through the downpour. "You got him, Hank! It took thirty years, but he's finally done!"

Chapter 5

Morning mist hung thick and heavy among the towering trees as Megan prowled the deep woods. The air was saturated with moisture from the overnight storm. Dew glistened and dripped from the leaves and needles. Rays of cool November sunlight streamed through the multicolored canopy of the sprawling forest.

As she did more often than she cared to admit, Megan had awakened on the couch before dawn, still fully dressed. Her guitar lay on the floor next to her. The bottle of bourbon stood on the coffee table—half empty.

Megan had lingered a moment, gazing absently at the bottle before snapping out of it. It was still too early for drinking—she hadn't hit that low yet. She still preferred to be on the functioning side of her alcoholism. The yellow light of the living room lamp seared her bleary eyes. Her mouth was parched, and her head pounded as she dragged herself to her feet and went to the kitchen to dump some coffee grounds into her French press.

While the coffee steeped, Megan's first task had been to

formulate her requisition for a DEC dive team to search Grindstone Bay. It was a tricky thing. The standard protocol for human remains mandated the involvement of state police resources, not the DEC. Megan understood Sam's desire to keep this quiet, and avoid handing the case over to the state troopers—this was a personal thing for both of them. After what had happened with his own father, if anyone was going to solve the mystery of Graham Danforth's disappearance, it was going to be Sam.

But what justification did Megan have to request an environmental conservation team? Without a plausible cover story, she would have a hard time explaining herself when the divers inevitably found human bones in the exact spot she'd directed them to.

Megan had toyed with a variety of excuses before settling on a combination of truth and fiction: after the discovery of human remains in a remote part of the lake, she was concerned about the potential for long-term environmental damage caused by a possibly decades-old sunken and leaking motorboat. To sweeten the story, she'd added a detail about traces of oil or gasoline being spotted on the surface of the water in Grindstone Bay.

It worked. The dive team would meet her at the town boat launch at dawn the next morning.

Megan texted Sam to give him the update. There was a tremor in her fingers as she typed. What happened tomorrow could change everything. Sam's forensic analyst was going to determine if the bones were that of Megan's father at the same time that divers tried to locate the rest of the victim's skeleton.

Victim…

The word gave Megan a shiver. It was hard to imagine her father being a victim of anyone but himself.

She sipped her coffee on the back porch, watching as the first rays of sunlight conjured mist from the chilly water of the lake. She'd need a distraction if she was going to make it through the day. She wasn't scheduled for a patrol rotation, but she'd head back into the woods to work on her personal project: the wolves.

No one had seen a wolf in the Adirondacks since the early 1900s, when the last of the wild packs disappeared as a result of nearly a century of logging and unregulated hunting. Most believed the last wolf had been shot sometime in the 1890s.

Then something strange happened a few years ago.

The DEC started getting reports of wolf sightings east of Malone at the northern limits of the park. At first, they were dismissed as cases of misidentification; large dogs and coyotes were often mistaken for wolves. But the reports kept coming, not just from up north, but from places down around Balsam Lake as well. The witnesses all insisted they knew a wolf when they saw one, but no one could provide any proof.

The idea of wolves somehow naturally returning to the Adirondacks captivated Megan's fascination. She became determined to find them.

In her spare time, she met with anyone who reported a sighting, taking down details and coordinates to track the pack's movements. So far, the best evidence she had of the presence of wolves in the area was a mutilated deer carcass found near White Lily Pond. Still, it confirmed her belief that the pack existed. With enough time and effort, she would prove it.

Now, dressed in snug hiking pants, a warm fleece sweater, and a puffy down vest, Megan was two hours from the nearest trailhead. The White Lily Pond trail wasn't maintained, and it was little more than a vague herd path snaking through some of the most unforgiving backcountry in the region. No one came out here anymore, and with good reason. Here, the firs and spruces crowded so close together, moisture couldn't escape through the thick canopy. Mosquitos and black flies swarmed the air in all but the coldest months. Gigantic boulders, scraped from the bedrock and strewn everywhere by the glaciers of the last ice age, made navigating the woods even more treacherous.

Megan was only here to follow up on a wolf sighting someone had reported while kayaking along the shoreline of the nearby lake. The trail used to intersect a path from the old Wright Great Camp to the water, but the Wright family had abandoned their once majestic ancestral retreat decades ago. For a time, curious hikers ventured out here, ignoring trespassing warnings to explore the ruins, but flooding from Hurricane Irene swept away the only bridge on the trail. All that remained now was a tangled labyrinth of smaller paths left over from disoriented hikers struggling to find their way through the impenetrable forest. Cellphone coverage was non-existent out here, and it took some serious proficiency with a GPS or map and compass to keep to the main trail.

Mosquitoes danced around Megan's head and she swatted them away. Her Deet worked to repel them, but they were still irritating in her eyes and ears. She picked her way around the boulders, careful not to wrench a knee. It was a miserable trek. She'd begun to second-guess her decision to come out here when she spotted something that froze her in place and made it all worthwhile.

There it was. A wolf's paw-print in the mud.

Several of them, actually. A whole track of prints leading up the indistinct trail before veering off into the brush.

Megan's heart skipped a beat as she stared at them, a sense of elation dispelling the gloom that had fallen over her since she'd received Sam's text about the bones. She crouched to get a closer look at the impression in the mud. It wasn't fresh, likely even a few days old. The edges had been eroded by last night's heavy rain, but Megan could still make out the four symmetrical toes and pronounced claws that were the telltale signs of a canine. She unslung her pack and rummaged for her measuring tape. The paw-print was about five inches long and four inches wide; much too big for any dog or coyote. Megan studied the trail of prints stretching away from her. Their path was direct and purposeful, not the energy-wasting, meandering route of a dog.

Megan stood, her mind racing with the magnitude of her discovery. She fumbled for her phone to take photos of the tracks, only to discover a low battery warning. Her phone had less than four percent charge left.

"Shit…" Megan winced. She'd passed out on the couch without thinking to charge her phone.

Megan snapped as many photos as she could before the battery died. She got more than she needed; any of them would prove wolves had indeed returned to the Adirondacks.

When she was done documenting the tracks, she plucked a worn and warped notepad from her pack. The pages were filled with the notes and geographical coordinates she had accumulated in her hunt for the wolf pack. Using her handheld GPS to pinpoint her location, she jotted down the coordinates before continuing on. Was there more evidence to be discovered deeper in the forest? Might she even come across the pack itself?

The thought ignited Megan's heart and got her blood racing. Adrenaline spiked her veins as she picked her way through the trees. She pushed into the hollow and halted when the unmistakable stench of rotting flesh hit her nostrils.

The carcass of a large snowshoe hare lay crushed in the jaws of a steel trap.

Megan's eyes narrowed as she approached. Judging by its state of decomposition, the animal had been there for at least a few days, maybe more. Its eyes were gelatinous holes and its fur was matted with blood and dirt. Ropy lengths of shriveled entrails spilled from the gaping wound where the sharp teeth of the big trap had almost cut the hare in half. Flies buzzed in the air around the rotting flesh.

Megan felt a knot form in her stomach. Trapping hares and rabbits weren't uncommon, but it was usually done with snares. This trap was an obsolete steel-jaw variety, the kind that hadn't been legal in the Adirondacks in years and was only good for one purpose—trapping wolves.

An uneasy apprehension took root as Megan examined the deadly mechanism closely, trying not to disturb any evidence. Something about it didn't sit right with her. The trap was old and rusted, clearly not in use for some time. So why was it here, in this black and forgotten stretch of forest, and who had set it? In her years as a conservation officer, she had never come across an illegal trap this far from the nearest trailhead. Poachers had never been a problem in these parts, and as far as she knew, she was likely the first person to come out here in months.

Megan rose from her crouch and grabbed a long and sturdy stick to search the area for evidence. She advanced slowly, surveying her surroundings as she scanned the leaf-strewn ground for any sign of disturbance. Something glinted in the sunlight near a fallen log. She approached cautiously and poked it with the stick.

WHAM!!!

A second steel trap sprang shut, snapping the wood into splinters. Megan continued on and found three more traps before she was done, all set with expert precision. Her unease turned into anger and disgust. Whoever had set these traps was not only breaking the law, but also posing a danger to the local wildlife and potentially to the rare person who visited this remote stretch of forest. Who else knew the wolves were even out here? And why would they want the animals dead?

Megan set herself to dismantling the traps when she discovered the footprint.

It wasn't that of a wolf. This one was made by a man with a large boot. But what really piqued Megan's curiosity was that there were no other tracks. Just this single footprint in the mud. It was recent, the impression still well-defined despite the rain.

Megan peered deeper into the forest. Ahead, the land rose steeply to a solid blockade of granite boulders. They loomed in a knot of dense trees like the battlements of a medieval fortress.

Megan stiffened.

She was no longer alone.

Years of abuse at her father's hands had given Megan an almost preternatural sensitivity to her environment. As a girl, she knew she was in for a beating by the particular slam of her dad's car door when he pulled into the driveway. The sound of his keys being hung on a peg versus being tossed on the table sometimes meant the difference between a black eye and a good night's sleep. The creak of a specific floorboard in the hallway told Megan to brace herself.

Now, the woods had gone silent.

And she could feel eyes on her.

Something was out there, watching her from the depths of the forest.

The feeling of not being alone washed over Megan as she revolved in a slow circle, eyeing her surroundings. "My name is Megan Danforth!" she shouted. "I'm an environmental conservation officer with the DEC!"

Her voice echoed loudly through the forest.

"Steel-jaw leg traps are illegal for land use in the Adirondack preserve! So is killing endangered wolves! I catch your ass and you'll never hunt again!"

Something cold fluttered her hair.

Megan flinched. An icy tingle prickled her skin, and the hairs rose on the back of her neck. It was a strange sensation, one she had never experienced before. The woods were her home and refuge, the one place where she felt the most safe. She'd encountered black bears with cubs, and been caught in whiteout blizzards high above the tree line on the High Peaks, but she had never been afraid out here. Even the possibility of encountering a pack of wild wolves had given her a thrill.

Yet she sensed something sinister here.

Whatever was out there meant to harm her.

Megan waited, her heart thudding uncomfortably in her chest. Her muscles clenched into tight knots. She wished she had brought her pistol, but part of her wondered if it would do any good. It seemed insane, but whatever was out there didn't feel like any person or animal she had ever encountered. It felt like… what? Megan couldn't put a name to it, but she could feel its shadowy presence, lurking just out of sight, its malevolent energy seeping into the air around her.

Megan let out a shuddering breath and puffs of white bloomed from her mouth. It wasn't her imagination. The woods had grown colder around her. It was darker too, wasn't it? As if the forest had narrowed its eyes to glare at her. The trees seemed to crowd in around her, the shadows elongating and reaching out like twisted fingers. She could feel the malevolent presence filling the woods with a suffocating sense of dread. It was closing in on her. She could almost feel its cold breath on the back of her neck.

Sweat sprang to Megan's palms, and the spit dried up in her mouth. She tried to force herself to remain calm, to convince herself she was just imagining things, but she felt an irresistible impulse to turn and run. And yet, she was afraid whatever was out there would hunt her down before she made it very far.

And then it was gone.

Megan felt the malign presence suddenly vanish, as if some terrible pressure had been released without warning. Sounds rose among the trees, the chirps of chickadees and the chatter of squirrels. Even the sunlight filtering through the boughs seemed slightly brighter, as if the forest itself had momentarily fallen under a shadow.

Megan hesitated, the debilitating terror still gnawing at her gut. Never in her years of roaming the backcountry had she ever experienced such fear. She checked her GPS for the route back to the trailhead. Ordinarily she would have enjoyed relying on her map and compass to navigate, but now she just wanted to leave this place and return to her pickup as quickly as possible.

As she neared the trailhead hours later, a faint sound caught Megan's attention: the distant whine of a police siren echoing across the vast wilderness.

* * *

Deputy Noah McCrae was waiting for Megan in his cruiser when she pulled into her long driveway. It was mid-afternoon, and the November sun was shimmering on the lake behind her cabin.

Noah waved Megan down through his open window. An old, melancholy folk song played on her pickup's radio as she slowed and pulled up beside him. She killed the music and lowered her window.

"Megan! Chief's been trying to reach you all day." Noah was unusually animated. Something had him rattled.

Megan held up her phone and shrugged. "Dead. I texted Sam this morning. The dive team's gonna—"

"That's not what this is about."

Megan's face grew dark, alarmed by the uncharacteristic

expression on Noah's face. "What? What is it?"

"We finally caught him."

"Who?"

"Spooky."

Chapter 6

The man known as Spooky hunched at the table in the interrogation room. Without his bulky jacket, he looked thin and frail in his blue flannel checked shirt and jeans. His face was drawn and gaunt behind his thick glasses. Matted ropes of gray hair tumbled down to his shoulders and the bushy mess of his beard grazed his upper chest. His skin was powdery pale and creased with age lines.

Sam sat across the table from him, tired and frustrated. It had been a long night. A glance at his watch revealed it was now almost two in the afternoon. He ran a hand over the stubble on his cheeks and chin.

"Fourteen hours," he said. "Not a single word. You're stubborn, I'll give you that."

The strange man said nothing. He just stared over Sam's shoulder, his piercing blue eyes focused on nothing in particular, as if he was meditating with his eyes open or replaying the scenes of a movie in his head.

Sam sighed and stood from his chair.

The station house's tiny interrogation looked nothing like

52

anything he'd ever seen on TV. Sure, the walls were bare, and the room was devoid of anything a prisoner could use as a weapon. But it was really just a conference room about the size of a spare bedroom. There was no two-way mirror, just a video camcorder Sam had mounted on a tripod. The table was wooden and plain, about three-by-four feet. No impressive steel surface fitted with a loop to secure shackled prisoners here, not in Balsam Lake. Sam and the man sat on folding chairs. Streams of cold daylight sliced through the blinds of a small window. Another window looked through the plain office door into the hallway. The fluorescent lights hummed, and there was a whiff of pine disinfectant and burnt coffee in the air.

Sam straightened his uniform. "You've been terrorizing this community for over three decades. Nobody's been safe. Hell, my father was the goddamn chief of police and you stole our canoe when I was seven. He spent his entire career chasing you, like you were some kind of phantom. Do you know how many homes you've broken into over the years?"

The man remained stubbornly silent, his blank stare unwavering.

"That was a question," Sam pressed. "How many homes have you robbed?"

Still no response.

"You averaged about twenty-six a year—and that's just what was reported. That's over eight-hundred burglaries in your career."

Silence. The man's bearded face was an impenetrable mask.

Sam leaned across the table and stared the man in the face, trying to pry his attention away from wherever it was. "Right now, you're about up to your chin in shit. You don't start talking, I'm gonna make sure it piles up way, way over your head. Now tell me, who are you? Where are you from?"

No response.

"Here's what your future holds," Sam went on. "You haven't requested a lawyer, and we're under no obligation to provide you with one until you go to court. I've got forty-eight hours to file formal charges against you, but that doesn't include the weekend. So I'm going to take my sweet-ass time with you for four full days until you start talking. Once I file charges on Monday, you're going to be transferred to the Essex County Jail. Makes this place seem warm and cozy. If you're still uncooperative, there's a good chance they'll toss you into solitary just to loosen you up. Given the number of charges we'll be bringing against you, it's a certainty you're going to die in prison—unless I can convince the D.A. that you've been oh so very, very cooperative. You can start by telling me your name."

At last, there was a reaction. The man's eyes flicked sideways to peer over Sam's shoulder.

Sam swiveled around.

Megan and Joanna watched through the window in the door. The man's attention was fixed on Megan. The blankness was gone from his gaze. There was something new there. Recognition?

"Her?" Sam prodded. "Do you know her?"

The man remained silent as he stared at Megan.

Sam went for the door.

"Its gotta be him, right? Spooky?" Joanna asked as soon as Sam stepped into the hallway.

Sam frowned and shut the door behind him. "Maybe."

Joanna glanced at Megan. "You don't looked convinced either."

"The break-ins could be anyone, Joanna," Megan replied. "Kids bored out of their minds. A pissed-off local with an axe to grind against the rich city people and their giant lake houses."

"Like hell." Joanna snorted with derision and showed Megan her phone. "My kids can't even work a screwdriver thanks to these. Besides, what about the people that've gone missing?"

"Did you notice the way he's looking at you?" Sam cut in. He stood with his back to the door as he gave a subtle nod over his shoulder toward the window. "Stares at the same spot on the wall for fifteen straight hours until you show up. Now he can't take his eyes off you."

"So?"

"It's as if he recognizes you."

Megan peered through the window. She frowned and shook her head. "Never seen him before."

Sam let out a weary breath. "Well, I've been banging my head against him all night and half the day, and you're the only thing that has sparked any reaction. Why don't you go in there and see if you can get him to open up?"

"What? No way."

"Just give it a try. I just need you to get him to start talking. Get a name, a hometown—anything."

Megan looked from Sam to the man in the room behind him. She swallowed hard before cracking the door open.

The man's gaze followed her as she crossed the room and

sat across the table. The metal chair squeaked beneath her. His icy eyes shifted back and forth, refusing to meet Megan's as she faced him.

Minutes crawled by and they remained sitting in silence. Megan didn't push him. She just remained there, letting him get used to her like an animal in captivity. The silence lengthened between them. But those damned fluorescents were scratching at Megan's nerves, conjuring unwanted images of those nights in the garage, alone with the punching bag and her father. She couldn't endure them any more. She got up and flipped the switch by the door.

The lights flicked off, and the man seemed to ease a bit.

Megan caught his reaction. "I hate them too."

The man offered a slight nod. At last, here was a breakthrough in communication. A slant of late afternoon sunlight fell across his shoulder in the otherwise dim room.

"Can you tell me your name?" Megan asked.

The man's eyes stopped bouncing as he focused on a thought.

"Take your time," Megan said.

The man seemed to think it over. He still refused to make eye contact; his gaze focused just over Megan's shoulder from behind his scratched glasses. He opened his mouth, closed it. Opened it again. His voice took a heartbeat longer to catch up.

"Thoreau," he rasped. His voice was hoarse and gravelly like a mummy risen from a centuries-long slumber.

"Thoreau?" Megan repeated. "That's your name? Like the writer?"

The man nodded and kept his eyes averted.

"Are you able to answer some questions for me, Mr. Thoreau?"

No response, but Megan sensed it wasn't a refusal. "When were you born?"

Thoreau's thin eyebrows knitted together. He needed a moment to think about it.

"Nineteen-seventy."

Now that his voice was warming up, it came out as a deep baritone. But the cadence of his speech was strange, out of rhythm, as if his vocal cords had somehow atrophied.

"Do you know what date?" Megan asked.

"March… 17th."

"St. Patrick's Day."

The man named Thoreau shrugged.

"What is your address?"

"Don't… don't have one."

"You're homeless?"

"I have a home. It has no address."

"Where have you been living?"

Thoreau hesitated, as if unsure how much he wanted to reveal. "The forest."

"The forest?" Megan gave him a doubtful look. "You've been living out there in the woods? For how long?"

Thoreau thought about it. "When did the Berlin Wall come down?"

"That was nineteen-eighty-nine," Megan replied. She leaned back in her chair and completed the math in her head. "You've been out there for over thirty years? How did you survive? Where did you live?"

"A tent."

"You must've taken shelter indoors at some point. Maybe somebody's cabin?"

Thoreau's face darkened. "No. Not once."

Megan shook her head in disbelief. "What year is it?"

Thoreau shrugged.

"Jesus, what have you missed?" Megan wondered in disbelief. "Mr. Thoreau, do you know what the internet is?"

Thoreau blinked at her.

"Emails? Texts? Nine-eleven? Obama? Trump?"

The names meant nothing to the man. "Am I going to jail?" he asked.

"You might," Megan replied.

The man looked down at the table.

"Mr. Thoreau, where is your campsite?"

A change came over him. Thoreau's eyes came alive and starting twitching from side to side.

"Can you show me on a map?" Megan persisted, but she pushed it too far. Thoreau shut down and went silent.

"Mr. Thoreau…" Megan prodded.

No response. He was done talking.

Megan rose and studied the strange man before heading for the door. Sam and Joanna were waiting for her in the hallway.

"No way in hell that's his real name, is it?" Sam asked.

"Probably not," Megan agreed. "Henry David Thoreau was a nineteenth-century writer. He withdrew from society for two years to live in the woods."

"You believe him?" Joanna asked. "Is it possible he's been living out there?"

Megan shrugged. "Minus-forty winters? Just surviving a couple of weeks out there would be astonishing. An entire season, damn near impossible. Thirty years? It'd make him the toughest son of a bitch alive."

"You think he's dangerous?" Sam asked.

"I'm just the conservation officer," Megan sighed. "I can gladly tell you when an animal is going to be aggressive or violent. But humans? They're an entirely different beast." She glanced back at Thoreau through the window. "If he is telling the truth, what could have driven him to live like that?"

"I don't know and I don't care," Sam said. "The only thing we have on him is a single count of criminal trespass and burglary. We need more hard evidence if we're going to prove he's our Spooky."

Just then, Noah came hustling over. "Sam!"

Sam turned. "What is it, Noah?"

"A call just came in. A little girl's gone missing near Stag Rock Falls."

Chapter 7

Becky Flynn looked like she had been crying for hours. Her pert nose was raw and her watery blue eyes were swollen and bloodshot. She was holding it together by a thread as she sat on the edge of the bed in her room in the Timber Lodge motel. Her tears had ceased, but she had grown so used to them spilling down her face she still wiped her cheeks every few seconds.

"What time did you notice Piper was gone?" Sam asked. He had pulled up a chair to sit facing Becky and her husband, Kurt. Megan stood further back, her arms crossed over her chest as she leaned with the backs of her thighs against a small desk. Joanna hovered near the door.

Most of the room was occupied by two double beds. The worn carpet filled the air with a musty scent. Framed landscapes by a local photographer who had died over a decade ago decorated the outdated wood panelling.

"Around three in the morning," Kurt replied. He was in his early thirties and taller than average, with an athletic build and a growth of sandy stubble that matched his tousled hair.

"I woke up and realized she wasn't in the tent. I thought she must've gone out to pee, so I waited a bit. When she didn't come back, we went out to look for her."

Kurt struck Sam as a guy who felt more at home in the woods than the usual weekend warriors the area attracted. He was doing his best to be strong for his wife, to keep her mind from imagining the worst, but Sam could see the strain and fear lurking behind the man's taut features.

"Do you have any idea how long she'd been gone for?" Sam asked.

Becky sniffled and shook her head, her loose blonde ponytail swaying in the air. Her hands trembled and her fingers were restless as they kneaded the rumpled tissue she held between her knees. She kept glancing at the digital clock on the stand next to the bed, as if unable to keep herself from counting the minutes. "She woke me up to tell me she needed to pee sometime in the middle of the night. I don't know what time it was, but the rain hadn't started yet."

"So sometime before midnight," Sam said. "Piper might have been gone for about three hours before you noticed."

A pained look flashed across Becky's face. She choked on a sob as if some invisible hand had constricted her throat.

"I didn't mean that as a criticism, Mrs. Flynn," Sam said, his voice low and reassuring. "None of this is your fault. We just need to establish a clear timeline of events. The average person can travel about two miles an hour through the forest —much less in the dark and last night's rain. Knowing when Piper went missing can help the forest rangers with their search radius. What happened when you looked for her?"

"The rain made it impossible," Kurt replied. "We kept

looking for a few hours once it stopped and the sun came up, but any tracks she might've left got washed away."

"And I'm guessing you had no phone service out there?"

Kurt shook his head. "We just thought we'd be able to find her eventually, you know? I mean, how could she just disappear? She had to be somewhere nearby. We kept expecting her to just turn up. Once we realized we needed help, it was a three-hour hike back to the car. We left the tent and all our gear there in case Piper came back. Becky wanted to stay behind to wait, but we decided we couldn't risk something happening to me on the trail if I went for help alone. We called you as soon as we could, and your deputy told us to meet you here for our report."

Sam nodded. "You'll be more comfortable waiting here while we search."

Becky sniffled and her voice quaked in her throat. "I can't believe I did that—leaving there without my daughter, knowing she was out there alone in the woods. Oh God, she must be so scared. She—"

"We'll find her, Mrs. Flynn," Sam said with conviction. "I can't imagine how hard it was, but you did the right thing. If your husband had been injured or lost on the way out, you'd have no way of knowing. Now I have to ask you some routine questions. Did you see anybody else out there yesterday?"

"Just a few people heading back to the trailhead as we headed in," Kurt replied.

"Any chance someone followed you?"

"I don't think so. I mean, there was a young couple, and a dad with his teenage son."

Sam leaned back in his chair and pivoted to Joanna.

"Follow up on the names at the trail register."

Joanne nodded and vanished out the door to the parking lot as Sam swung back around to the Flynns. "Anybody else? Maybe someone who came up the trail after you?"

Kurt followed where Sam's questions were going. "You think someone might have taken her?"

"It's not likely, but we have to check all the boxes," Sam replied. "How about Piper? Any unusual changes in behavior lately? Any indication she might have wanted to run away?"

"Of course not," Becky snapped. "She's a very happy girl."

"Any problems at home?"

"I mean, we have fights like anybody else, but—"

"Nothing serious?"

"No. Just stupid things."

"Anything Piper might have witnessed?"

"No, we—"

"She heard us," Kurt cut in.

Becky threw him a puzzled look.

"That night last month," Kurt went on. "I'm sure she heard us while she was in her room."

"Okay, fine," Becky conceded. "But that doesn't mean she'd want to run away."

"No, of course not," Sam said. "Like I said, these are just questions I have to ask. Let's move on. Do you have a recent photo of Piper?"

Kurt dug in his pocket for his phone and scrolled through the images until he stopped and showed Sam the screen. "I took this one yesterday afternoon while we made camp. We couldn't find that blue fleecy this morning, so she must have been wearing it when she disappeared."

Sam looked at the photo. Piper Flynn was an unassuming girl whose face hinted at the pretty teen she was destined to become. She smiled with her eyes, which were the same clear blue as her mother's. They sparkled with life in the sunlight. Her summer freckles had faded away during the fall, but a few tiny dots were still visible on her snowy skin. She had Kurt's straw-like hair, and she wore it in a long braid. Her cheeks were round and soft, her lips plump but not full, and her chin was a rounded point like the bottom of a strawberry. Her expression in the photo was that of a vibrant girl, filled with curiosity, who delighted in new discoveries.

"Can you send me this picture?" Sam asked. "With your permission, we'll post it on all our social media feeds." He gave Kurt his number and checked his phone to make sure he received the photo.

"Does Piper have much experience in the woods?" Sam asked. "Would she know not to wander around and stay in one place if she was lost?"

Kurt nodded. "She's been out camping with us dozens of times. We're both Forty-Sixers and Piper is on her way to becoming one, too."

Sam nodded. The Forty-Sixers were a club of hikers who had reach the summits of all forty-six Adirondack peaks above 4000 feet. It wasn't an easy accomplishment. Many of the mountains had no maintained trails and required backcountry skills to navigate through dense and rugged terrain.

"Okay, here's what happens next," Sam explained. "Federal law requires us to file Piper's info with the NCIC Missing Persons File. Conservation Officer Danforth here has already alerted her colleagues at the DEC Forest Rangers in Ray Brook. They will be in charge of the search and rescue."

Becky blinked a few times and Sam paused. She had a vacant look that told him she wasn't able to process the information fast enough. She wasn't entirely present; her thoughts were still out there in the forest with her daughter.

"The Rangers will be out there within the hour with all of their resources, including a canine team," Sam went on, more slowly now. "Over a hundred people get lost in the Adirondacks every year, and the Rangers find them all. "

"Chief…"

Megan motioned her head for Sam to step away from the room to speak privately.

"Excuse us a moment." Sam got up and joined Megan outside on the second-floor gallery overlooking the parking lot. It was about five o'clock, and the last of the daylight had already dwindled from the sky. Dusk was casting its gloom over the land. Maybe it was the chill in the air, but the scent of pine mingling with the musky-sweet smell of dead leaves seemed stronger this evening.

"The nights will be close to freezing out there soon," Megan said, once the Flynns were out of earshot. "If Piper's clothes got wet in last night's storm…"

"Hypothermia. I know." Sam's lips pressed into a grim line. "The Rangers can search past nightfall, right?"

Megan nodded. "The dark won't stop them. But there's something else you should know, Sam."

"What is it?"

"From what I gather, their camp was about five miles upstream from White Lily Pond. I found wolf tracks near there this morning."

Sam's expression grew even darker as he stared at her. "Christ… Are you serious?"

"You want me to show you the photos?"

Sam let out an exasperated sigh. "How many wolves are we talking about?"

"I can't say for sure, but lone wolves are the exception to the rule. If there's one in the area, there's likely a pack around too."

"Would they attack the girl if they came across her?"

"Probably not. Wolf attacks are extremely rare. Most happen when wolves become used to human food. Still, just the fact that they are *here* makes this pack unpredictable."

Sam drew a breath and let it out again. He glanced back into the room at the couple perched side-by-side on the edge of the bed. Becky was crying again. Her shoulders were hunched over and her slender frame trembled with her quiet sobs. Kurt was rubbing her back and whispering something reassuring in her ear, but his face didn't look like he believed his own words.

"They don't need to know about this," Sam murmured.

Megan gave a nod. "I'll still alert the Rangers."

They fell quiet, each consumed by their own misgivings. Sam stared across the parking lot at the wall of trees on the other side of Route 30. The land climbed steadily toward the tall peaks in the distance. Somewhere out there, a scared little girl wondered if she'd ever see her parents again.

A hollow pit opened in Sam's gut. The exhaustion of recent events overtook him, and it occurred to him he hadn't slept in more than a day. His eyes burned and a dull throb was building between his temples. Still, something told him there would be more sleepless nights in the coming week.

"Doesn't it seem like all of this town's skeletons are spilling out of the closet at the same time?" he said after a moment. "First the bones in the lake, then Spooky, and now this?"

Megan chewed the inside of her cheek and said nothing. She'd been thinking the same thing.

A pickup roared by on Route 30 on its way into town.

Sam's phone vibrated in his pocket. He checked the text message. "Ah, shit…"

"What is it?" Megan asked.

"The village board called an emergency town hall meeting."

"When?"

Sam checked his watch. "In two hours. Looks like word's gotten out about our friend Thoreau."

Chapter 8

Sam's palms were sweaty, and his throat was dry. He sipped from a water bottle as he stood behind the lectern on the small stage at one end of Balsam Lake Elementary's gymnasium. He hated public speaking—always had. To make it even worse, he knew what these people said about him when he wasn't around.

Roy Hayden's boy ain't fit to be our police chief, not after what his ol' daddy did…

"The girl's name is Piper Flynn, and she is ten-years-old," Sam said into the microphone. The PA speakers boomed off the gym walls. "She has been missing for approximately eighteen hours, and was last seen at her family's wild camp at Stag Rock Falls. She is about four feet tall and weighs fifty-seven pounds, with light blonde hair and blue eyes. We've posted a photo of her on the town's social media pages."

Sam paused, painfully conscious of the hundreds of eyes staring at him, waiting for him to go on. He couldn't remember the last time he'd seen so many citizens at a town hall meeting. Maybe never. The gym was packed from end to end, and the organizers had run out of folding chairs to accommodate everyone. Gritty locals and wealthy city people stood in the side aisles, leaning against the wooden climbing bars fixed to the walls. More people crowded the doors and spilled into the hallway. The whole town had turned out to hear what Sam had to say. A camera fixed to a tripod in the centre aisle live-streamed the meeting to the few residents who chose to remain at home.

"Search and rescue efforts are already underway under the direction of DEC Forest Rangers with the assistance of Adirondack Mountain Rescue," Sam continued. "My office will liaise with the mayor's and the state police will provide aerial search helicopters and medevac if necessary. If she isn't found by morning, we'll be asking for volunteers to form a search party and sweep the area."

A hand shot into the air. It belonged to Dick Mayfield— "Big" Dick Mayfield, they called him, for reasons Sam didn't care to imagine—and he didn't wait to be acknowledged. "Aren't you supposed to put out an AMBER alert, chief?" he asked with a scowl plastered across his craggy face.

"Only in cases of suspected abduction," Sam replied. "At this point, we have no reason to suspect anything criminal. Based on her parents' account, Piper left the tent in the middle of the night to relieve herself and never returned. Our working assumption is that she got turned around and lost in the dark."

"What about the guy you arrested last night at Camp Whippoorwill?" Mayfield pressed. "Is it him? Is he the one who's been robbing us blind all these years?"

Sam noticed a few people in the crowd had their phones

out, taking videos. The capture of the local boogeyman was a generational event that many in the small community wanted to document. Sam chose his next words carefully. Whatever he said would be tweeted and shared online within seconds. He glanced side-to-side across the stage.

Megan stood in the wings with her arms folded, watching the proceedings from off-stage. Mayor Dwight Hough sat at the folding table to Sam's left, a rakish man in his sixties who looked like he should be wearing an apron behind the counter of the town general store instead of occupying the mayor's office. Wade Ramsay, the president of the village board, sat immediately to Sam's right. He was a boisterous, middle-aged developer who probably still saw a star athlete when he looked in the mirror, and not the beefy, ham-fisted lout he had become. He owned one of the largest properties on the lake, a glass and chrome monstrosity that stood like a middle-finger to its natural surroundings. The village board had only approved it for construction because of how much Wade could intimidate his fellow trustees. He would never win an election, but everyone knew Wade was the town's unofficial mayor.

"The suspect in custody is being questioned and will be transferred to the county jail if and when charges are filed," Sam answered evenly. "We're not pursuing any additional suspects at this time. We're confident he worked alone."

"So who is he?" The question came from further down the table. Bev Morrell was the only woman on the Board and the only local resident. The other three trustees were weekenders like Wade.

"We haven't yet established his identity," Sam replied.

"In other words, you don't know jack." Wade Ramsay finally rose to his feet next to Sam. He wore a ridiculous pair of designer glasses that were too small for his round face. Blotches of sweat stood out like dark little islands on the back of his expensive polo shirt. There was no need to stand, but as with everything Wade did, the gesture asserted his dominance in front of the huge audience.

Sam swallowed. "We'll be releasing a photo to solicit the public's help in identifying—"

"Our help?" Wade scoffed. "*You're* the cop here! Where's all our stuff? He broke into my house dozens of times. He must have a whole stockpile somewhere. Hank Morrison says he's some kind of hermit. Why aren't you out there looking for his camp?"

"Right now we're devoting all our resources to finding Piper Flynn," Sam replied with an edge in his tone. Christ, this guy got under his skin. He grit his teeth and struggled to keep his cool; he wasn't about to let Wade get the better of him in front of all these people. "We're talking about thousands of acres, Wade. Once the girl is found and home safe with her parents, we'll coordinate with DEC to mount a search of the park for our suspect's camp. But it's gonna take some time. Please be patient and let us do our job."

"I've been patient for half my goddamn life!" Wade exclaimed. "I wanna know what's going on. How you still have a job is a joke!"

There was a stirring in the crowd. A murmuring of hushed voices rippled through the gym and rolled up toward Sam.

"We're pursuing every lead," he said. "We'll have answers soon."

"You've been saying that for years! You're as useless as your old man was, Hayden. He chased Spooky for the better part of twenty years and still came up with squat. What's it gonna take to get some real cops around here?"

Sam's face darkened angrily as the crowd erupted with shouts of agreement.

"That bastard did more than rob our homes!" Wade went on, sensing the crowd was on his side and relishing the power it gave him. "He stole our peace of mind! He scared the crap out of us!"

"He stole my Halloween candy when I was eleven!" A middle-aged man in the audience shouted.

Wade turned to the crowd, not bothering with the mic. "Who else has been robbed by this guy?"

Hundreds of hands flew into the air.

"Who's ever felt like someone was out there watching? Waiting for you to leave home?" Wade was really turning it on now.

"Yeah! People have vanished out there, chief!" Another voice shouted. "What about Charlie Dix? Avery Burke? That couple of missing hikers from Chestertown?"

"There's no evidence to suggest any of them were victims of foul play," Sam countered.

Wade's voice cut through the din. "What about the body you pulled from the lake, chief?"

A hush settled over the crowd as the upraised voices suddenly went quiet.

"Was that foul play?" Wade pressed.

Sam hesitated and glanced across the stage at Megan. She stared back at him, her expression growing uneasy.

"That investigation is still ongoing and I won't be discussing details," Sam said. "It's been a long day, folks. That's all the info I've got for tonight."

He left the lectern and crossed the stage while the crowd erupted with more shouted questions. Mayor Hough took the podium and struggled to be heard over the din. His reedy voice squawked through the speakers. The sound in the gym really was horrible. No wonder the kids' Christmas choir never stood a chance.

Sam paused next to Megan on his way through the wings. "My guy will be here first thing in the morning to examine the bones. I can stall Thoreau's transfer until Monday. That gives you two days to get him talking. If there are more bodies out there, I want to find them. And if he has anything to do with Piper Flynn's disappearance, we need to know about it before these people do."

His insinuation sank in.

"You think Thoreau might have—"

Megan was talking to the air. Sam had already slipped out the side door.

Chapter 9

Megan stood in her snug home office, examining the impressive collection of books she had collected over the years. It was late, and darkness pooled outside the room's only window. Dust drifted through the yellow beam of the desk lamp that illuminated the book spines.

Megan's eyes roamed over the titles, looking for one in particular. She had always been an avid reader. Books were free at the school library, and they were portable enough to be carried with her during the long hours she'd spent hiding out in the woods until darkness forced her to return home to her father. Since graduating, her office had become her own personal library, filled with volumes on subjects ranging from botany to folk art and music history. They represented her interests, her passions, and often, her thirst for escape.

She kept the shelves curated and organized to her liking, and she quickly found the section dedicated to the American transcendentalists. Her gaze passed over the works of Emerson, Hedge, Fuller, Whitman, and—

"Son of a bitch..." she murmured.

An empty space stood between two thick volumes where another book was missing. Megan's jaw hung open.

Her copy of Henry David Thoreau's *Walden* was gone.

She tried to remember the last time she had seen it, but it had been a while. Could she have misplaced the book herself? She couldn't be sure. She searched the shelves again, slowly this time. No matter how many times she looked, she still came up with nothing. Her copy of *Walden* was definitely missing.

Megan stood back and frowned at the empty spot on the shelf. Books didn't just vanish on their own. At some point in time, someone had come into her home and taken it. And from what she could tell, Thoreau's classic account of his years alone in the woods was the only thing stolen.

A creeping sense of unease crawled up the back of Megan's neck. Had the mysterious hermit in Sam's jail cell known about this missing book? It couldn't just be a coincidence. Did he remember stealing it? Is that why he called himself Thoreau? Why he spoke to her? Did he somehow recognize her? And even more chilling: had he been in the house with her?

Megan's thoughts remained troubled as she grabbed her guitar from its stand and snapped the desk light off.

Out on the back porch, the soft glow of the Coleman lamp stood between Megan and the darkness. A thick fog was rolling across the black expanse of the lake toward where she sat in her rocking chair. It was a thick, heavy mist that seemed to swallow everything in its path as it creeped closer to the porch. Ghostly rays of moonlight shimmered through its swirling depths.

Megan's mind was still too dark to notice. She tried to focus on the chord changes while she strummed the guitar, but echoes of the town hall meeting kept reverberating in her mind.

What about the body you pulled from the lake? Is it Graham Danforth?

In the morning, that question would finally be answered.

Megan's F barre chord came out wrong, and the dissonant tone jarred her back to the present. She stopped and sipped from the bottle of bourbon sitting on the apple crate next to her. That F chord always gave her a hard time, and she once again wondered about her choice of guitar.

The acoustic had belonged to her aunt, and Megan had picked it up after moving in with her in her early teens. Her father had been missing for months at that point, and her aunt had stepped up to be her legal guardian. Over the following weeks, Megan had slowly taught herself how to play the discarded instrument. By the time she was ready to move out and start university at UMass Amherst, her aunt figured Megan might as well take it with her. It became one of the few possessions she held on to as she bounced from the university dorms to cheap, off-campus apartments, and, finally, back to Balsam Lake.

Frustrated with the chords, Megan gave up and started picking something else. Her fingers danced across the strings, pulling out a melody that was both haunting and beautiful. The night air was cool and still, the only sound her melancholy notes and the creak of her rocking chair on the wooden planks. The fog seemed to embrace the cabin, wrapping it in a cocoon of mist and mystery. It swirled and eddied around the porch, as if drawn to the sound of the guitar.

Megan closed her eyes and tried to lose herself in the music and the quiet, ethereal world of the fog.

What about the body you pulled from the lake?

Like the imposing presence of Dick Mayfield himself, the man's words insinuated themselves back into Megan's thoughts.

Is it Graham Danforth…

* * *

Megan is thirteen that summer morning. She and her father are on a secluded stretch of shoreline somewhere far down the lake. The evergreens crowd close to the water's edge, bending around a short sliver of tall reeds and sand. Megan stands watching while Graham sorts the fishing lures in his tackle box. He expects her to pay attention, to learn the pros and cons of each lure. But it's hard to focus when Megan's nose is so swollen and her eyes are black and blue.

It's July the Fourth and school has been out for over a week. Graham will make sure no one sees her until she's healed.

"You see this one?" Graham shows her a lure that resembles a small, stubby fish. It's light blue on top, with a silver belly and iridescent yellow stripes down its sides. The two treble hooks dangling from its underside rattle as Graham holds it up in the air. "This one's called a crankbait. It's meant for shallow water like this. This square bill here makes it move like a panicked baitfish when you reel it through the water."

Megan reaches for the lure to take a closer look, but Graham snatches it back. "Oh, hell no," he says with a disdainful chuckle. "These fuckers are expensive. Can't have you getting it snagged on those reeds and losing it. You're using stick bait." He selects a bright green rubber worm from his tackle box. Its wriggling motion is almost lifelike as he fixes it to the hook at the end of Megan's line.

While Graham attaches the crankbait to his own line, Megan carries her rod to the water's edge. The sandy shore pitches steeply down into darkness beyond the toes of her worn-out sneakers. The sun has just risen and steam rises in curling tendrils from the lake. It was cool overnight, but the day is already warming up despite the early hour. It's going to be a hot one, and Megan's happy for the cutoff jean shorts, yellow tank top, and thin flannel shirt she chose when her father woke her up before dawn.

She doesn't know where they are, only that it was still dark when they launched their battered canoe. They must have paddled for about an hour, and sunlight was peeking over the mountains by the time they reached this hidden inlet. The canoe now rests beached on the shore nearby. Graham's big styrofoam cooler still sits between the benches, loaded with beer. He'd cracked the first one as soon as they hit the water. He's already had four more since.

Megan hooks her fishing line with her forefinger near the reel and opens the bail, just like her father has shown her countless times. Except this time, she'll get it right. She draws the rod back over her shoulder and whips it forward again to cast her bait.

But she doesn't release her finger in time. The line hitches and catches in the air before the bait can go very far. The rubber worm plops into the water only yards from her feet.

Graham shakes his head and deflates a little as she struggles. "Fucking useless," he mutters.

Whatever hopes Megan has for the day are quickly evaporating. Her shoulders sag as she reels the line in for another attempt.

Graham goes to the canoe and pulls a couple of beers from the ice inside the cooler. Foam spills down the side of his can as he cracks it open and takes a swig. He tosses the other one to Megan. "Here…"

Megan catches the can and stares at it like it's a live grenade.

"Drink it," Graham orders.

Megan wavers. The expression on her father's face makes her uncomfortable. "Dad, I don't—"

"Have a goddamn beer with your dad. Christ, can't ya make me happy for once in your fucking life?" His tone is a low and menacing growl. No room for refusal. But there's something else there too, something buried deep beneath the venomous words. There's despair.

Megan knows that hurt wouldn't be there if she was a boy. She's already disappointed her father enough; she doesn't want to let him down again. She cracks the can open and grimaces as she gulps. A bitter, metallic taste floods her mouth. The bubbles tickle her nose and prickle her throat when she swallows.

Something like a smile cracks Graham's thin lips. He claps Megan on the back and a light flickers to life in the haunted houses that are his eyes. She hasn't seen that light since that snowy December night four years ago, when he'd swerved to miss that deer and slid into the crash that killed his wife and mother of his child.

Megan doesn't want that fragile light to ever go out again. She swallows another mouthful. And another, nearly finishing the can. She'll drink them all with him if she has to. They'll empty the cooler together. Anything to keep her father happy again, to make this delicate moment last.

Hours later, Megan is on her hands and knees, puking her guts out into the weeds at the water's edge. Empty beer cans litter the ground around her. Her fishing rod lies discarded nearby.

Graham hovers over her, drunk and bleary-eyed, watching helplessly as his daughter's retching gives way to painful dry-heaves. His feeble attempts at concern echo in Megan's ears.

"Hey... Hey, are you okay...?"

Megan's young body twists and contorts as she spits up bile. It scorches her ravaged throat, and she curls up on her side. She hugs her knees to her chest, wanting nothing more than to go to sleep so the world will stop spinning and the painful retching will end...

* * *

Megan took a long swig of whiskey straight from the bottle. She had been avoiding her memories of that day for years, but lately, they seemed to be closing in on her from all sides. She took another sip, letting the alcohol work its magic. It dulled the pain of the images still lingering in her head, just enough to make them bearable.

The fog had thickened around the cabin now. Maybe it was just her sense of violation at having discovered her copy of *Walden* missing, but something about the mist's silent, shifting tendrils made Megan's skin crawl. She set the whiskey back on the apple crate and glanced at her phone. It was almost eleven o'clock. She knew she would finish the bottle if she stayed up any longer. The DEC divers would meet her at dawn, and she needed her mind to be clear and alert for the day ahead. She snuffed the Coleman and carried her guitar by the neck. The old deck planks creaked beneath her feet as she crossed the porch to the door.

The warmth of the living room wrapped her in an embrace. The fire was dying on the grate, but it still cast a flickering orange glow through the room. Megan laid the guitar across the couch and stopped at the fireplace to scatter the embers. The firelight was nearly extinguished, and a gloom descended around her. She turned and took a few steps toward the stairs.

A sound thumped on the back porch.

Megan went rigid where she stood.

What was that?

She remained very still, ears pricked. Had something knocked her whiskey bottle over?

The hairs rose on the back of Megan's neck as she peered across the darkened room toward the picture window overlooking the foggy lake. She could see nothing in the swirling darkness of the fog beyond.

Another thump.

This time, there was no mistaking it.

A footstep.

Someone was out there on the back porch.

Megan tried to stay calm, but her heartbeat shot up as she made a slow turn in the sound's direction, listening as the footsteps grew louder and louder. There was something off about them, something not right. They seemed to move in a strange, erratic pattern, as if whoever was making them was struggling to keep their balance. She still couldn't see anyone through the window, but she could feel their presence out there, getting closer.

A loud squeaking filled the room, like fingertips being slowly drawn across wet glass. Megan saw five streaks appear on the picture window where the dew was being wiped away, as if by some invisible hand. Tiny beads of water dripped down the glass from the trails the unseen fingers left behind on the windowpane.

Megan still couldn't make out who was out there, but even in the dim glow of the embers, she was certain they could see *her*. Her heart drummed against her ribs as the footsteps drifted across the porch toward the back door. She had locked it behind her on her way in.

Or had she?

Megan stared hard, but the door was beyond the reach of the feeble light cast by the dying coals. She couldn't see if she had turned the bolt or not. She started across the room when a wave of horror washed over her and froze her in place.

Those heavy and menacing steps outside were familiar.

They were just like her father's.

No. It's not him. It can't be. Someone else is out there...

But who? A burglar? Any other night, Megan might have assumed it was the mythical Spooky. But the man who called himself Thoreau was now locked up in Balsam Lake's only jail cell. Sam had caught him in the act, burglarizing a place that had already been targeted dozens of times.

Still, what if Thoreau hadn't worked alone for all these years?

Megan fumbled for her phone. She had to call for help.

Before she could even dial, the slow tread of the footsteps halted at the door.

The dreadful silence was terrifying.

Cold sweat broke out on Megan's forehead. Her hand shook as she held the phone. Her gun was still in her belt, hanging by the front door, but she didn't dare turn her back on whoever was out there. She could only hold her breath, waiting for the door to burst open. She could hear nothing but the drumming of her own heart.

Something scratched at the wood.

An icy prickle crawled up Megan's spine. Whatever was out there wasn't human. A human would try the door handle, not claw at the solid door. She tried to convince herself it was just an animal, but she couldn't shake the feeling it was something far more sinister. It reminded her of the dreadful sensation she had experienced earlier that morning in the forest, that unshakable sense of malice that had overcome her.

Another loud scratch, harder this time.

And another. Over and over again.

The door shuddered and rattled in its frame.

Whatever was out there wanted to get in.

Megan's fighting instincts finally overcame her fear. She dashed across the room to the vestibule and grabbed her Glock from its holster. With a deft flick of the wrist, she pulled the chamber and cocked a round into place. The weight of the gun in her hand gave her courage as she marched to the back door and whipped it open.

There was nothing there but darkness and fog.

Megan hesitated in the open door, unable to shake the feeling that she was being watched. She gripped the gun with both hands and inched out onto the porch. The fog swirled around her, tingling her skin with moisture and dampening her hair. The light spilling from the door barely pierced the thick, ghostly mist.

Megan saw nothing in either direction. Her heart wouldn't stop pounding, and she found herself gripping the gun tighter as she turned to inspect her door.

Dozens of criss-crossing gouges scarred the wood, but they didn't resemble any claw marks Megan had ever seen. They were too deliberate, even in their frenzied haphazardness.

Megan peered into the fog again. The planks creaked beneath her as she took a tentative step across the porch toward the railing.

A bright flash of pain raced up from the bottom of her bare foot, and something tinkled across the deck planks. Megan jumped up and looked down at what she had stepped on.

Her blood turned to ice in her veins.

A blue and yellow fishing lure lay on the porch at her feet.

The air burst from Megan's lungs as if she had been punched in the chest. She staggered back against the doorjamb, staring at the crankbait in horror as if someone had left a human heart at her doorstep.

Chapter 10

The fog was thicker and even more impenetrable in the morning. It swirled around Megan as she stood by the water's edge, gazing at the rigid hull inflatable boat anchored in the middle of Grindstone Bay. It was a gray and dreary morning, the kind that shivered with the first brush of winter's chilly breath. A bitter wind cut through Megan's uniform and vest as it swept across the lake. Behind where she stood, there was nothing but miles of thick evergreen forest.

The hours had been long after the discovery of the fishing lure on her doorstep. Megan had snatched it up with trembling hands and retreated inside, throwing the door closed and bolting it shut behind her. The cold plastic of the crankbait and the clinking of its hooks made her skin crawl as she set it down on the coffee table.

She sank into the couch and remained awake for the rest of the night, unable to believe what she was looking at. It was like something from a nightmare had somehow manifested itself in reality. This was the same lure her father had shown her that fateful morning at the lake. She was sure of it.

Someone had deliberately left it on her doorstep—someone who could still lurk nearby. Megan kept peering out the window into the darkness, but all she saw was the fog staring back at her, taunting her with its secrets.

When dawn came, she was glad to get away. Her thoughts were still rattled when she had joined the DEC divers at the town boat launch. The team consisted of two men and a flinty woman named Nora, who seemed to be the veteran of the trio. After they put the RHIB into the water, Megan guided them southwest through the soupy fog to the isolated bay. They dropped her ashore to observe the dive from a distance while they conducted their search. When an initial sonar sweep failed to turn up any sunken boats, Megan feared they would call it a day. It was with some relief when she saw them prepping their air tanks for a thorough search of the lakebed.

Now, one man still remained in the boat while Nora and her partner continued to explore the cold depths below.

Megan kept her hands jammed into her vest pockets as she stood peering into the shifting gray of the fog, trying to shake the unease that had settled into the pit of her stomach. Images of the fishing lure sitting on her coffee table kept leaping into her mind like actors in a Halloween haunted house. She thought about the wolf traps she'd discovered the previous morning, that awful sense of being watched in the woods. Could someone have vandalized her door as some kind of warning or message? Or was this a cruel prank being played by one of the locals?

Neither explanation seemed possible. No one knew about that lure's significance to her. Megan and her father had been isolated and alone that day, miles away from anyone.

Hadn't they?

A footstep crunched in the woods to Megan's left and gave her a start. Her thoughts had been so distracted, she didn't notice Sam weaving toward her through the trees along the shoreline. She had heard a boat's motor approaching through the fog, but hadn't been able to make out who it was. Sam must have had the same problem locating her and found a spot to anchor somewhere further up the rugged shoreline.

"They said I'd find you out here," he said as he approached. He joined her and looked out toward the dive team. The fog had wrapped around them and veiled them in gray. "They find anything?"

"A few more bones wrapped in a ripped nylon tarp," Megan replied. "Other than that, nothing. Not even a belt buckle. Body was probably stripped naked and dumped here."

Sam's lips bent into a grim frown. "It's your father, Megan. Dental records confirmed it this morning. Forensics concluded the cause of death was massive head trauma, just as you suspected."

Megan's face was a grim mask as she gazed across the water at the shadowy shapes in the fog.

"I'm sorry," Sam said. "I know we've had our issues, but just the same, well… I'm sorry."

Megan chewed her cheek and remained silent, brooding.

"I imagine in some ways, it would've been easier for both of us to keep believing he got drunk and drowned, or—"

"Or abandoned me," Megan finished.

Sam frowned. "Listen, I know our past has been…

complicated. I don't blame you for what you think of my father. When you went away to school, I thought things might get better, but…" He shrugged. "I don't know why you came back to this town, and I don't know if we'll ever put what happened with our dads behind us. But right now, it looks like it's in both of our interests to work together on this."

Megan gave a distracted nod, her thoughts straying back to the fishing lure. During the sleepless hours she had spent on her couch, part of her had wondered if her father himself had returned after all these years. Had he been the one trying to get in through her back door? As unlikely as it seemed, it was the only rational explanation she could think of. Now, that possibility had just evaporated, leaving her with nothing.

"Megan, what do you remember about that day?" Sam asked.

Megan's chest heaved as she inhaled the crisp, cool air and let it out again. "Not much." She paused and slid her gaze toward Sam. "Nothing I didn't tell your dad. I'm sure it's all in his files. He was dead-set on proving I killed my father."

Sam said nothing. He kept his dark eyes focused on the spot on the water where Nora and her dive partner had just surfaced.

"They still haven't found Piper Flynn," Megan said after a moment. "She's been out there for two nights."

Sam lowered his head and gazed at the ripples lapping at the shore. "The damn rain washed away any chance of the dogs picking up a scent. We're putting the call out for volunteers for a search party. State troopers are going to get their helicopter in the air, too."

Megan turned from the water and looked him in the face. "You think Thoreau took that girl?"

Sam shrugged. "Let's consider what we already know. If this guy's telling the truth, he's been surviving out there by himself for thirty years, living off things he steals from local houses and cabins. No one ever catches a glimpse of him and he never makes mistakes... until now. He's robbed Camp Whippoorwill over a dozen times—but always in winter. Now, on the same night a little girl wanders away from her camp, he breaks his pattern and robs the camp just a few hours later. Why? What suddenly made him take such an uncharacteristic risk?"

Megan caught on. "He needed more food."

"Why?"

"He had another mouth to feed... Piper Flynn."

Sam nodded.

"You think he killed my father?" Megan asked.

"I think he's the one suspect that has never been questioned in your father's disappearance. And if he did kill your dad, there's a good chance he might've murdered others, too."

The low growl of a powerful outboard motor revved to life and rumbled through the stillness of the fog. Out on the lake, Nora and her dive partner were climbing back into their boat and shrugging out of their air tanks. The search was over. Nora looked at Megan from across the gulf and made a negative motion in the air with her hands. There was nothing left to find down there.

"Clock's ticking, Megan," Sam said. "Once Thoreau is transferred to county, he'll be appointed a lawyer and lost in the system. I'm betting if we find his camp, we'll find Piper

Flynn, too. For some reason, you're the only one he'll talk to. Let's finally get some answers and put these old ghosts to rest."

Chapter 11

As soon as Megan stepped through the doors of the station, Noah McCrae recognized the determination in her stride. He was at the reception desk, fielding calls on the station's Piper Flynn tip line, when she marched over, her hiking boots thumping across the wooden floor.

"Where are Thoreau's personal things?" she asked, her tone sharp and demanding.

Noah looked up at her, his eyes narrowed in confusion. "Evidence locker."

"The only thing he had on him at the time of his arrest was a duffel bag with some tools, and a book, right? I need to see it."

Noah hesitated for a moment, clearly unsure of how to proceed. He glanced around, as if hoping for some backup to appear, but the station was empty. Finally, he stood up from his seat and gestured for her to follow. "Come with me."

He led the way through the station to the evidence room. Megan remained in the corridor while he flipped on the fluorescents and went inside. She couldn't bring herself to look at her father's bones still laid out on the table inside the sterile room.

When Noah returned a moment later, he handed Megan a plastic evidence bag. Inside was the battered paperback Sam had found in Thoreau's jacket the night he was arrested.

Megan's heart lurched when she laid eyes on it: *Walden* by Henry David Thoreau. She tore the bag open.

"Hey!" Noah exclaimed. "You can't—"

"It's mine, Noah," Megan said. "This book is mine. Look…" She peeled the cover open and showed him an inscription scrawled inside:

To Angela,
Merry Christmas, 1991
Love, Graham

Megan snapped the book shut. "My father gave it to my mom when they were dating. Thoreau stole it from me. I need to see him."

Noah saw her looking at him with her arms folded over her chest, her face stony with resolve. There was no arguing when she was like this. He let out a sigh and ran a hand through his hair as he brushed by her on his way to Thoreau's cell.

Through the window, Megan saw the hermit sitting hunched on the edge of his bunk, staring at the wall with a blank expression. He stirred and snapped out of his trance at the sound of their footsteps approaching. He seemed to have aged overnight, his piercing blue eyes now dull and sunken, as if he were withering in captivity.

Megan waited for Noah to unlock the cell and swing the

door inward. Maybe it was because it was the only one in town, but Balsam Lake's jail cell was larger than most, at about eight by ten feet. Thoreau's bunk stood in the back corner, beneath a small window with bars. A stainless steel toilet protruded from the wall next to it. There were no other furnishings.

Megan took a step inside, but Noah placed an uneasy hand on her shoulder.

"It's okay, Noah," Megan said. "He won't hurt me. Will you, Mr. Thoreau?"

Thoreau just stared at a spot on the floor at Megan's feet.

Megan took a few steps into the cell and held out the paperback for Thoreau. He put his scratched glasses on and climbed out of bed to inspect it. When he recognized the book for what it was, he clutched it and retreated to his bunk. He opened the creased cover and picked through the pages like they were sacred parchment. He went straight to a specific chapter and passage and read aloud, murmuring to himself.

"*I find it wholesome to be alone the greater part of the time. To be in company, even with the best, is soon wearisome and dissipating. I love to be alone. I never found the companion that was so companionable as solitude...*"

Satisfied the book didn't present any danger to either his prisoner or others, Noah started to back out of the cell when Megan stopped him.

"Can we turn those off?" She motioned at the harsh fluorescents overhead.

Noah gazed at her a moment before nodding and leaving them alone. The cell clanged shut, and the lock engaged with a clink.

Megan remained by the door and let Thoreau adjust to her presence until the fluorescents flicked off an instant later. The morning light slicing through the window divided the cell in two where it hit the floor. Thoreau's hunched form was a silhouetted shadow on the other side of the pale beam.

Megan took out her phone and hit a recording app before setting it down on the edge of the cot. Thoreau looked up from his book and glanced at the device from the corner of his eye. He had no idea what it was.

"Must be hell in here compared to the wide open wilderness," Megan remarked.

Thoreau said nothing.

"My name is Megan. Megan Danforth. I'm a conservation officer with the DEC."

Thoreau's gaze shifted away from her face.

Megan picked up on the cue and averted her eyes to avoid contact. Instead, she focused on the book in Thoreau's lap. "You stole that book from me. I don't know how long ago. I didn't notice it was gone until yesterday."

Thoreau studied Megan's face and seemed to conclude she was no threat. "Wasn't anything personal," he murmured.

Megan took heart at the communication breakthrough. "Thoreau must have meant something special to you. You didn't take anything else."

His frown faded, and his expression brightened. "Thoreau's masterpiece encompasses the entirety of human resilience and absurdity. There is no purer account of the roots of human suffering."

A heartbeat went by. Thoreau had nothing else to say. His

attention wandered back to Megan's phone.

"It's called a cellphone," she explained. "It goes everywhere and does everything."

He studied the device with a mixture of curiosity and contempt. "Doesn't leave much room to be alone with your thoughts."

"You'd be surprised, Mr. Thoreau. In a lot of ways, people are more lonely now than they've ever been."

Thoreau lowered his gaze and scratched his beard.

Megan tried a different approach. "I'd like to know more about your time in the woods, Mr. Thoreau. Can you tell me about your home? What was it like living out there for all those years?"

Thoreau's eyes zigzagged, unsure how to respond. "I watched a mushroom grow on the trunk of an oak for years. It's one of the more humbling things I've seen."

"You've probably seen a lot of things the rest of us haven't," said Megan.

"Probably."

"Can you tell me about it?"

Thoreau closed his eyes. His mind drifted, his thoughts going elsewhere.

Back to the forest.

"*I went to the woods because I wished to live deliberately,*" he said, quoting his namesake again. "*To front only the essential facts of life, and see if I could not learn what it had to teach, and not, when I came to die, discover that I had not lived…*"

***

It's early autumn in 1989. The sky is a deep indigo in the blue hour before dawn. The moon is still out, a ghostly crescent veiled behind a scrim of clouds.

Thoreau wears the same bottle-thick glasses he wears in Balsam Lake's jail cell over thirty years later. He drives a mud-spattered Jeep through the empty streets of Balsam Lake to the edge of town, and veers onto one of the backcountry roads that threads like a black vein through the forest.

Autumn leaves flutter in the early morning breeze and skitter across the road ahead. The branches of the giant trees on each side of the road form a tunnel of golds and reds through which the Jeep passes until it arrives at the pull-off for a remote trailhead.

Thoreau rumbles the 4x4 to a stop and throws it into park. He gets out but leaves the keys in the ignition. He's not coming back for it.

With a heavy backpack strapped to his shoulders, he peers into the dark depths of the misty forest sprawling out before him. He hesitates for a moment, looking back over his shoulder at the safety and familiarity of the road behind him. But the magnetic allure of the forest is too strong. Before he knows it, he is stepping off the road and into the mist.

The trees seem to close in around him as he walks, their branches reaching out like fingers trying to hold him back. The mist swirls around his feet, making it difficult to see more than a few feet ahead. But he presses on, drawn by an unseen force he can't explain. The air is cool and damp, the ground soft and spongy under his feet. He can hear the rustle of leaves and the whisper of the wind, but no other sound breaks the silence.

Gravel and pine needles crunch beneath Thoreau's hiking boots as he veers off the trail and pushes into the seemingly impenetrable wilderness. Fallen timber, moss, and foliage cover the forest floor as he vanishes into the unexplored forest. Despite his misgivings, Thoreau feels a sense of excitement and wonder growing inside him. He has no idea what he will find in the misty forest, but he knows it will be something special.

As he walks deeper into the trees, he feels a sense of peace and solitude wash over him. He is completely alone in this dark and foreboding place, but for some reason, he doesn't feel afraid. He doesn't know where he is going, but feels like he is exactly where he is meant to be.

Thoreau is too captivated by the thrilling freedom of his aimless wandering to notice the smoldering clouds rolling across the sky. A storm is brewing. Before long, howling winds whip through the forest and the heavens open up.

Thoreau huddles under the green canopy of a giant pine, trying to stay dry as the rain pounds down on the boughs above him. He knows he should have checked the weather forecast before setting out, but he had been so focused on the exhilaration of leaving his life behind that he hadn't stopped to consider the potential for bad weather. He sinks deeper under the cover of the tree and wraps himself in his ragged rain coat.

The punishing downpour is relentless, and as the rain continued to fall, Thoreau realizes he has to find some kind of shelter. He can't stay huddled under the tree all night, and he can't risk getting hypothermia in the cold, wet conditions. He glances around, trying to get his bearings. He has no map and no compass—these things are only for people with a destination, and Thoreau's only intent is to be lost. Now, he can't even see more than a few feet in front of him, the rain and fog making it impossible to distinguish anything beyond the trees.

Despite his fear and uncertainty, Thoreau has to keep moving. He can't just sit there and wait for the storm to pass. So, with a deep breath, he pushes himself to his feet and searches for shelter.

He walks for what feels like hours, his feet soaked and his clothes clinging to his skin. Giant boulders loom like hulking monsters in the rain as he roams the woods. He squeezes through a tight maze of truck-sized rocks and scrambles up a slick ridge onto even ground.

A dark canopy of massive balsams blocks out the rain in a small grove. They're woven so tightly together, it would be impossible to locate this spot from overhead. It's a needle in a haystack, a secret refuge hidden from the rest of the world.

Thoreau stands beneath the shelter and drops his pack, relief flooding through him. He collapses among the dirt and pine needles, his breathing ragged and his heart racing, grateful to have finally found this sanctuary.

This is home.

Thoreau loses track of the days as, slowly but surely, he teaches himself the art of survival. There are times when he is lost in the dense forest, unsure of which direction to take. There are times when he is bitten by poisonous insects, and attacked by wild animals. And there are times when he goes days without a meal, his stomach constricting painfully with hunger.

He learns to forage for berries, and experiments with different ways to trap and fish—trying and failing and trying again. He snares a rabbit or two, and nets the occasional perch or bass at the base of the giant cliff known as Witch's Rock. But nothing ever yields enough food to sustain him. It's as if the wilderness is determined to see him wither and fail. One rainy morning in late-October, he trudges from the forest to a backcountry road where he finds a meal to satisfy his starving body—a roadkill partridge.

He knows he can't go on like this. Winter is coming, and with it, the icy winds and snow that will make it nearly impossible for him to leave his hidden refuge. He'll never survive if he doesn't find some way to get more food.

As the days grew shorter and the nights colder, Thoreau can't shake the feeling of dread that settles over him like a heavy cloak. The forest floor is a carpet of fallen leaves mixed with a dusting of snow. Thoreau's breath blooms white in the air as he wanders through the forest. The winds are picking up, and the tree branches bend and sway, as if trying to escape the icy grip of the season.

Desperation has pushed Thoreau to explore further and further from his camp, and now he's the farthest he's been in weeks—a few miles, at least. He claps his hands together for warmth and huddles in his thin rain jacket. It's way too inadequate for this sort of cold.

A man's voice suddenly cuts through the forest. Faint. Indecipherable.

Spooked, Thoreau crouches low and assesses the situation. He scans the surrounding woods and perks his ears.

Another voice. Female. Are they arguing?

Instead of fleeing, curiosity takes over. Thoreau hasn't seen or heard another person in three months. He creeps forward and pushes through the underbrush until he spies a charming lake house. He hides in the shadows, watching unseen as a young couple gets into a luxury SUV in the driveway. Thoreau doesn't know it, but it's Wade Ramsay, and he has just purchased the property that he'll eventually tear down to erect his modern eyesore. The woman is his first wife, one of many that he will trade in for younger models over the years.

"Don't backtalk me, Hailey!" Wade growls. "Get your skinny ass in the truck and shut your goddamn mouth."

Doors slam. The truck revs to life and speeds off.

Thoreau focuses on the lake house. Empty. Unprotected.

It's surprisingly easy to get inside.

Thoreau gluts himself ravenously. He guzzles margarita mix. Gorges on Twinkies and cupcakes. Chugs a bottle of peach schnapps. Polishes off a bag of cookies. Peels the foil from a stick of butter and takes a bite.

An hour later, he treks back through the forest, huddled in the warmth of Wade Ramsay's bulky new winter parka.

The heavy weight of a large propane tank dangles from his hand.

Back in the safe confines of his camp, Thoreau opens the gas line on a stolen Coleman stove. It ignites. He warms his hands over the flame and dumps the contents of a new duffle bag. It's all food. Winter has arrived, and Thoreau knows he will have to fatten-up to survive. He'll have to steal all he can.

So he does. And a local legend is born.

* * *

Thoreau opened his eyes and found Megan gazing at him from across the cell. She waited for him to go on, but got only silence.

"Why did you go into the woods?" she asked. As she had listened to his tale, she couldn't help but feel a sense of sympathy for the man. Despite his reputation as a notorious thief, he seemed kind and gentle, and Megan could only wonder what had led him down a path of isolation.

Thoreau's expression remained vacant, as if he was lost somewhere in his own thoughts. Megan sensed their window of dialogue was closing. These were likely the most words the man had uttered in decades. The strain of conversation seemed to drain him of energy. If she had any chance of gleaning any insights into Piper Flynn's disappearance, it would have to be now.

"Mr. Thoreau, I want to ask you about a little girl who went missing the night you were arrested."

Did something flicker in Thoreau's bouncing eyes? A spark of recognition? Megan couldn't be sure. His gaze was too restless to read.

"Her name is Piper," she went on. "She's ten-years-old, and she's been alone out there in the wilderness for almost forty-eight hours. Do you have any idea where she might be?"

Thoreau kept his stare averted. "I'd like to be alone now."

Damn...

Megan deflated with disappointment, but she knew when to quit. She retrieved her phone and headed for the door, where she knocked and waited for Noah to return.

"*He* has her." Thoreau suddenly blurted.

Megan spun around and stared at him. "Who? Who has her?"

For the first time since she had entered his cell, Thoreau looked her in the eyes, his gaze cold and unreadable. "Do you believe in ghosts?"

Chapter 12

An icy tingle crawled like a spider up Megan's spine to the base of her skull. "What do you mean, Mr. Thoreau? What ghosts are you talking about?"

Thoreau's intense gaze stayed locked on hers, piercing right through her. For a fleeting moment, she finally saw a glimmer of emotion behind his eyes—fear. The chilling expression on his face made Megan shudder.

And then the connection was broken. Thoreau turned his back on her and curled up on his bunk, his face toward the wall.

Megan's muscles clenched with frustration. "Thoreau, you have to tell me what you know. *Who* has Piper? Is she safe?"

It was no use. Thoreau had gone silent.

Megan fought the urge to march across the cell and yank the man to his feet to force him to speak. She couldn't believe that this man, the one person who could help save a young girl's life before it was too late, was refusing to talk.

There was a clink of metal scraping against metal, and the cell door swung open. Noah wore a look of concern as he stood waiting in the open space, drawn by the sound of Megan's raised voice.

Megan's blood still simmered as she marched from the station to her pickup. The morning fog had started to lift, but airy wisps still floated through the streets. Megan inhaled the crisp air deep into her lungs and forced herself to calm down. After a couple more breaths, she realized Thoreau's words could have been meaningless. He'd been talking about ghosts, for God's sake. There was a very good chance his sanity wasn't intact after thirty years of isolation.

Still, if he knew anything about Piper Flynn's whereabouts…

Megan decided she needed a drink or the familiar solitude of the forest to quiet her thoughts. She decided on the more productive of the two options and opened the truck's tailgate to do a quick check of the backpack she kept stashed there.

Sam's SUV rumbled to a stop a few parking spots over. He got out and ambled over. "You done with him already?"

Megan nodded and slammed the door. "He's done talking."

"You get anything useful out of him?"

"I think he might know something." Megan didn't see any point in mentioning what Thoreau had said about ghosts. "He said somebody else has Piper, but he won't say who. I got the impression he wanted to say more, but it's gonna take some time to build that kind of trust."

"Time's not something we have a lot of right now."

"Feel free to take over if you think it'll be quicker," Megan snapped.

Sam picked up on her irritation and let it drop. "We gotta talk." He made a motion with his head back toward the station.

The thought of going back inside made Megan's skin itch. "I'm starving," she said, and opened her truck's door. "Follow me to Brenda's."

* * *

Megan had never seen Brenda's Diner so deserted. The whole town seemed to have joined the search for Piper Flynn. Except for Ol' Rory, a grizzled local who never seemed to leave his stool at the long formica counter, Megan and Sam had the place to themselves. It was so strangely quiet, Megan could actually hear Brenda's radio playing through a pair of tinny speakers. The diner was usually so bustling and noisy that she'd never even noticed the music before.

Brenda appeared from the kitchen as they sat across from each other in a booth by the window. A plump woman with huge round glasses and a smile that tickled the corners of her eyes, she had been waiting tables and cooking at the diner for well over fifty of her seventy-six years. She woke up every morning at four to take the curlers out of her hair, apply a tasteful amount of makeup, and shimmy into her uniform— pink with mint green collar, cuffs, and apron.

Brenda didn't bother bringing them menus, and she had no need of the pad and pen she kept tucked in her apron; they both always ordered the same things. Megan asked for a club sandwich and Sam took the full breakfast, despite the fact that it was well past noon.

"What about your father's murder? Anything?" Sam asked, while Brenda headed back to the kitchen.

"I didn't bother getting into it yet," Megan replied. "My dad's been dead for over a decade. A couple more days won't make a difference."

Sam sighed with frustration. "It's already been two days and we've still got nothing. I can't stall forever. We've got forty-eight hours. On Monday, I'm gonna have to release him or transfer him over to the state boys to be formally charged."

"I'm doing my best," Megan grumbled testily. "You see what he's like."

"What you're doing's not working. Maybe it's time we tried a different approach."

Megan glared back at him. "Go ahead. See how far you get with him."

Sam's jaw muscles bunched as he bit back an impatient remark. "So, what do you make of him?"

Megan thought it over. "I don't know. He doesn't have a clue where our world begins or ends."

"What I want to know is why he went out into the woods in the first place," Sam said. "What would drive a guy to do something like that? To leave everything behind and live in total isolation for over thirty years."

"He's not the first," said Megan. "History is filled with people who've simply dropped out of society. The real world —the one you and I live in—it's a hard one. Filled with teeth and claws. Is Thoreau really so crazy for walking away from it?"

"Just like that kid in *Into the Wild*?"

Megan arched an eyebrow. "You read that?"

"Saw the movie."

"Great soundtrack."

"So Thoreau can't relate to people," Sam went on. "Turned his back on society altogether. How far would someone like that go to protect his privacy? To keep his anonymity?"

"What are you getting at?"

"If someone discovered him out there, would he kill to keep his hideout a secret?"

Megan shrugged. "I don't know. But I have a hard time thinking he could kill someone. He's too fragile, too damaged."

"Maybe that's what he wants you to think. Crazy as a fox and all that shit." Sam gave her a knowing look. "We released his photo to the public. No leads yet on who he might be."

"I still can't figure out why he chose to speak to me," Megan said.

"He's been living out there like a wild animal for thirty years. If anyone can understand him, it's you. It's what you do day-in and day-out. Maybe he senses that about you, a kindred spirit with an insight into how he thinks."

Megan chewed her lip and didn't respond.

"We're going to see if he'll consent to a psych evaluation this afternoon," Sam said. "Why don't you have another go at him afterward?"

Megan shook her head. "I'm heading out to White Lily Pond. Still got a day job to do."

Sam frowned. "What's so important out there?"

"Following up on a hunch."

"A hunch?"

"Some asshole's trying to trap the wolves. My guess is Wade Ramsay."

"Well shit, that's a helluva lot more pressing than our little serial killer investigation." Sam couldn't resist the sarcasm.

Megan gave him an irritated look. "There hasn't been a wolf in these mountains in over a century. You know what happens when natural predators disappear from an eco-system?"

Sam shrugged his indifference.

"Without natural predators, the white-tail deer population explodes. All those cute little Bambies need to eat. The forest composition changes as sugar maple and yellow birch saplings disappear. Canopy and sub-canopy dominance are compromised. Plants like ferns and trilliums are unlikely to recolonize. Without undergrowth shrubs to shelter in, songbird populations decrease while parasitic insect numbers rise. The dominoes continue to fall until the entire fucking eco-system collapses."

Sam whistled and sat back in his seat, impressed in spite of himself. "They taught you a lot at UMass."

"Yeah. So now that wolves have somehow started to repopulate naturally, I'd prefer if Wade Ramsay would stop trying to trap them in my backyard." Megan frowned. "Besides, with Piper Flynn somewhere out there by herself, we'd better find the pack before they find her."

Brenda returned with their orders. They ate in silence until Megan glanced over at the short stack of file folders Sam had deposited at the end of the table, next to the hot sauce and the salt and pepper shakers.

"What're those?" she asked.

"Missing persons reports since we started keeping track in '71," Sam replied between mouthfuls of bacon. "I pulled 'em out this morning to brush up on the details." He reached for the first folder and flipped open the cover. "The first recorded case was Timothy Wright, the ten-year-old grandson of Grayson Wright."

"The timber baron," Megan said.

"You got it. One of the wealthiest industrialists to ever exploit these forests. On the morning of July 8, 1980, Timothy left the family's summer Great Camp to play in the woods and never returned. The Wrights had been vacationing there for twenty years and Timothy was known as a mini woodsman. With the temperature dropping, state police and locals from town searched throughout the night, but found nothing. The next morning, DEC Rangers joined the search with their dogs. The Air Force base in Plattsburgh even sent planes with heat-detecting infra-red. Nearly a thousand volunteers scoured the woods for miles around the Wright Great Camp, but there was no trace of Timothy. Six weeks later, the state police called off the search. It wasn't long after that the Wright family abandoned their Great Camp and never returned."

"Timothy was ten when he went missing?"

Sam nodded. "The same age as Piper Flynn."

"But that happened in 1980. Thoreau only went into the woods in '89."

"So he says. We have no idea who he is or even how old."

Sam tossed the folder onto the vinyl seat next to him and grabbed the next one from the stack. "Ten years later—one year *after* Thoreau says he went into the woods—a local hunter named Charlie Dix heads out the first week of November in search of a big-game buck. He never returns. Charlie's a heavy guy in his mid-fifties, so the suspicion is he died of a heart attack while backpacking over the rugged terrain with heavy gear. But his body is never found, despite the fact that he was known to hunt the same area year after year."

Sam reached for the next folder. "In 1996, Neil and Amanda Bailey, a married couple from Chestertown, sign in at the Panther Mountain trailhead for an overnight hike of the Seward Range. They're never seen again. It's their first night away from their two-year-old boy, and they've left him at home with his grandparents for the weekend."

"In other words, they had everything to live for," Megan said. Like anyone else who had grown up in Balsam Lake, she knew all about the people who had gone missing over the years. But now that Sam was laying all the details of each case out for her, it was hard to argue there wasn't something sinister at work.

Sam nodded and took another folder. "Things are quiet around here for almost ten years. Then, in 2003, twenty-three-year-old college student Avery Burke goes missing while solo hiking to Raquette Falls along the East River Trail. It's her Spring Break from Syracuse and she's only a few months away from graduating."

Sam didn't bother opening the next folder in his hands. They both knew what it contained. "July 4, 2010. Local man Graham Danforth vanishes while fishing with his thirteen-year-old daughter, Megan." He gave Megan a sideways look, but her expression remained stony, her gaze focused on her plate.

Sam added the folder to the others next to him on the bench and reached for the next one. "And finally, sixteen-year-old Ethan Berry's car is found abandoned at the Corey's trailhead on October 28, 2017. He has a history of mental health issues, including severe depression. His family still believes he went into the woods to kill himself, but his body has never been recovered."

Megan wiped her mouth with her napkin and nodded at the last folder remaining on the table. "What about that one?"

"This one's for Piper Flynn." Sam flipped open the cover to show her it was empty. "This morning, I promised Becky Flynn we'd make damn sure it stays this way."

Chapter 13

The lake sparkled with the golden embers of the setting sun. Megan stood at the railing of her back porch and watched the placid water turn a molten red as the great fiery orb sank ever deeper behind the distant peaks. The mountains on the other side of the lake seemed to go on forever, their rugged peaks etched against the orange and pink hues spreading across the sky.

Megan closed her eyes, letting the cool evening breeze wash over her. She could hear the gentle lapping of the water against the shore and the chirping of the birds as they settled in for the night.

Do you believe in ghosts?

Thoreau's cryptic words echoed in Megan's mind. What did he mean? She couldn't help thinking of that chilling sensation that had come over her the last time she'd hiked the White Lily Pond trail, that dreadful feeling of being watched by something dark and predatory. She thought of the people who had vanished without a trace over the course of forty years.

And yet, Megan still doubted Thoreau was capable of murder. After all, he'd offered no resistance when Hank Morrison had cornered him, and he was nearly twice Hank's size.

But what if there was something *else* out there? Something so malevolent it had darkened nature itself in her presence?

And what if it had taken Piper Flynn?

Megan knew it didn't make sense, but she couldn't shake the feeling that something was wrong with those woods. The disturbing possibility led to another. Could something have followed her home from that place? Some unseen *thing* that latched on to her and left the painful memento of the fishing lure on her doorstep? It sounded insane, even to herself, but Megan could think of no other explanation. She had always been a skeptic, never believing in the supernatural. But now, she remembered the local legends her aunt used to tell her about ghosts and otherworldly creatures that roamed the woods and valleys. For the first time, a crack formed in Megan's disbelief.

The same disturbing thoughts kept swirling around her head until a man's shout grabbed her attention and jolted her back from her contemplations.

Russ had rounded the point and was paddling toward her in a canoe. "Hey! I gotta take a dump! Can I use your can?"

Megan frowned as he leapt ashore and hauled the canoe up onto the bank. His face was pinched as he clambered up the steps to the porch.

"Upstairs," Megan said.

"I brought beer." Russ deposited a couple of four-packs of tall cans on the apple crate next to her before disappearing inside.

When he re-emerged a few minutes later, Megan was lugging her backpack to her pickup.

"Whew! Thanks and apologies. Do *not* have Brenda's famous burrito before heading out on the lake." Russ was still wringing his wet hands when he noticed the gouges ripped across Megan's back door. "What the hell happened there? A wolverine try to get in or something?"

For an instant, Megan considered telling him about what had happened in the middle of the night. But she decided her father was a subject she didn't want to bring up. "There aren't any wolverines in the Adirondacks. Must've been raccoons."

"Raccoons, huh?" Russ gave the door a skeptical look.

Megan glanced at his canoe, still beached on the shore, and changed the subject. "Do you even own a car?"

"In this town, if I can't get to it by boat, it ain't worth visiting—as evidenced by this evening's ill-fated foray to the diner." He grinned and nodded at the pack slung over Megan's shoulder. "You heading out?"

Megan nodded and shut the tailgate. "White Lily Pond."

Russ retrieved the packs of beer from the apple crate. They were from one of the many craft breweries that had popped up in the region. "Care for some witty conversation and the company of one helluva fine looking guy?"

A refusal sprang into Megan's mouth. But after her experience in the woods the previous day, and the unexplainable events of last night, the thought of being alone after dark gave her a shiver. She opened the passenger door.

The warm glow of the sunset lit their faces through the pickup's windshield while Megan drove. The melancholy melody of an old Neil Young song played on the stereo.

"Spent the day with the search party up near Stag Rock Falls," Russ said. "No point keeping the bait shop open with everyone out looking for Piper Flynn. Figured I'd take your advice and see some of this fine wilderness I've been missing."

"Any news?" Megan asked, though she already knew the answer.

Russ's expression darkened. "Nothing yet. I've got a bad feeling that poor girl is going to be spending another night out there by herself." He looked at Megan. "How long do you think she can last?"

"There's plenty of water to drink out there, and a healthy girl like her can probably go at least two weeks without food. But it's the cold I'm worried about. Without a shelter and some way to make a fire…"

They went quiet a moment, the music filling the silence of the cab. Megan turned onto the access road that twisted through the woods toward the trailhead. The Ford bounced over the deep ruts of the muddy backcountry track, rocking her and Russ from side-to-side in their seats.

"Hey, I got partnered-up with Tad Eames for the search," Russ said. "Guy's a walking history book on this area. Did you know an entire logging village fled in the middle of the night during the War of 1812? Left everything behind 'cause they thought the place was cursed after a bunch of villagers killed themselves for no apparent reason." Russ gazed out the window at the dense wall of trees crowding the dirt road on either side. "Makes you wonder, huh? All these miles of trees and mountains? What's happened out there that we don't know about?"

Megan said nothing as she pulled into the trailhead. The conversation was too much of an eerie echo of her own thoughts.

The sun had dropped below the horizon and lit the undersides of the clouds with crimson radiance when Megan and Russ started down the overgrown trail. Pinesap and decaying leaves were redolent in the crisp evening air.

"You ever hear of the Aokigahara Forest?" Russ asked, looking around at the shadows gathering among the trees.

"That woods in Japan where people go to kill themselves?"

Russ nodded. "On the side of Mount Fuji. Hundreds have committed suicide there over the years. They say it's cursed, that there's something evil lurking in that sea of trees. But what if it's the other way around? What if that forest somehow absorbed the suffering of those who died there and grew *into* something evil?"

Russ brought his attention back to Megan. "Speaking of mythical beings… word is, you've been visiting ol' Spooky."

Megan shot him a look.

"No secret's safe in Balsam Lake," he grinned.

"You'd be surprised," Megan muttered.

"Well, not out with the search party. Locals around here gossip more than old ladies with hemorrhoids." Russ chuckled. "Did he talk to you?"

"In pieces." Megan told him about Thoreau's vacant expression and strange mannerisms, his aversion to eye-contact, his flat and monotone way of speaking, his apparent inability to interpret the nonverbal communication of her facial expressions.

"Sounds to me like some kind of autism," Russ remarked.

Megan glanced at him from the corner of her eye.

"I taught elementary school before moving out here," he explained. "Had to take training to work with kids with special needs."

"Why'd you quit teaching?" Megan asked.

An unexpected shadow crept across Russ's bearded face. He looked Megan in the eyes and gave her a tight smile that told her the subject was one he didn't want to talk about.

Megan didn't push it. So he had painful secrets of his own.

"Thoreau must've been living close to town to have robbed so many places," Russ said. "How hard can it be to find his campsite?"

"Thirty years hard."

"You think he's dangerous?"

Megan shrugged. "Hayden seems to think so."

"What's Hayden's deal, anyway? Sounds to me like he's treating Thoreau like he's the Unabomber or something. All he did was steal some shit to survive. It's not like he trashed the places. Most of the time, nobody even knew he'd been there until months later."

Megan frowned. "It's more complicated than that."

"How?"

"It's a small town. The smaller the town, the bigger the secrets."

"Please enlighten."

"Sam's father was the police chief here twenty years ago. There was a scandal involving a woman he picked up for DUI. She accused Sam's dad of sexually assaulting her late one night while she was in his custody. Sam's old man denied it, of course, but he didn't know his deputy had brought my father in for drunk and disorderly earlier that evening. My dad said he heard the whole thing from his jail cell. The state police got involved and my dad was gonna testify against the chief, but when he disappeared, they dropped the charges for lack of evidence. Naturally, everyone suspected Hayden killed my dad to shut him up. He spent the rest of his days in disgrace, swearing he had nothing to do with it, until he shot himself ten years ago."

Russ whistled.

"Now that Thoreau's been caught, I'm guessing Sam sees him as another plausible suspect," Megan explained. "If he can prove Thoreau killed my dad, he'd finally be able to clear his own father's name."

"You think he might be right?" Russ asked.

"I don't know."

"Whew… and I thought my hometown was fucked up."

"Where are you from, anyway?"

"South Side Chicago."

Megan couldn't stifle her laugh.

The trail broke away from the forest as it skirted around the long oval of the pond. It was getting darker now. Megan pulled a headlamp from her pack and handed another to Russ. Their beams lit the way until Megan drew to an unexpected halt. Her light revealed a huge print stamped on the muddy shore.

"That's twenty minutes old," she murmured. She touched the print.

"Deer?" Russ asked.

Megan nodded and looked around. "We'll wait here."

"Wait for what?"

"Just sit."

They hunkered on a fallen log on the bank of the marsh. Russ handed Megan one of the beers he'd brought along and watched as she took her first sip. "Good?"

"Just what I needed."

Megan gulped another mouthful while Russ cracked open a can for himself. The citrusy scent of fresh hops filled his nose as he took his first sip. They drank their beers and peered up at the millions of stars in the treeless sky above. Before long, Megan drained her can and reached for another.

"That's a double IPA," Russ cautioned. He'd barely started his own can. "It's got about twice the alcohol as a regular beer."

"Perfect," said Megan. These days, she'd drink anything with enough alcohol to keep her from confronting her memories. She filled her cheeks with another gulp.

They sat in silence, drinking their beers, while a cool breeze whispered through the forest around them.

"You asked why I quit teaching," Russ said unexpectedly, his tone suddenly somber. "One of my students was shot and killed on her way home from school. She was twelve." He took a long sip and swallowed. "Her older brother had come to pick her up, and that was the day his rival gang set out to get him. They didn't care that his little sister was there with him."

Megan didn't know what to say. "That's awful," she murmured and instantly regretted how trite it sounded.

"Her murder ripped us apart," Russ went on. "I tried going back to normal, but every day when I walked into the classroom, I didn't see vibrant little kids anymore; I saw walking corpses. It was paralyzing. How was I supposed to teach them that the world was a great and wonderful place when I didn't believe it myself? My one rule as a teacher was that my students should leave my room better than when they walked in. When I couldn't do that for them anymore, I knew it was time to walk away."

Russ took another swig and gazed across the pond, where the color was draining from the sky. "I sometimes still feel like I abandoned them. That's why I don't like to talk about it. They needed me, and I should've been stronger for them. But I just… couldn't."

This time, Megan knew she was better off saying nothing.

A bone-chilling howl echoed through the forest.

Russ froze mid-sip, his eyes growing wide as he looked at Megan. "What the hell was that?"

"Wolves," Megan murmured excitedly. She had her ears perked, listening intently. "They're hunting."

Russ cocked an eyebrow. "Wolves? Here?"

Megan nodded, her face alight. "My theory is they migrated down here from Algonquin Park in Ontario. There are a few hundred of them up there."

"That's a long way for them to go, isn't it?"

"Yeah, a couple hundred miles northwest. But we know wolves from Algonquin range to within fifty miles of the New York border. It wouldn't be unheard of if they dispersed further. Two wolves were shot in Vermont not long ago. They'd migrated south from Quebec. And these are just the ones that we know about. Wild ways still exist, and animals like wolves do like to roam."

"Okay, say they did wander down here from Canada. Why

are you so obsessed with finding them?"

Megan sipped her beer. "In 1995, scientists released fourteen wolves in Yellowstone National Park. There hadn't been a wolf there in seventy years and the deer population had destroyed the local flora."

"So the wolves ate them."

"Nope, but they forced the deer to be more careful about where they ate. They avoided sections of the park and the vegetation began to thrive. Within six years, the number of trees had increased fivefold and coastal erosion of the rivers stopped. But no one expected what happened next. Beavers reappeared to build dams. The new ponds they created became breeding grounds for ducks, muskrats, and fish. The wolves also intimidated the coyotes, which led to an increase in hares and mice."

"Which then became food for other predators?"

"Exactly. Hawks, ferrets, and foxes all returned to the park. Not to mention the bears that fed on scraps left by the wolves. Nature needs predators. It's a known fact that they increase biodiversity in an area, from coral reefs to savannahs. Yellowstone is a little over two million acres. The Adirondack Park is over six million. If wolves could have such a profound impact on the ecosystem there, imagine what their reappearance would mean here, in such a sprawling habitat. I've been trying to get the DEC to reintroduce wolves here for years, but they want to focus their resources on protecting existing species. If I can prove wolves have begun to repopulate on their own, the DEC would have no choice but to develop a recovery plan."

"So this all comes down to—"

"*Shhh...!*" Megan held a finger to her lips and pointed across the marsh. There was a deer there by the water's edge, limned in the dying twilight against the black backdrop of the forest. It was a mature buck, with a full set of antlers, thick neck, sagging belly, short legs, and a slight hump over its front shoulders.

"That one's old," Megan whispered. "Six or seven years. It's an easy target."

The buck panted heavily, its immense chest heaving as it stood rigid and alert with its head raised and ears pricked. There was danger nearby.

Without warning, there was a rustling explosion among the trees and an immense shape burst from the forest. The deer panicked and bolted as a huge gray wolf lunged for it, snarling and snapping hungrily at the buck's shoulders and flanks. Three more wolves sprang from the woods, cutting off the terrified deer's escape before it could get very far. The pack had separated and surrounded their prey, shepherding it toward the pond and trapping it between them and the water.

One of the wolves leapt for the buck's rear, its black lips peeled back from its vicious fangs. The deer swung its great head around and raked the attacker with its sharp antlers, nearly goring it. In the same instant, another wolf struck and sank its teeth deep into the buck's nose. The deer let out a strangled whimper loud enough to be heard across the pond as the wolf whipped its head savagely from side to side. Flesh ripped away and blood poured freely down the buck's face as the rest of the pack swarmed like a small mob. The buck flailed and struggled beneath them before they brought it crashing to the ground.

The fearsome brutality of their attack was shocking. Within minutes, the deer would be dead of blood-loss. One of its legs still spasmed in the throes of death while the ravenous pack dragged its bloody carcass away to be devoured in the woods.

An eerie silence fell upon the pond and forest. For long moments, Megan and Russ remained in dumbstruck silence, their hearts thundering with the intense rush of the savage violence they had just witnessed.

Megan turned to Russ and gazed into his deep blue eyes. They seemed evanescent in the twilight. Something came over her, something more than just the beer or the adrenaline shooting through her veins.

She grabbed him and kissed him, her tongue dancing with his as she pushed him down onto his back by the water's edge. She straddled him, her mouth not leaving his as she fumbled with his belt. Russ's touch was electric as he explored her body with his hands. She had let no one near her in so very long, and his fingers sent shivers of desire down her spine. She let out a soft moan, surrendering herself to the moment as the moonlight danced across the water.

Chapter 14

Thoreau huddled on his bunk in the corner of his cell with his knees up against his chest. Night had fallen, and shadows filled the station house. Noah had locked up hours ago, and the awful silence of Thoreau's cell was smothering.

This was the second night he would spend indoors in over thirty years. The first night had been unbearable. He had spent the time pacing back and forth in the small, cramped cell. He'd grown accustomed to the wide open spaces of the wilderness, the freedom to roam and explore as he pleased. Now he felt suffocated and trapped; the walls closing in around him.

If Thoreau didn't find a way to cope with his confinement, he would lose his mind. He took out his copy of *Walden*, trying to find solace in the words of his idol. But as he read and reread the familiar lines, the sense of peace and escape he so desperately craved kept eluding him.

The familiar sounds of his life in the woods were gone. There were no crickets or tree frogs or pine boughs rustling in the wind. There was only the awful silence of four cinderblock walls and Thoreau's own ragged breathing in his ears.

A crushing sense of claustrophobia coiled around Thoreau's chest and constricted his lungs. He squeezed his eyes shut and opened them again, gasping for air like a drowning man. The panic in his chest kept rising, threatening to overwhelm him. He tried to focus, drawing in deep lungfuls of air to calm his racing thoughts. But it was no use. The walls continued to press in on him, strangling him with their unyielding presence.

And then... a sound.

It was faint and distant. Almost imperceptible.

Thoreau recognized it at once.

An owl.

Thoreau rose to his feet and moved to the small barred window, pressing his face against the cold metal. All he could see was a sliver of the sky, a teasing reminder of the vast world beyond these four walls.

The hoot of the owl grew louder.

Thoreau closed his eyes and listened to the wild, letting its soothing song melt his terror. He'd grown used to solitude in his decades of isolation, but this... this was different. Out there, he had never really been alone.

He had been there with him...

* * *

A sheet of ice covers the winter landscape. Snow drifts across the frozen lake, and the sky is a grey and desolate void. Walls of icicles hang like stalactites from the edges of the giant tarps

Thoreau has strung over his camp. It's just past sunrise, and a thermometer dangling on a string reads minus four Fahrenheit.

Huddled in Wade Ramsay's stolen parka, Thoreau uses a pine branch to brush the newly fallen snow from his makeshift shelves of food. The rough-hewn planks are mostly empty now. Only a few cans of beans remain. With the lake frozen solid, he can't paddle north to the more inhabited areas to pilfer food. He's now emaciated, down to nothing, and too weak to make the long trek through the snow around the frozen shoreline.

Thoreau grabs one of the last cans of beans. He's been rationing for days and he can feel his stomach devouring itself, cannibalizing whatever calories he has left in him. Tremors shake his hands as he opens the can. The beans are frozen hard. They slide from the can in one big, frosty clump and clang against the bottom of the pot perched on Thoreau's propane camping stove. Tiny blue flames flicker and dance on the burner, but within a few minutes, they shrink. At these frigid temperatures, the liquid propane doesn't vaporize very well. Thoreau gives the tank a shake to rouse the gas and get it flowing again. The flames leap up, but they only last a moment before sputtering out.

Thoreau checks the element on the stove. Turns it on and off. The problem isn't that the propane is cold; it's that the tank is empty.

The ravenous ache in Thoreau's stomach won't be put off any longer. He looks at the beans, just starting to melt apart from each other and soften in the pot. It will take too long to heat them. Thoreau snatches the pot from the burner and slurps the beans down cold, viscous liquid and all.

With his stomach no longer holding his mind hostage, Thoreau can think again. He goes to the edge of his camp and unties a nylon cover stretched across his propane stash.

There's only one tank left.

Thoreau stares at it and does the math in his head. He's gone through two in four months and buried the empties in the forest to avoid discovery. How is this one tank supposed to last him the rest of the winter?

There's no other choice. If he wants to live, he'll have to traverse the frozen lake.

A gentle dusting of snow continues to fall by the time Thoreau stands at the seam where the forest meets the ice. He surveys the barren landscape. If he had a radio, he'd know the snowflakes are the beginning of a savage Nor'easter headed his way, the kind that dumps almost two feet of snow into the mountains and knocks out power for miles.

But Thoreau doesn't know it as he stares across the ice toward the trees on the distant shore. His only concern now is getting across and finding more propane to keep his monstrous hunger from consuming him. He's got a big pickaxe in his gloved hands. It's not a proper ice axe like he read about in those mountaineering books he devoured as a kid, but it's the best he's got. With any luck, it just might keep him alive.

Thoreau takes his first tentative steps onto the ice. He's watched the lake slowly freeze over with each passing day, but it's still early in the season and he doesn't know how thick the ice is out where the water is deepest. He moves slowly, one foot inching forward after the other. The ice emits a hollow *thud* as he tests it with the butt of the pickaxe to ensure it will bear his weight. The wind rages unimpeded here, and spindrifts of snow lash at Thoreau's face.

He looks back over his shoulder. He's a long way from solid land now. The merciless wind is already eroding his tracks behind him. There's no chance they'll lead anyone back to his camp.

A sharp, thunderous *CRACK!* resonates across the width of the lake.

Thoreau feels the surface shudder beneath his feet. He freezes where he stands and grips the pickaxe, keeping his weight distributed evenly between both boots. He has to leave the ice. *Now!*

Slowly, carefully, he inches back toward the safety of the shoreline.

CRAAACK!!!

The ice collapses beneath him.

Thoreau plunges into the frigid lake. The water steals the breath from his lungs and stabs like needles into his flesh. It fills his mouth, and it feels like his throat is being packed with ice. He flings a hand upward through the churning water as visions of being trapped beneath the ice and suffocating flash through his mind. His fingers graze the edge of the broken ice shelf, and he grips hard to keep from going under. But the unbearable cold is stripping him of his strength. His muscles cramp so painfully it's as if they're being twisted in a vice. The soaked goose down of his heavy parka feels like he's got the weight of a bear on his back, dragging him downward.

Thoreau sputters for air as he struggles. He swings the pickaxe over his head, intent on driving the spiked end into the ice.

No luck. It rebounds off with a spray of ice shards.

Submerged from the waist down, Thoreau kicks and thrashes his legs below the surface. It won't be long before he's hypothermic. If he doesn't find some way of dragging himself from the water, his nervous system will give out and he'll sink down, down, down into the icy depths.

Thoreau wields the pickaxe again, harder this time, putting all of his remaining strength into it. The spike digs into the ice and anchors deep.

Thoreau grips the handle with both hands. If the spike breaks free of the ice, there will be nothing to keep him from plunging back under water. Cramps torture his muscles as he slowly hauls himself from the freezing water onto the ice.

The winter storm is merciless. Snow piles up quickly as Thoreau trudges back to his camp. He prays for the strength to keep putting one foot in front of the other as the cold bites into his bones. He's exhausted and trembling violently by the time he finally makes it. The blizzard engulfs his refuge; the snow assaulting it inside and out.

Thoreau's teeth chatter in his mouth as he crawls into the tent. Drenched and shivering, he closes the flaps and zips them shut. The canvas walls shudder and shake from the pummeling. With frozen fingers, he struggles to untie his laces. Eventually, he manages to wriggle his boots off. He removes his socks.

His feet are purple.

Thoreau squeezes his toes with his fingers. He flicks them and pinches them, but they've gone numb. Is this permanent? Oh God, does he have frostbite?

Still shivering all over, Thoreau slips into a pair of thermal underwear and wraps a blanket around himself. He's desperate to get warm.

Outside, the storm howls like a ravenous predator as night sets in.

Thoreau rolls onto his side on his cot, defeated. For the first time since he walked into the woods almost four months ago, he regrets what he has done. He knows he should try to stay strong, to remain focused on the task of survival. But as the blizzard rages outside, he can't help but feel a sense of despair wash over him.

Winter was always going to be a time of hardship, a time to be endured rather than enjoyed. But this? This feels like an insurmountable challenge, and Thoreau knows he no longer has the will to survive it. He wishes he were some place indoors and warm, not out here, alone and shivering in this brutal cold. He's going to die here. Tonight. Even now, he can hear Death's beckoning whisper in his ear. It sends frost into his heart. He's so terribly lonely, and so very, very afraid.

A voice reaches into the tent for him.

Thoreau's eyes snap open and his heart leaps into his throat. It's impossible. Nothing can cut through the incessant roar of that winter wind.

But Thoreau is certain he heard it.

Someone is out there in his camp.

Or at least, that's what Thoreau thinks it is. He can't be sure; his tortured mind and body are betraying him. Death is already taking him apart piece by piece. Fear tightens its tentacles around Thoreau's chest and makes it even harder to breathe. He remains very still, listening for the voice in the wind.

There it is again.

A hissing whisper coming from the other side of the tent.

Closer.

Thoreau's head whips around. The hairs rise on the back of his neck. Whatever is out there is approaching the tent. He can feel its presence out there in the storm. He keeps his eyes fixed on the eerie sound. The wind screams and howls like a freight train derailing. Thoreau's heart slams against his ribs as he waits and waits. He struggles against the dread that comes with knowing he's too weak to defend himself if he needs to.

Very slowly, the canvas wall of the tent begins to distort. Vague shapes materialize on the surface: five ghostly impressions that turn into fingers.

A hand is pressing into the fabric from the outside.

Terror sweeps over Thoreau and sends him recoiling across the tent.

Another hand bulges through the canvas.

Still trembling with cold, Thoreau scrambles up against the door. The pain in his chest is too much to withstand. He fumbles with the zipper, his hand shaking so badly he can hardly get a grip on it. Finally, he spills out into the teeth of the raging blizzard.

The wind is so strong it almost knocks him off his feet. Swirling snow and ice blow into his face and sting his eyes. He has to squint to see as he creeps through the darkness, inspecting his camp for the intruder.

There's no one there.

The bitter cold bites deep into Thoreau's flesh. His chattering teeth are like tiny pile-drivers in his head. If he stays out here much longer, he'll collapse with hypothermia. Intruder or not, he has to get back beneath the blankets in his shelter before it's too late. He turns around.

There's a fresh trail of footprints in the snow. They're too small to be his.

And they lead into his tent.

Pinpricks of fright shoot down Thoreau's spine. He stares at the tent, and it occurs to him that he's been lured outside. The open flaps whip in the wind, the zipper jingling maddeningly. He doesn't want to know what's waiting for him in there. But he doesn't have a choice.

Thoreau's frozen fingers tremble as he slowly reaches for the flap. His nerve almost fails him, but the agony of the cold gnawing at his bones pushes him on. He brushes the flap aside and peers inside.

A scream rises in his throat, and his heart constricts painfully.

The face of a young boy stares back at him.

A boy he watched die years ago.

Chapter 15

The whirling helicopter blades chopped through the air high above the vast expanse of the Adirondacks. Sam sat in the rear of the state police Bell 407, behind Sergeant Greg Barnard and their pilot, Trooper Andre Slade. They were heading south, away from Adirondack Regional Airport in Saranac Lake, where Sam had met Barnard and Slade early that morning for takeoff. The brown, gold, and green forests of the Adirondacks rolled out beneath them. To the east stood New York's highest mountain, Mt. Marcy, rising like a fang at the end of the long chain of peaks known as the Great Range. Further in the distance, the slate-gray expanse of Lake Champlain separated New York from Vermont.

"We're making our way over the High Peaks Wilderness territory." Barnard's voice crackled through Sam's headset. "Lots of dense forest. Low visibility. No trace of the girl so far."

Barnard was a burly man in his mid-fifties, with close-cropped gray hair, soft hazel eyes, and a shave so close to the skin his cheeks gleamed.

"What are we hoping to see up here?" Sam asked through his headset microphone.

"Smoke. Any indication the girl might be trying to signal us. If she's down there, just hearing the helicopter and knowing that we're out here looking for her could be enough to keep her hanging on until we find her."

Sam nodded and turned his attention back out the window. As far as he was concerned, this whole ride-along was a waste of his time. The state police search and rescue team was perfectly fine without him, and he sensed they resented his presence as much as he disliked being there. His time was far better spent back in Balsam Lake, where he could help coordinate the ground search along with the forest rangers. Sam had told Mayor Hough as much, but Hough had insisted he accompany the state police as a liaison. Sam interpreted that to mean it was to keep up appearances with the locals more than anything.

Since cajoling his way into the position of president of the village board, Wade Ramsay had made it his mission to see Balsam Lake's local police force disbanded in favor of outsourcing law enforcement to the state police barracks in Ray Brook. Not that Ramsay had any real personal enmity for Sam; just a deep-seated, self-serving desire to cut his own tax bill. But Sam just couldn't bear to see the old station house shuttered. It wasn't just for the sake of his job; it was the long list of unsolved mysteries that would be filed away as cold cases and forgotten once the local force was gone. No one at the state police would care as much about the decades-old missing persons cases as Sam did. As far as he was concerned, Balsam Lake's police had unfinished business, and he was determined to see it ended with himself.

With the helicopter's rotors roaring overhead and nothing but endless miles of trees and rocks beneath him, Sam slipped his phone from his pocket and popped a couple of earbuds into his ears beneath his headset.

On his way up to Saranac early that morning, he'd received an email from Dr. Diana Rose, the state-appointed psychiatrist who had attempted to evaluate Thoreau the previous afternoon. She had attached a video of the interview, and Sam had downloaded it before takeoff. The whole clip was just under half an hour. Now, Sam hit *Play* and kept the volume low enough to still hear Barnard through his headset if he needed to.

In the video, Dr. Rose sat across the table from Thoreau in the station's interrogation room. Rose was an efficacious woman in her late-fifties. Her hair was a gleaming silver, and she wore it twisted into a bun without a strand out of place. She wore a stylish pant-suit that she accessorized with a colorful scarf draped around her neck. Sam cringed at the sight of it, recognizing the scarf for the strangulation hazard it was. He'd have to talk to Noah about being more vigilant.

The first few minutes of the video consisted of Dr. Rose attempting to coax Thoreau into talking. From the looks of things, she had never encountered a patient quite like him. She tried her best to keep her voice soft and sincere and naturally calming, but Thoreau resisted whatever she threw at him.

Sam scrubbed through the video until it looked like there was some kind of breakthrough.

"People used to tell you that you're impolite. Agree or

disagree?" Rose asked.

Thoreau didn't answer.

"Mr. Thoreau, you need to understand that I'm no threat to you. My only purpose here is to help you, to listen to you. You don't even need to speak. You can simply tap with your right hand for yes and left hand for no. Can you do that?"

Thoreau's gaze rose and focused on a spot just to the side of the psychiatrist's face. She interpreted the gesture to be a silent affirmative.

"You prefer to do things the same way over and over," she stated.

Thoreau's right hand tapped. *Yes.*

"You often notice small sounds others don't."

Right hand tapped.

"You usually notice license plate numbers or similar strings of information."

Right hand tapped.

"You know how to tell if someone listening to you is getting bored."

Thoreau hesitated. He had to think about the question.

Dr. Rose moved on.

"In school, they designated you for special education. Agree or disagree?"

Right hand tapped.

"When you were young, you used to enjoy playing games with other children."

Three hard taps with his left hand. *NO! NO! NO!*

"Your parents treated your siblings differently than you."

Thoreau squeezed his fists anxiously.

"You had a good relationship with your father."

A switch flipped in Thoreau. He went cold.

Rose caught on and followed up. "Your father had a bad temper."

Thoreau squirmed.

"You have an irrational fear of authority."

He looked at Rose without expression. It was no use.

"Okay, let's move on to something else," she said. She slid a sheet of multiple-choice questions across the desk, the kind that are often used to test IQ.

"Do you think you can answer these for me?"

Thoreau blinked an affirmative.

"Let's see how many you can complete in thirty minutes."

Thoreau's restless eyes scanned the questions on the page. He picked up the pencil Rose nudged across the table for him. Again, Sam cringed at how the writing instrument could be used as a weapon. There was nothing but the wooden desk between Thoreau and the psychiatrist.

Unlike the verbal qualitative segment, Thoreau whipped through the written test. Within minutes, he slid the paper back across the table and resumed his blank stare at a fixed point on the wall.

Dr. Rose reviewed his answers. When she was done, she seemed neither surprised nor impressed by Thoreau's performance. Judging by her reaction, Sam got the impression she'd expected him to be successful.

The video clip ended. Sam returned the phone to his pocket and stared out at the mountains looming on all sides of the helicopter.

Back on the ground in Saranac, Sam got into his truck and poured himself a black coffee from the thermos he'd left on the passenger seat that morning. It was about a half hour drive back to Balsam Lake, and he was surprised to be able reach Dr. Rose on the SUV's hands-free system as he drove.

"Dr. Rose? This is Sam Hayden. I'm so sorry to bother you on a Sunday, but I had a look at the video you sent and we don't have time to wait for your full report. Do you have a minute to discuss?"

"Sure." Rose's voice was deep and cool through the truck's speakers. "From what I could tell from yesterday's very brief interaction, your suspect has some cognitive behavioral issues to work through. Definitely autistic spectrum, most likely what we used to call Aspergers."

"Aspergers?" Sam repeated with a note of skepticism.

"It's a form of autism, a developmental disorder often characterized by high intelligence, difficulties in social interaction, and restricted or repetitive behavioral patterns."

"Sounds like a sociopath to me. You've seen him; it's empty behind his eyes."

"It's not his fault, Chief Hayden. If I'm right in my diagnosis, your suspect is likely incapable of emotional reciprocity. He simply cannot recognize the feelings of others, the same way a color-blind person cannot distinguish hues. He is highly intelligent, but struggles with abstract concepts and personal interactions. Whatever social skills he might have had before entering the woods would have merely been memorized behavior—awkward at best. Added to which, he now hasn't spoken to a human in what? Thirty years?"

Sam sipped his coffee. "Thirty years in the woods just made it worse. What made him go out there in the first place?"

"I'm afraid it'll take a lot more than just one session to get an answer to that one."

"Any chance he could be violent?"

Dr. Rose's voice stiffened. "People with a condition like that tend to be the victims of violence, not the perpetrators."

"What if you knew he had taken that little girl? What would you think of him then?"

There was a pause on the other end. "I have another appointment, chief," Rose said. "I'll have my full report ready tomorrow afternoon. Am I sending it to you or to the state police?"

"Send it directly to me."

Rose disconnected.

Sam didn't turn the radio on. The silence and the low hum of the truck's tires helped him think.

Chapter 16

The bell above the entrance to Brenda's Diner jingled a cheerful ring as Megan entered and headed for the counter. The smell of bacon grease, singed toast, and strong coffee washed over her. Ol' Rory was perched on his usual stool, reading the *Adirondack Daily Enterprise* while his cup of coffee went cold on the formica surface in front of him. Most of the other locals avoided the diner on Sunday mornings. It was too crowded with out-of-towners stuffing themselves with breakfast and coffee before hitting the road back to their lives in the city.

But Ol' Rory refused to be chased away.

Brenda spied Megan through the service window that separated the dining room from the kitchen. She signaled for Megan to hold-on while she bagged her breakfast.

Ol' Rory didn't look over from his paper as Megan leaned against the counter next to him. She surveyed the dining room while she waited. A conversation at a nearby booth cut through the din and caught her attention. She glanced over. Vanessa Ramsay was there with another chic city woman.

Megan always tried hard to find a fault with the way Wade Ramsay's wife looked, but she never could. Vanessa was nearly half her husband's age, and whatever work the twenty-something-year-old had done was imperceptible. Her breasts were just the right size and height, her lips were not too plump, and her nose was just narrow enough. Her luxuriant hair was a blonde that could only come from an expensive bottle, but she wore it too naturally to be questioned. Hell, even her impossibly long fake eyelashes somehow looked liked she'd been born with them. Vanessa's only flaw was being married to Wade Ramsay—which spoke volumes about her character.

Both women were distracted by their phones while they sat across from each other at the booth.

"…doesn't surprise me," Vanessa was in the middle of saying. "Hayden's been obsessed with finding Spooky ever since that scandal with his father."

The other woman—a slim brunette with a trendy cut—barely glanced up. Her manicured nails clicked against the screen as she swiped on her phone. "Did you hear Megan Danforth's been visiting him in jail?"

"If you ask me, she's just like that crazy hermit," Vanessa scoffed. "What kind of woman spends all her days alone in the woods?"

Maybe it was the weight of Megan's glare burning into her that made Vanessa look up from her phone. When she saw Megan glowering at them as she approached their table, Vanessa shut up and broke eye contact.

"Morning, Vanessa," Megan managed through clenched teeth. How many other gossipy residents had Vanessa had this same conversation with? She was Wade's wife; people trusted whatever she said. "Mind passing a message on to Wade for me?"

"Sure," Vanessa sneered.

"Tell him adding a wolf skin to his trophy collection isn't worth going to jail for."

"What the hell are you talking about, Danforth?"

"I know Wade's been trying to trap wolves in the park."

Vanessa rolled her sparkling blue eyes. "Wolves? What wolves? Wade's been working in the city. He hasn't been up here in weeks, except for Friday night's emergency meeting."

This was a twist Megan wasn't expecting. She stared at Vanessa, trying to sniff out a lie.

A bell chimed and Brenda appeared in the service window, dangling Megan's bag of takeout in the air.

With one last icy look at Vanessa, Megan turned her back and crossed the dining room. She could feel the heat of the women's glares on her back as she went. They'd no doubt add this encounter to every retelling of their gossip. Brenda gave Megan a smile as she collected her food and coffee and turned for the door.

A bony hand clamped on her wrist.

Megan jumped and nearly spilled her coffee as she whirled around. Ol' Rory was peering at her from his perch at the end of the counter.

"You been talking to him, ain't ya?" He stabbed a finger at an article in the *Daily Enterprise* about Thoreau's arrest. "Your daddy's bones ain't the only ones out in that lake."

Megan eased her wrist from his grip. "What are you talking about, Rory?"

"I seen a skeleton washed up on the shore near Witch's Rock, jus' after Irene came through. That bitch of a hurricane dumped nearly a foot of rain on the mountains. All that water rushing down stirred up the lakebed and all manner of things came floating up. I was out collecting flotsam in the boat after the storm when I seen them bones heaped there in the sticks and leaves by the water. Fetched Roy Hayden to show him what I found, but by the time we got back to Witch's Rock, them bones were gone. Chief figured I must'a seen a bunch o' sun-bleached driftwood."

Rory's watery gray eyes squinted to piercing points as they drilled into Megan. "I know what folks say 'bout me 'round here. Ol' Rory's as crazy as a soup sandwich. But I know what I saw out there by that rock, and it weren't no driftwood. I ain't imagined that pale white skull staring back at me on the shore. Too small to be a man's. It was that Wright boy, I'm telling you. His bones were there, and *he* took 'em." Rory pounded a finger into the newspaper article again. "You been talking to him. You go ahead and ask him yourself."

Rory peered at her a moment longer before turning to catch Brenda's attention and gesturing for another coffee refill.

"Sure thing, Rory," Megan muttered uneasily. "I'll ask him."

Outside, Megan paused on the sidewalk and sipped her coffee. She stared at the vacant building across the street as she considered Rory's claims. Had he really seen a skeleton washed up on the shore beneath Witch's Rock? The landmark was a towering rock cliff overlooking the water on the eastern shore of the lake. It got its name from two jagged promontories that resembled a witch's hooked nose and protruding chin when viewed from the lake.

Rory's story wasn't impossible. The flooding from Irene had been enough to turn brooks into raging torrents powerful enough to wash away boulders and tear scars in the mountains themselves. But Ol' Rory now had enough trouble remembering to pay his tab at Brenda's, let alone what he thought he'd seen there on the lakeshore over a decade ago.

A more pressing thought elbowed its way into Megan's head. If Wade Ramsay wasn't responsible for the illegal traps she had found near the old Wright Great Camp, then who was?

Megan knew it could be anyone in town, but her instincts still told her it had to be someone like Wade, someone who would think nothing of killing a threatened animal for the sake of a personal trophy.

Megan fished in her pocket for her keys as she went to her pickup. Vanessa Ramsay's new gunmetal-gray Jeep Rubicon gleamed next to its neighbors a few spots away. The hulking monster was loaded with more after-market bells and whistles than Megan could count. The suspension had been lifted to accommodate the outlandishly oversized tires, and the grille was even outfitted with a winch. What the hell was Vanessa Ramsay going to do with a winch? She'd never let this beast off its leash. The Jeep wouldn't be venturing near anything even remotely off-road. For Vanessa, it was nothing more than a vanity piece. Its sole purpose was to convey her from her chic condo in Connecticut to her expansive lake-house in the straightest possible line. Vanessa could have had her husband buy her something more practical and luxurious, but she liked to believe the rugged Jeep helped her fit in with the locals. Megan suspected she actually got off on flaunting her toy in front of her envious neighbors.

Megan skidded to a sudden halt next to her pickup.

The Jeep…

An idea slammed into her, one so clear, she cursed herself for not having thought of it sooner.

She yanked the truck's door open and tossed her bag of greasy takeout on the passenger's seat. It wasn't for her, anyway.

Right now, she had to get to the station house.

* * *

Joanna was working the reception desk and looked up from her paperwork when Megan barged in.

"I need to see police reports from 1989," she said. "Where are they? Town archives?"

Joanna gave her an uncertain look and shook her head. "They're still in the basement."

"Take me to them."

"Uh, I don't know, Megan." Joanna hesitated and squirmed. "I—"

"Call Sam if you need to," Megan said with thinly veiled impatience. "I'll wait."

Joanna looked at her. "This have something to do with finding Piper Flynn?"

Megan nodded.

Joanna wavered a moment longer before giving in. "Ah, shit. C'mon…"

Megan followed her down the back corridor to the locked door that guarded the stairs to the basement. Joanna flicked the lights on as they descended the creaking wooden steps. To Megan's relief, they were industrial incandescents, not fluorescents.

The cramped space beneath the station house smelled dank and moldy. Rows of metal shelving units held hundreds of boxes of files. Joanna turned one corner, then another, before indicating three boxes all labelled *1989*. "Here they are."

Megan opened the first box and started perusing the files.

"They're mostly moving violations," Joanna explained. "Listen, Megan, I gotta get back up to the desk. Nothing leaves this room, you understand?"

Megan gave a distracted nod, and Joanna ascended back up the stairs.

The old papers rustled beneath Megan's fingers as she walked them slowly through the police reports, scanning the dates on the entries.

March, April, May…

The files in the box ended. Megan pulled open the lid on the second box and continued her search.

June, July, August, September…

Still nothing.

Megan let out a sigh, her confidence faltering as she reached for the last box. She felt the weight of the situation weighing down on her. Three nights had now passed since Piper Flynn had gone missing—three nights alone in the cold, dark woods. And they still had no leads, no clues, and no reason to believe they would ever find the girl alive. Megan had been so hopeful that these files might finally yield a break that could lead them to her. But as she sifted through the files, she couldn't help the sinking feeling in her stomach.

October, November…

Something caught Megan's eye, and she stopped rummaging. Was this it? She plucked a report from the box, her breath quickening as she scanned the details.

"Got you…" she muttered.

Megan's heart raced as she grabbed her phone and called Sam. Her foot tapped the stone floor impatiently while she waited for him to pick up.

"Hey, Megan." Sam's voice was buried in background noise on the other end. He was on the road somewhere.

"Sam! I've got a lead on who Thoreau is."

"What? How? The tip line?"

"No. He told me he drove to a trailhead one morning in '89 and ditched the car when he left his life behind and went into the woods. If he was telling the truth, the abandoned vehicle would eventually have been reported. Right?"

"Yeah. It couldn't have just sat there forever."

"I'm digging through the station's records right now and I found a match. In November 1989, a 1977 Jeep Wrangler YJ was towed from the Old Forge trailhead after sitting there for over a month. It was registered to a woman named Margaret Singer. She'd never reported it stolen and had to pay a fine when she came to pick it up."

"Singer? You think they're related?"

"Could be. Thoreau's sister? Mother? Wife? Who knows? But it's the only lead we've got. According to the address on the Jeep's registration, she lived near Long Lake, about half an hour away."

Megan gave him the address and Sam went quiet on the other end. She could hear a faint tapping as he punched the details into his truck's computer.

"I'll be damned, Megan. According to Margaret Singer's most recent license renewal, she still lives at the same address." Sam could barely contain his exhilaration. "I'm heading there now."

"Send me the address," Megan said. "I'll meet you there."

"No. You keep Thoreau talking. Don't let him know we're onto him."

Chapter 17

Sam's truck rumbled over the overgrown lane. Trees crowded the ditches on either side. Their creeping limbs threw heavy shadows across the withered weeds sprouting between the muddy wheel ruts.

Sam wondered just how far back into the woods the Singer residence sat from the turnoff. He'd been on this bumpy, twisting lane for at least a quarter of a mile now. He felt like it was leading him deep into the heart of the mountains when, at last, the trees opened up ahead of him.

The farmhouse at the end of the lane had to be at least a century old and looked like a wreck of its former self. It was a Folk Victorian with a gable roof and brick chimneys on each end. Dingy white paint flaked and peeled in curls from the weatherbeaten siding. Three windows faced Sam from the second floor. They were covered in drab curtains and there were no lights on in the rooms beyond. The front porch slumped away from the house and brown vines snaked around the railing's balustrades. Parts of the rail had rotted away, the pieces still visible where they had fallen into the weed-choked flower beds surrounding the house's foundation. The porch's rickety columns leaned like they would collapse under the weight of the roof at any moment.

Dense forest encroached on the property on all sides. An unkept field of waist-high grass grew between the house and the trees. The tall grass was yellow now, and it swayed in the lonesome breeze whistling across the dreary homestead. Further back on the lot, a large barn had been converted into a two-door garage. From the look of its crooked angles and the holes in its tin roof, it was just as in need of repair as the house.

Sam felt a creeping sense of foreboding as he mounted the uneven porch steps. The warped planks were soft and rotting beneath his feet. He crossed to the front door and rang the bell, glancing around uneasily while he waited. There wasn't a neighboring house for at least a mile in either direction.

Sam wondered if he should have waited for Megan to join him after all, or brought one of his deputies along. Margaret Singer had no police record, and there was no reason to believe she might be violent. But out here in the middle of nowhere, anything could happen to him and no one would know.

When there was no response, Sam pulled on the flimsy screen door and rapped his knuckles on the heavy wood.

Still nothing.

Sam hesitated a moment longer before moving to the nearest window. He cupped his face with both hands against the dirty glass, and peeked through a hole in a plaid curtain. The fabric was so thin it was nearly translucent. Sam still couldn't make out anything in the gloom, but a nagging intuition told him the house wasn't empty. Someone was inside.

Sam left the porch and rounded the house toward the big barn. His attentive gaze roved his forlorn surroundings, scanning for potential threats. He was sure he felt unseen eyes watching him as he went, but when he stole a glance at the house's darkened windows, he saw no one there.

There was a chicken coop between the house and the garage. A few pitiful hens pecked around on their side of the rusty wire fence. Someone had recently scattered handfuls of cracked corn for them. Sam was right; the house wasn't deserted. Whoever was in there was avoiding him.

Or waiting in ambush.

One garage door stood open, gaping like a mouth with a missing tooth, as Sam approached the converted barn. He couldn't be sure, but he thought he caught a hint of movement within. He slowed and poked his head inside.

A battered Dodge pickup was parked in the space inside the open door. It was at least twenty years old. Occupying the second space in the garage was a broken-down Jeep Wrangler.

Sam's flesh tingled at the sight of it. It had to be the same one Thoreau had left behind at the trailhead thirty years ago. Sam fought the urge to creep inside and inspect it for clues Thoreau might have left behind. Without a reason to suspect a crime, he had no justification to enter. Any evidence he found would be useless in court.

The rest of the cavernous space was crammed with decades of accumulated junk. A rickety set of wooden stairs on one side led up to an unused hayloft that hung obscured in the shadows above.

The hairs suddenly stood up on the back of Sam's neck.

He wasn't alone.

Sam turned around.

A hard-looking woman stood outside the garage. She glowered at him with narrow eyes. Her skinny arms were folded around a Browning hunting rifle.

"There a reason you're skulking around my property?" She rasped with the ravaged voice of a lifelong smoker.

The woman wasn't aiming her rifle at Sam, but its presence in her hands was enough to convey an unspoken sense of menace that put him on edge.

"Margaret Singer?" he asked.

The woman tilted her head in a slight nod. Margaret was in her late-sixties, and her weathered face bore a line for each year of her hard life. She had a pair of black cat's eye glasses perched on her thin nose. Her eyes were butcher-knife gray and her long hair was frizzy with split ends. She wore a knitted woolen sweater over a threadbare cotton dress. Below her knobby knees, a pair of rubber boots protected her feet from the mud.

Still wary of the rifle, Sam kept his guard up as he stepped toward her and extended a hand.

"Ms. Singer, I'm—"

"I know damn well who you are, Hayden," Margaret snapped.

Sam withdrew his hand. "Have you been expecting me?"

Margaret scowled. "Ever since I saw my brother's face on the news." She turned her back and walked away. Her bony hand waved through the air, beckoning him to follow her toward the house. "Let's get it over with, then."

Margaret led Sam through the front door, across the foyer, and into the house's parlor. The floorboards creaked and groaned beneath them and the room smelled of dust and mildew.

Margaret leaned her rifle against a wall and eased her stiff bones into a rose-colored armchair. The side table next to her was cluttered with empty soda cans, and an ashtray sat piled high with ashes and butts. Margaret reached for a chipped china teacup and emptied the contents of an open can of soda into it. She didn't offer Sam anything, but motioned for him to sit on a threadbare couch across from her.

Sam looked around. The room's furniture appeared as old as the house, a collection of antiques that might have been worth something if they weren't so worn-out and shabby. There were lamps with nicotine-stained shades on the side tables, but Margaret didn't light them. The pale afternoon light filtering through the curtains made the space feel more cold and damp than it already was. Dusty family photos hung on the walls. Sam recognized a much younger Thoreau sporting the same thick, wire-rimmed glasses he still wore. He was with Margaret and an older couple, who Sam assumed to be their parents.

There was nothing joyous about the portraits; just four people standing together with sullen faces.

Margaret followed his gaze. "We grew up in this house. Didn't always look like this, you know. Pop was a foreman down at the mill until Lou Gehrig's took his legs out from under him back when we was little. Things started coming apart after that. Ma passed a few years back. Mesothelioma from the asbestos down at the paper mill. Shame she couldn't last long enough to see Garrett alive. Most of us assumed he was long dead, but Ma never gave up hope."

"Garrett?" Sam asked. "Is that your bother's name?"

Margaret nodded.

"He calls himself Thoreau now," Sam said. If he was expecting the name to spark some kind of reaction from her, he didn't get it. Margaret just gave a disinterested shrug.

"Garrett's gonna be transferred to the county jail over in Lewis tomorrow," Sam went on. "There will be a trial, and considering the evidence we have against him, he's sure to be found guilty. He was carrying a knife at the time of his arrest, so the prosecutor will argue a case of criminal trespass and burglary in the second degree—a Class C felony with a minimum sentence of three and a half years. If he's lucky, he'll serve his time nearby in Adirondack Correctional, but there's a good chance he might end up somewhere worse, like Elmira or Clinton. He won't survive there."

Margaret let out a grim sigh. "No, I imagine not. Poor bastard's not built for those kinds of walls."

Sam spied a childhood photo of Thoreau and his father on the side table. The older man stared back at the camera from the leather seat of a wheelchair.

"Have you ever heard of Graham Danforth?" he asked.

"Uh, huh. Who hasn't?"

"Your brother's a person of interest in his murder. We need to get through to him if we're going to help him. Anything you can give us would be a big help."

Margaret sipped her soda and lowered the dainty teacup back into her lap. "When I seen Garrett had taken the Jeep, I knew he didn't want to be found. He could've just walked right out that door and into the woods behind the house if he wanted to. But he didn't. He made it harder to find him on account he knew I'd come looking for him." Her eyes wandered around the room. "This was the furthest thing from a home for him. He's spent his entire life living in the harshest conditions—both in here and out there. Like he had a choice. Garrett was cut off from the town because of how poor we was. He had it bad growing up around here. Stick around long enough, you'll hear the ghosts in the hallways."

Margaret got up and went to one of the family portraits hanging on the wall. "I stood up for him as much as I could. Only other friend he had was that Wright boy. And when he went and got lost in the woods… well, Garrett had no one then, didn't he?"

Sam sat up straight in his seat, feeling like she'd just smacked him across the face. "Hold on. Garrett was friends with Timothy Wright?"

"Uh, huh. Except they never went nowhere where anyone might see 'em together on account of Wright's family being such uppity pricks. Them boys couldn't be seen together in public, not with Garrett being the way he was and all. They had to sneak around them woods together to have their fun."

"You know what happened to Timothy, don't you, Ms. Singer?" Sam asked. "He went out into the forest one day and never came back. Being poor doesn't excuse the things your brother might have done out there. Graham Danforth was murdered. Seven others have vanished without a trace since your brother went out into the woods, including his childhood friend and a little girl who might be freezing to death at this very moment."

Margaret's thin lips curled. "The way I remember it, your pop was balls-deep in that whole Danforth mess, too. Whole county knows your daddy's story, Hayden."

"Ms. Singer—"

"You know what people around here say, don't ya Hayden?" Margaret leaned forward in her seat. "They say your daddy raped a girl and killed Danforth to shut him up."

Sam felt the blood rush to his face. "That's a lie," he growled. "My father swore he had nothing to do with it."

"He swore, huh?" Margaret sneered. "And why's his word worth any more than my brother's?"

Sam was too overcome by rage to manage a response. These same damn lies had plagued him his entire adult life. They had ruined his father's career and turned him into a broken shell Sam didn't recognize. And in the end, they had been the reason Roy Hayden had put his pistol into his mouth and blown his own brains across the kitchen linoleum.

Margaret seemed to sense she had touched a nerve. She sat back, satisfied. "I'll tell ya this, Chief. Person of interest, murderer—I don't know nothing about all that. Don't give a shit neither. Way I see it, after the hell Garrett went through as a little one, he deserved a little peace and quiet out there on his own. And if that degenerate Graham Danforth happened to get in the way, then I'm square with whatever happened to him, too."

Chapter 18

Thoreau sat cross-legged on the floor of his cell, concentrating on his copy of *Walden*. He had been up all night and looked like hell. He was so engrossed in the book he didn't hear the footsteps approaching in the hallway. Only when the cell door squeaked open, and shadows knifed across the book in his lap, was he startled back to reality.

Megan and Noah's silhouettes filled the open doorframe.

"Not till we have lost the world, do we begin to find ourselves, and realize where we are and the infinite extent of our relations." Megan's voice detached itself from her backlit figure. "One of my favorite Thoreau quotes."

She entered and waited for Noah to close the door behind her. The lock engaged automatically. While the deputy's footsteps receded down the corridor, Megan offered Thoreau her paper bag of takeout. "I brought you brunch."

Thoreau eyed the bag for a moment before uncoiling from his spot on the floor to take it from her. The brown paper crinkled in his gnarled hands. Inside was a fried egg with cheese on an English muffin, and two greasy hash-browns.

"I had to make some stops on the way here, so they got a little cold," Megan said.

Thoreau didn't seem to care as he tucked into the breakfast sandwich with a ravenous appetite.

"I brought you something else, too." Megan reached into her pocket and produced a short, fat pinecone.

Thoreau nearly dropped the breakfast sandwich back into the paper bag at the sight of it. He reached for the pinecone and cradled it in his palm reverently before raising it to his nose and inhaling deeply, savoring the scent of the pinesap.

"Smells like home…" he sighed.

"I'll have to take it with me when I go," Megan said. "But I can bring it back later… if I'm welcome back."

Thoreau nodded absently, still delighting in the woodsy aroma.

Megan gave him a moment, then asked, "Mr. Thoreau, why were you out there?"

Thoreau peered at her, and Megan feared he was about to withdraw into himself again.

"I know there's something wrong with me," he mumbled. "There always has been. My father thought he could cure me…" His thoughts wandered off to somewhere unpleasant.

"Did your father hurt you?" Megan prodded.

Thoreau's face tightened. "He wanted me to act normal. When I just couldn't, he'd lock me in the crawl space beneath the house for hours on end. My sister would find me down there, all curled up and sweating and unconscious. One time I lashed out. Pop tied me to the bed and Ma prayed over me for three days straight, neither one of us eating or sleeping. Turns out, she couldn't exorcise the strange out of me."

"Is that why you left? Why you went out into the woods?"

Thoreau chose not to answer. He returned his attention to the pinecone and ate his breakfast sandwich.

"Why didn't you light a fire while you were out there?" Megan asked

Thoreau shrugged while he chewed. "Couldn't give away my camp. I'd worked too hard to disappear."

"The lake is surrounded by houses and cabins. You must have encountered other people over the years? Hunters? Hikers?"

"A few. They didn't see me. Still, I noted them in my journal."

"Journal?" The revelation hit Megan like a sack of bricks. "You kept a journal?"

Thoreau lowered the egg sandwich and eyed Megan suspiciously, as if she suddenly couldn't be trusted. "I'd like to be alone now."

Megan didn't move. "Mr. Thoreau, there's something important we need to talk about. Chief Hayden thinks you might have hurt some people while you were out there."

Thoreau's eyes darted from side-to-side with agitation.

"It's why he's trying so hard to find your camp. He wants to find evidence to use against you. But there's nothing there to find, is there?"

Thoreau's knee pistoned up and down anxiously.

"I don't think you hurt anyone, Mr. Thoreau. Help me prove it."

Thoreau rose from the bunk. He kept his gaze averted and fixed on the floor as he crossed the cell toward Megan.

She took a wary step backward toward the door.

Thoreau stopped… and offered Megan the pinecone.

Megan took it, frowning with disappointment. It was her cue to leave. "Mr. Thoreau, I just need—"

Just then, the door whipped open. Sam stormed into the cell, his mood seemingly as dark as his expression.

"Let me jump in here," he snarled.

Megan stood aside, surprised by Sam's aggressive demeanor. "Chief, I—"

Sam's hand flashed out to silence her. He loomed over Thoreau and crossed his arms over his chest. "This area holds its share of unsolved mysteries. I have no doubt you're behind most of them, but here's one that concerns me most. On July the Fourth, 2010, Graham Danforth went fishing just like he did every year. Except he never made it home. Just disappeared. You know anything about that, Mr. Singer?"

Sam let the man's real name hang in the air.

Thoreau's knee stopped bouncing, but he still refused eye contact.

"That's your name, isn't it? Garrett Singer?" Sam said. "How about all the people that've gone missing while you were out there, Singer? You know anything about them? What about a little girl named Piper Flynn?"

"Chief, I'd like to finish with Mr. Thoreau," Megan cut in. "Alone, please."

Sam persisted, undaunted. "You're our only lead in thirty years, which makes perfect sense to me. You disappear in 1989; one year later, a hunter goes missing. Was he your first victim, Singer?"

Thoreau's eyes darted nervously around the cell.

"Or was it Timothy Wright?"

Thoreau's gaze stopped jittering. The blood drained from his face.

"Look at me, you son of a bitch," Sam growled. "I see through your bullshit. You killed that boy, didn't you? And then when you went back into the woods years later, you picked up right where you left off."

"Chief!" Megan interjected. "Can I speak with you outside?"

Sam brushed Megan off. "You killed that hunter. He stumbled across you and your camp and you killed him for it —just like you killed Graham Danforth. Then you stole his clothes and dumped his body in a distant corner of the lake where you thought no one would ever find it. But there are a couple of things you didn't see coming. The first was the Raquette hydro dam. The second was global warming. Combined, they've dropped the lake level by about three feet... just enough for a fishing hook to snag that tarp and reveal what you did."

Sam leaned close, his face flushed with anger. Veins stood out like ropes in his neck. Thoreau cringed and retreated across his bunk until his back came up against the cinderblock wall.

"Chief!" Megan tried again. She had never seen Sam like this. What had gotten him so worked up?

"Admit it!" Sam persisted. "You murdered those people because they got too close to your camp! Open your goddamn mouth and talk to me! What have you done with that little girl?"

Sam glared at Thoreau while he cowered on the bunk.

"Sam!" Megan's angry shout finally got through to him. He

turned and glowered at her, his jaw clenched tight with frustration.

Tension filled the tiny space until Sam stormed from the cell.

Megan followed him into the hallway and slammed the cell door shut behind her. "Jesus Christ, Sam! What is wrong with you? You know threatening him won't work!"

Sam whirled on her, still fuming. "Come here…"

He ushered her further down the corridor to the portraits of Balsam Lake's former police chiefs. He stopped at the space where one photo had been removed.

"You see these? My father's face should be up there! They took it down 'cause he supposedly raped a girl and murdered your father to cover it up. I have to look at this empty space every fucking day. Do you have any idea what that's like? To be Roy Hayden's kid?"

Megan glared at him, her eyes icy cold. "Yeah, I think I do, Sam. My father was the town drunk, remember?"

"Right. The drunk who'd say anything to keep himself out of jail, including pointing his finger at a good cop who'd done nothing wrong."

Joanne and Noah had appeared in the background now, drawn by the shouting.

Megan lowered her voice. "Are you so determined to clear your dad's name you'd risk hanging a murder on an innocent man?"

Sam took a deep breath and willed himself to cool down. "I got a call from the Public Defender's Office," he sighed. "Singer's lawyer will be here with the state police at nine tomorrow to transfer him over to the county jail. When he goes, so will our only chance of finding Piper before it's too late."

Megan shook her head with exasperation. "And now, thanks to you, he won't say another goddamn word."

Sam scowled and grit his teeth. She was right. He'd let Thoreau's sister rattle him, and now he'd made a grave mistake by letting his anger and resentment get the best of him.

He stalked off to his office and slammed the door behind him, furious at himself as much as the world.

Chapter 19

The Trail's End Pub was nearly empty. A couple of steadfast regulars had come in to watch the Sunday night football game after spending the day searching for Piper Flynn. Otherwise, Megan sat alone, hunched on a stool at the bar. After that afternoon's disaster between Sam and Thoreau at the station, the only thing that offered any comfort was the tumbler of bourbon sitting between her hands on the bar-top.

With the Beer n' Bait still closed while Russ scoured the woods with the search party, the Trail's End was the only place Megan could find a drink on a Sunday night. Aside from the glow of the large-screen TVs, the pub's lighting was dim and cozy. The dark, wood-paneled walls were covered with fishing trophies, and kitschy vintage posters advertising the area's most popular activities of hiking and skiing. A billiards table occupied the center of the space, and a colorful jukebox radiated its light at the far end of the room.

Beyond the neon glow of the signs hanging in the pub's large, street-front windows, the season's first snowflakes were fluttering lazily through the night. Like so many things in

Megan's life, they wouldn't stay and would be gone in the morning. But somewhere out there in the dark forest, Piper Flynn was spending her fourth night in the cold. As much as Megan tried not to imagine the worst, any hope of finding the girl alive was melting as fast as the snow. The only way she knew how to deal with that heart-wrenching fact was to drown herself in the amber liquid.

She picked the tumbler from the bar and tossed its contents back. The whiskey burned the back of her throat as it went down, but it was a good kind of sting. Megan had lost count of how much booze she'd already consumed. The edge had fallen off long ago, and her mind was now hazy enough to keep her thoughts from conspiring against her. She knew she should stop, but she couldn't bear the idea of thinking about that scared little girl sober.

Past the taps of cheap beer further down the bar, Danny Dugger was toweling large plastic beer pitchers. The bartender was a lanky guy in his mid-twenties, with shoulder-length blonde hair and a seemingly endless collection of black concert T-shirts. Megan waved to get his attention and motioned for another. There was something disapproving in Danny's eyes as he slung the towel over his shoulder and reached for the whisky bottle.

Megan waited and watched while he poured. Now and then, the regulars threw furtive glances her way from their table, but they kept their distance. They knew who she was. Distracted by the football, they barely spoke to each other as they drank their beers and helped themselves to the free popcorn machine.

Danny plunked the whiskey down in front of Megan just

as she became conscious of a new presence by her side.

"Evening, Megan," Joanna said. "Ain't planning on driving tonight, are ya?"

Megan's gaze slid from the deputy to Danny. "Did you call her?"

The bartender played dumb and raised his hands in mock defense.

"Don't do this to yourself," said Joanna. She nudged the glass back across the bar. "Just the tab, Danny."

Megan gave her a searing look. There was a storm brewing inside her. Her hand flashed out and seized Danny's wrist as he reached for the glass. "Keep it coming," she growled.

The bartender paused and glanced at them both.

"I'm taking her home," Joanna insisted.

"The fuck you are," Megan said, her voice laced with fury. She was in no hurry to return to the secluded cabin where unseen prowlers left painful mementos of her past at her doorstep in the middle of the night.

"Megan, let's just go…"

The storm struck. Megan slapped the shot of whiskey from the bar. It smashed on the floor.

"Megan!" Joanna shouted.

Danny reached across the bar and laid a gentle hand on Megan's shoulder. "Hey, c'mon…"

Megan's fist became a wicked left hook aimed at the side of the bartender's head. In the same instant, Joanna yanked her backward before the blow could connect. Megan's fist shot through the empty air just inches in front of Danny's nose.

One of the regulars leapt to his feet. Megan eyed him menacingly, daring him to make a move on her. He was big, but she was never one to be intimidated by a fight.

Joanna sensed the violence about to erupt and jumped between them. She grabbed Megan by the arm and hauled her toward the exit.

A big trophy bass mounted above the door caught Megan's hazy attention.

She squinted up at it.

The fish triggered something in her, a dim memory of that fateful day by the lake…

* * *

Thirteen-year-old Megan wakes up on the shore, the warm sand beneath her cheek. The sunlight is blinding and sears her eyes. She squints and grimaces at the pain in her head, an aching throb that pierces like a nail driven right into the center of her skull. How long has she been asleep? She props herself up on her elbows and looks around in confusion.

And that's when she slowly becomes aware of a sticky, warm sensation covering her skin. She looks down and sees that she's covered in bright red blood. Her face, clothes, hands.

Everything.

Panic starts to set in. Megan searches herself. Her shirt's undone, but she's not hurt. The blood isn't hers.

She lurches to her feet, but her legs are weak and unsteady. She stumbles to her knees, her heart racing. The ground around her is soaked a dark crimson. Empty beer cans litter the area. Her fishing rod lies discarded in the reeds nearby.

The canoe is gone and her father's rod is lying on the ground.

There's no sign of him.

As she struggles to her feet, Megan hears a rustling in the woods. She freezes, her eyes wide with fear.

"Dad?" she shouts.

There's no response.

"Is someone out there?" she calls again. The panic makes her voice shake.

Still nothing.

Megan waits at the water's edge as the echo of her cry fades into nothing. Clouds have moved in since she passed out; ugly grey smudges that hang in the sky with the promise of a downpour. Megan's insides twist into a tight knot. Did he leave her there alone? Or did something happen to him? She looks around frantically, searching for any clue of her father's whereabouts. He must have just gone off into the woods to take a leak. But why is the canoe gone? It doesn't matter; he'll reappear at any moment and they'll sort this all out.

Except he doesn't.

Megan waits and waits. She's trembling all over now. Her skinny knees knock together below the frayed hems of her bloody cutoffs. What happened out here? Where did all this blood come from?

"Dad! Where are you?"

Still nothing. An eternity passes until Megan comes to a chilling realization.

Her father's not coming back.

Megan's breaths come hard and fast. She looks down at her blood-soaked clothes. Horrified, she wades into the cold water and crouches low, doing her best to wash herself clean.

Her eyes are round and tearful, on the verge of hysterics. The blood runs in watery streams from her skin.

Shivering, and with her teeth chattering from shock, Megan retreats to where her backpack rests on the shore. She strips off her clothes and changes into a clean set from the pack. She throws her wet and bloody shorts and shirt far into the woods.

The sun is just starting to dip behind the mountains when Megan hefts the pack and slings it around her shoulders. She glances around one more time, hoping against hope that her father will reappear.

Silence.

Megan gathers all her strength and forces herself to run, her feet pounding against the hard ground as she races through the trees, leaving the lake and all that horrible blood behind…

* * *

Megan's eyes popped open. She was flat on her back on her couch under her wool blanket. She winced at the grey light of morning streaming right into her eyes through the slit between the curtains. The worn couch springs creaked as she rolled over and pulled the blanket up to her chin. Her head felt like it had been run over and her mouth was pasty, as if she'd swallowed a spoonful of baking soda.

The low thump of footsteps upstairs drove her upright.

Someone was in her house.

The room whirled around her, and her stomach roiled as she tried to focus. She had a flash of Joanna dragging her from the pub, but the ride home was a hazy blur. Was Joanna still upstairs? The footsteps sounded too heavy. Megan's vision shifted in and out of focus as she scanned the room. Where had she left her gun?

The footsteps grew louder as they moved across the second floor. An instant later, Russ came down the steps with a glass of water in one hand and a couple of Tylenols in the other.

Megan stared at him with bleary eyes as he handed her the pills. "How the hell did you get in here?"

"Back door was unlocked," he replied. "A friend down at the station suggested I drop by to check on you."

"Ugh, Joanna…" Megan sighed as she gulped down the painkillers. Instead of being refreshing, the water tasted stale and metallic in her parched mouth.

"She said you swung a pretty good right hook at Danny down at the Trail's End," Russ added. He dragged a chair over to sit across from her.

Megan raised her fists listlessly, nodded up at the boxing trophy on the fireplace mantle. "Golden Gloves Champion."

"I thought your boxing years were behind you."

Megan cocked an eyebrow. "You know about that?"

"I heard." Russ didn't feel the need to tell her about the video he'd found online. After their encounter in the woods, he couldn't help wanting to find out more about the woman who had so captivated him. Megan didn't seem to have any social media presence, but it had surprised Russ to discover dozens of articles about her boxing career while she studied on an athletic scholarship at UMass. It wasn't long before he came across the clip of her championship match, titled "THE BEST KO OF THE 2017 GOLDEN GLOVES".

In the video, Megan was dressed in red trunks, shirt, and headgear. Her opponent wore blue and was a full head taller than Megan, with the arm reach of a polar bear. For the first thirty seconds, the woman in blue pummeled Megan mercilessly. Megan's lip had been cut in a previous round and blood dribbled down her chin from her lip. She responded with a few furtive jabs of her own, but Russ got the impression she wasn't making much of an effort to dodge or defend herself as her opponent assaulted her with one skull-rattling blow after another. It was as if Megan didn't mind being hit, like she was used to it.

And then the whole match changed in the blink of an eye.

Sensing her advantage, the woman in blue got too confident and overextended herself with a right hook, leaving herself open. Megan struck with the speed of a cobra. Her left fist rocketed out and blasted her opponent straight in the jaw. The woman in blue was already wobbling on her feet, but Megan didn't notice. Something had come over her, something brutal and violent. She landed three more swift and vicious blows before the woman staggered sideways on rubber legs and crashed to her knees near the ropes.

Megan went to her corner and glared across the ring while the referee rushed to her fallen opponent's side. An instant later, he waved his arms, and the match was over.

A close-up replay of Megan's sudden burst of fury revealed a look in her eyes that gave Russ a chill. The clip ended and left him stunned, trying to reconcile the primal aggression he'd just witnessed with the withdrawn woman he knew.

Megan shrugged as she sat slumped on the couch. "I guess fighting's a tough habit to break. My dad always wanted a boy. When my mom died, he started treating me like one. Said he'd toughen me up whether I liked it or not. The bruises I got from boxing helped disguise the ones he gave me."

"He beat you?"

"He preferred to call it *training*." Megan winced against the pounding in her skull. She sat back on the couch, tilted her head back against the cushion, and closed her eyes. "It wasn't his fault, not really. He was behind the wheel when we had the accident that killed my mom. Stone sober at the time. He only really started drinking after that night. Eventually, the booze just made him angry and mean… and I kept trying to make him happy. He was dealing with his own pain, you know?"

"He was your father. He should've been there for *you*, not the other way around."

Megan opened her eyes and looked at Russ. "I'm not some restoration project, Russ. You're not going to fix me."

"Oh, I kinda like you just the way you are, drunken bar fights and all."

Megan made a feeble attempt at a smile. "I've been a drinker a long time, but I've never let it go that far—not like last night. But lately…" She trailed off.

"Lately, what?"

"I've been getting flashes of the day my dad went missing. They're just fragments, likes pieces of a broken mirror. The thing is, I don't even know if I can trust them. I don't know if what I think I'm remembering actually happened, or if my mind is just filling in the blanks."

"What do you remember about that day?"

Megan shook her head. "Not much. He'd taken me fishing somewhere on the lake. I couldn't catch shit, but I still wanted to make him happy, so I started drinking his beers with him. He pushed me into it, one can after another, until I couldn't take anymore."

"You were thirteen?"

"Like I said, he was a shitty father. I took it too far and blacked out. When I woke up, he was gone, and I had no idea where we were or how to get home. The rest is a blur. My childhood therapist called it PTSD. I wandered the woods until a couple of hikers found me. The next thing I knew, I was being questioned for my father's murder. Sam's dad always suspected I killed him."

"Wait. Hayden's dad? The guy everyone thinks murdered your father to keep him from testifying?"

Megan nodded and chewed her cheek for a moment. "Ever since we found my dad's bones, I've been haunted by him."

Sitting there, seeing the concern and affection in Russ's eyes, she suddenly had the irresistible impulse to unburden herself to him. The words spilled out of her as she told him about the sinister presence she'd felt stalking her on the White Lily Pond trail, and the inexplicable appearance of the fishing lure at her back door. And she told him what Thoreau had said about believing in ghosts.

"It's crazy, I know," she admitted. "But I don't know how else to explain it. What if Thoreau wasn't alone out there all these years, Russ? What if there was something out there with him?"

Russ stared at her when she was done. "Or he's just losing his mind after decades of isolation," he returned. "Isn't it more likely that whatever voices or evil presences Thoreau talked about are all in his head? That his subconscious made up these imaginary characters to keep himself company in the long years he spent out there by himself?"

Megan frowned and chewed the inside of her cheek. "I didn't make up the fishing lure outside my door, Russ. It's sitting in my office right now." Still, Russ had a point. Three decades of isolation could have driven Thoreau to invent any number of figments of his fevered imagination.

"There's something else," Megan said. "Something I've told no one."

"What is it?"

"When I woke up next to the lake that day, I was covered in blood."

Russ's eyebrows arched. "His? Your dad's?"

Megan shrugged. "Maybe. It wasn't mine. Even when people started talking, saying he'd abandoned me out there, I couldn't tell anyone about it. I was too afraid of what it might mean."

Russ swallowed. "Do you think you could've done it? Killed your father?"

"I don't know. I mean, I blacked out, but that doesn't mean…"

And that's when the memory hit her.

A clear vision flashed in her mind, a forgotten snippet snatched from the dark corners of her subconscious. She remembered being on all fours, vomiting violently into the reeds by the water's edge. Her father hovers over her, mouthing his pathetic attempts to care for her wellbeing. His voice reverberates off the walls of her skull, and the world won't stay in one place around her. God, how much can she possibly throw up? If she doesn't stop heaving, something vital is going to tear free from her insides and rush out between her teeth.

After long, agonizing moments, her retching comes to a merciful end. Megan slumps to the ground and topples over onto her back, just a few feet from her reeking puddle of puke. The sun is too bright in her eyes. She closes them against it, but not before she catches a blurry glimpse of a giant rock outcrop towering over the lake behind her father's tall silhouette.

It's very, very familiar.

And there is a shadowy figure perched atop it.

Stunned by a sudden revelation, Megan sat up on the couch and gaped at Russ. "Oh God. What time is it?"

Russ checked his phone. "Just past eight."

"There's still time. I gotta go…"

Megan got up and snatched her keys from the table.

"Wait!" Russ shouted "What—"

He leapt up and dashed after her.

The door slammed behind them.

Chapter 20

The cell door whipped open and clanged against the wall, jolting Thoreau awake. Megan stormed in as he scrambled up on his bunk, his flannel blanket tangled around his big frame.

"You were there," she said. Her green eyes blazed with a furious intensity.

Thoreau stared down at his feet and remained mute.

"Witch's Rock," Megan went on. "My father and I were fishing there the day he disappeared. You were there too. I saw you!"

Thoreau flinched, and Megan thought she caught a flicker of something in his inscrutable eyes.

"That's why you've been talking to me. You saw me there, and you recognized me all these years later. You know what happened that day, don't you?"

Thoreau kept his gaze averted. The tip of one thumb scratched at the fabric of the blanket.

"Do you know who killed my father?"

Thoreau's stare travelled over the blanket and upward toward Megan's face, coming as close as he could to making eye contact. He gave a grim nod.

A knot tightened in Megan's stomach. "Was it the police chief? Did he kill my father?"

No response.

"Don't fuck with me," Megan snarled. "What happened out there that day?"

Thoreau inhaled and waited, as if giving her a chance to change her mind. When she didn't, he said, "It was quiet…"

* * *

Thoreau doesn't know it's the Fourth of July. Later that night, he'll hear the concussive explosions of the county fireworks echoing across the lake. Their luminous colors will dance across the night sky far in the distance. But it's still morning now, and Thoreau's attention is focused on hacking up the big hemlock that fell during a recent storm. He's been waiting days for a break in the weather to clear it away. Now that the sun is shining, and the air is still, he needs to get to work.

Thoreau doesn't need the firewood—he has never once lit a fire in decades—but the tree has fallen right across the only path through the maze of giant boulders that keep his camp hidden from view. He knows hacking it apart is incredibly risky. The sound of his axe striking the timber will echo far through the forest and could attract unwanted attention. But he can't leave the giant trunk there, even if the task of cutting it up and moving it seems daunting. If he doesn't clear the hidden path, he'll be forced to find a way up and over the towering rocks whenever he wants to come or go—not an easy task when lugging stolen twenty-pound propane tanks.

WHACK! Thoreau brings the axe crashing down on the thick trunk with all his might. Splintered chunks of timber and bark spit from the trunk and land at his booted feet. The scent of freshly cut pine fills the air.

WHACK! Another chop. The gleaming blade of the axe lodges deep into the fresh wound in the wood with a satisfying crunch.

Thoreau pauses to catch his breath. The summer sun sneaks through the dense canopy of the treetops, and the air in the deep woods drips with humidity. Sweat glistens on Thoreau's brow and plasters his T-shirt to his broad back, but he doesn't mind the exertion. This is a task that requires focus and strength, and he has both in abundance. He can't help but feel a sense of satisfaction at his progress. There is something therapeutic about the physical labor, and he finds himself lost in the rhythm of it. Time seems to melt away as he hacks and chops, the only sound the ringing of metal on wood.

A man's voice suddenly cuts through the forest.

Thoreau perks his ears like a deer, instantly alert. At first, there is nothing but the chirping of birds and the rustle of leaves in the breeze. He wonders if he just imagined the noise. Nobody comes this way anymore, and he hasn't heard a voice in months, maybe longer.

There it is again. It sounds like… a shout?

Thoreau's heart races as he spins around, trying to locate the source.

It's coming from somewhere close. Near the lake.

Thoreau plants his boot against the trunk of the fallen tree and wrenches the axe blade free. His palms tighten around the axe handle as he creeps silently through the forest, picking his way around the trees toward the giant cliff that will give him an uninterrupted vantage of the lakeshore.

The voice grows louder and more distinct, rising from the lake down below as Thoreau scrambles up the incline and clears the trees. It's definitely shouting; a man is calling for help.

Thoreau sneaks up to the edge of the cliff, keeping low to avoid being seen.

He peeks over the precipice...

Sees...

* * *

The air was heavy with tension as Megan stared at Thoreau, hanging on his words. "Then what? Tell me!"

Thoreau closed his mouth and leaned back against the cinderblock wall, his eyes darting around the stuffy cell.

"Tell me!" Megan shouted, her voice shaking with desperation. "What did you see? Who killed my father?"

Thoreau fiddled with his hands and avoided her glare. He wavered a moment longer before looking up at a spot over her shoulder, his expression drawn and somber. "Don't you remember? *You* killed him."

All the color drained from Megan's face. "What?"

Footsteps echoed in the hallway. Loud. Ominous. Boot-heels marching with purpose.

Megan glanced at the window. Sam was there with Noah and two burly state troopers. The door swung open.

Sam's face was a grim mask. "Time's up, Megan."

The troopers entered the cell and hauled Thoreau from the

bunk. He wriggled between them as they slapped handcuffs around his thick wrists.

"No! Wait!" Megan protested.

Thoreau's eyes darted around the cell, the big man suddenly looking small and pitiful. "Where are you taking me?"

Megan spun to Sam, who remained at the door. "Sam, just a give us a few more minutes! He's gonna talk!"

"No. He's not." A slender Black woman barged her way around Sam into the cell. She was in her early thirties, with champagne-brown eyes, half-moon cheeks, and spellbindingly white teeth. Her conservative suit was a deep merlot, and a colorful headband kept the dense black mass of her Afro blowout pulled back from her forehead. A pair of stylish, black-rimmed glasses were perched on her nose.

"Who the hell are you?" Megan demanded.

"My name is Alanna Whittaker," the woman replied icily. "I'm Mr. Singer's court-appointed attorney, and I'm here to make sure this man's rights are respected." She looked at Thoreau. "Mr. Singer, please don't say another word to these people."

Megan shot Sam another pleading look. He sighed and shook his head in defeat. "Nothing I can do, Megan. This is the law."

Megan whirled to Thoreau as the troopers marched him to the door. "Thoreau, I need to know what happened out there! At least tell me where Piper Flynn is! Please! I know you're not this selfish! You won't just let a little girl die!"

Whittaker stepped in her way, insinuating her frame between Megan and Thoreau. "Mr. Singer has said all he's going to. From now on, any questions you have for him will come through me."

Megan resisted the urge to knock the woman flat and step over her to get to Thoreau. But the hermit was already gone. The heavy footsteps of the troopers receded down the hallway as they led him away.

Whittaker shot Megan one more look that was supposed to be intimidating before she turned and went after them.

Left alone in the cell, Megan spotted Thoreau's copy of *Walden* still lying on the bunk where he'd left it. She snatched it up and let out a furious curse as she hurled it against the wall.

Chapter 21

The stiff fabric of Thoreau's orange jumpsuit chafed uncomfortably against his skin as he shuffled down the row of cells in the Essex County Jail. A hulking guard trailed close behind him. His name-tag identified him only as PITTMAN. He was a heavily muscled man in his late-forties, with a heavy brow, a goatee sprouting from his granite chin, and gray hair shaved close to the scalp.

The intake process at the county jail had taken most of the day, and it was now late in the evening. After the hour-long ride in the back of the state police SUV, the troopers steered Thoreau through the sallyport into the squat, brown brick facility. Inside, they made him sit at a desk and handcuffed to a rail affixed to the adjacent wall. Alanna Whittaker had followed them in her car, but left Thoreau at the desk while she went to file paperwork.

The wait at the desk was tortuous. The jail's bullpen bustled with more people than Thoreau had seen in one place in thirty years. The cacophony of voices assaulted his ears, and a mechanical clinking somewhere in the building's ventilation system pounded his brain like a jackhammer.

There was no clock to gauge how much time passed before a harried man in a rumpled, button-down shirt arrived and sat across the desk from Thoreau. The corrections officer read several questions from a form regarding Thoreau's health and state-of-mind: *Do you currently believe that someone can control your mind by putting thoughts into your head or taking thoughts out of your head? Are you currently taking any medication prescribed for you by a physician for any emotional or mental health problems? Have you ever been in a hospital for emotional or mental health problems?*

Thoreau couldn't focus on anything other than the oily yellow ring around the upper rim of the man's white shirt collar. Whittaker had returned by then, and she stood by Thoreau's side, encouraging him to cooperate. She explained the health screening was a standard procedure to protect the jail population and that they could refuse entry to someone who is unstable at the time of intake.

When Thoreau continued to sit in stony silence, the oily officer simply wrote *REFUSED* next to each question on his questionnaire and moved on. He snapped a pair of latex gloves over his unusually long fingers and produced a sterile syringe from the drawers next to his desk. Thoreau had panicked then, and it took the two state troopers to hold him still enough for the injection that tested for tuberculosis.

Once the health screening was over, they separated Thoreau from Whittaker. She promised to return in the morning for his arraignment before they led him to a holding cell, where he joined about a half dozen other inmates awaiting processing.

The hours crawled by until an officer escorted Thoreau into a drab room down a corridor. There, he was told to remove his clothing, including any piercings. He felt more small and vulnerable than he ever had in the wild as he endured the humiliation of a search of his ears, mouth, and genitals for contraband. With the full body search completed, he was issued his jumpsuit and photographed. A bracelet was printed and fixed around his wrist. It bore his name, along with an identification number and a bar code. Thoreau was vaguely aware of the officer explaining the code would be scanned every time he was issued a meal or moved from one place to another. He was too distracted by the sight of his real name printed in plain black letters on the yellow plastic. He hadn't been Garrett Singer for decades, but now the identity was thrust back upon him along with all the dark memories that came with it.

Thoreau was given a coarse woolen blanket folded into a tight square, and he carried it with him when he was led to yet another holding cell. More hours crawled by. An officer scanned the bracelet when he brought Thoreau something pre-packaged to eat. It sat untouched until Pittman finally arrived to escort Thoreau to his cell.

Now, Thoreau felt the cold stares of the other inmates drilling into him from behind the bars. Pittman's looming presence kept them quiet, but he wouldn't stay by Thoreau's side all night. In another few hours, it would be time for lights-out; an entire night of darkness lay ahead for them to amuse themselves by torturing the fresh fish.

"Here," Pittman grunted.

A cell door stood open to Thoreau's left. He stopped and

peered inside. Dingy cinderblock walls. A stainless steel bunk and a toilet without a seat. Nothing else. The cell was as cold and smothering as a coffin.

Thoreau's eyes grew wide and fearful as he remained by the open door to the cell. Pittman gave him a shove and Thoreau dug his heels into the floor, resisting. "No! Please! Don't put me in here!"

Pittman's hard glare crackled with the promise of violence as he slammed the door shut in Thoreau's face.

Thoreau trembled as he lowered to the ground and curled into himself. The sharp buzzing and crackling of the jailhouse gnawed at him. Disembodied voices echoed down the cavernous halls of the cell block—snoring, shouting, and the occasional bout of laughter. They made the hair on the back of his neck stand on end. He shut his exhausted, bloodshot eyes and tried to imagine the forest and his life of solitude.

Eventually, the jailhouse chaos faded away...

* * *

The nicest name the other boys have for Garrett is The Poor Kid. He's even heard his teachers call him that when they think he's out of earshot. When the other boys really want to be mean, the cruelty of their words cut through Garrett like scalpels.

But Timothy's different. He's from out-of-town, somewhere down near the city where the houses are as big as hotels and the people aren't so stupid. He only comes up for a few weeks each summer, and he doesn't know the other boys. One time, he'd begged his parents to drive him to town to make friends and play ball. But it turns out that among the insular local boys of Balsam Lake, being The Rich Kid is almost as bad as being The Poor Kid.

Garrett hopes Timothy's path will never cross theirs again. He can't risk the other boys changing their minds about Timothy. He's the only friend Garrett's ever had.

He came across Timothy by the lake's edge one afternoon near the middle of June. Timothy was alone, trying to catch bullfrogs, but he was going about it all wrong. Garrett showed him how, and soon enough, they were building a tree fort out of sturdy sticks and pine boughs.

Timothy kept asking Garrett about things like his favorite comic book or *Scooby-Doo* episode. Garrett didn't have an answer for anything like that, but he did know which mushrooms would kill them if they ate them. That's impressive enough for Timothy, and the two misfits have been meeting up to explore the dense forest near his family's Great Camp ever since. It doesn't matter that Timothy lives almost two miles away. Garrett will walk any distance to be with his friend.

It's already a hot July day as Garrett makes his now almost daily trek north through the woods that stretch between their properties. The trail snakes through the forest, twisting and slinking around the massive glacial boulders. Soon, Garrett spies Timothy through the trees ahead. He's perched on the huge trunk of a fallen tree by the side of the trail, hunched over a comic book.

Timothy glimpses Garrett trundling up the trail toward him and springs to his feet from the giant log. "Geez, where've you been, Garrett? The mosquitoes are like vampires out here." He grins and his teeth are slightly too big for his mouth.

Timothy's the same age as Garrett and a head shorter, but only because Garrett is so big for his age. He's got bright blue eyes, a small, upturned nose, high cheeks, and a curly mop of sandy hair bleached by the summer sun. He's wearing blue running shorts with a white trim, and white socks with thick green stripes he's pulled up all the way to the mid-calf of his skinny legs. His top is a new T-shirt. It's light gray and emblazoned with the stylized logo for *Star Wars: The Empire Strikes Back*. There's an illustrated image of a young man waving a glowing blue sword, staring at Garrett from Timothy's chest. The man is surrounded by robots and spaceships shooting lasers and a tall hairy man-thing and another man and a woman who look like they're about to kiss. Looming over them in the sky is the head of a sinister-looking figure wearing an intimidating black mask and helmet.

Garrett guesses it must be the bad guy. "I like your shirt," he says.

Timothy looks down. "Yeah. Cool, right? Mom bought it for me after we went to see it in the theater when school got out."

Garrett just blinks and Timothy realizes the boy has no idea what he's talking about. "You know *Star Wars*, don't you? Luke Skywalker? Darth Vader?"

Garrett frowns and shrugs.

"Jesus, Garrett. Haven't you ever been to the movies?"

Garrett flinches at his friend's blasphemy. At the same time, it's why he loves hanging out with Timothy. Together, they do forbidden things. Dangerous things.

"I'll talk to Mom," Timothy says. "Maybe you can come with us next time."

"Yeah. That'd be great," Garrett responds with no genuine hope of it actually happening. He's only ten, but he knows why he and Timothy only meet to play in the woods; why his friend has never invited him inside his family's enormous country house to watch cartoons or play Atari. Timothy's parents don't like The Poor Kid. He and Timothy are not allowed to be seen together.

"C'mon," Timothy says. He waves his comic book for Garrett to follow him before he rolls it up and stuffs it into his waistband at the small of his back.

Before the comic disappears into Timothy's shorts, Garrett sees it's part of a series called *Supernatural Thrillers*. This issue features "The Living Mummy", and the cover depicts a mummy with one bandaged arm hooked around a man's throat. There's a torch falling from the man's hands and he looks terrified as the mummy chokes the life out of him. A blurb written in ghoulish yellow letters screams, "The Tomb of the Stalking Dead!" Garrett even sees the comic's price is twenty-five cents. He notices all of this with just a passing glance, yet he'll still be able to recall the details months later.

"Where're we going?" Garrett asks. He falls in behind his friend and they leave the trail behind, tramping into the woods.

Timothy glances over his shoulder. There's an excited gleam in his eyes. "A secret place."

They walk west for about half an hour, swatting at the buzzing mosquitoes, and the black flies that swarm their eyes, and the evasive deer flies that just won't quit hounding them until they're smacked flat. Timothy fills the time as they go. By the time they reach their destination, Garrett has a basic idea of what happens in *Star Wars*, but he's still fuzzy on how exactly the Force works. He says nothing though, because now the land is inclining upward at a steep angle beneath their feet. Soon, the trees open up and Garrett finds himself standing atop a massive cliff rising high above the lake.

Garrett sucks air between his teeth and his knees go a little wobbly at the dizzying panorama. He's never seen the lake this way before. It's vast and unknowable as it stretches out before him, reaching far back toward the vanishing point of the mountains. The yellow sunlight sparkling off the water is enough to make Garrett squint. He can make out the indistinct shapes of a few boats in the distance. Somewhere up there to the north is the town of Balsam Lake. It doesn't look like there's anything but forest between here and there.

As they reach the edge of the cliff, Garret can't help but feel a twinge of apprehension. He holds back a few steps.

"Come on, Garrett," Timothy says with a grin. "Don't be such a chicken. The view is amazing."

Garrett hesitates for a moment before reluctantly joining his friend at the edge of the precipice overlooking the water below.

"They call it Witch's Rock," Timothy says. "Wanna know why? It's cause they killed one here two hundred years ago—a real *witch*."

Garrett gives him a sideways look. "No, they didn't. There were no witches around here."

"They did too!" Timothy insists, his eyes gleaming

mischievously. "The townspeople dragged her from her house and brought her up here to die. They forced her down on this rock and tied up her wrists and ankles here…" Timothy gestures at a gnarled tree root growing out of the granite. "And there, and there, and there…" He points to three more spots around the periphery of the cliff. "And then you know what they did?"

Garrett shakes his head.

"They left her here to be eaten by the crows."

Garrett swallows. He doesn't like this story, and he wishes Timothy would stop making things up.

"We're standing right on the spot where she died," Timothy whispers gravely. "They say if you stay really quiet, you can still hear the echo of the crows pecking at her." Timothy's lips spread into a devilish grin and his teeth seem even bigger than before.

A cool breeze tickles the back of Garrett's neck and goosebumps ripple across his skin.

"*Peck! Peck! Peck….!*" Timothy suddenly sticks a finger into Garrett's arm.

Garrett jumps. He can't stand being touched—by anyone. The sensation feels like spiders crawling all over his skin. "Hey, stop it!"

Timothy doesn't stop poking him.

"*Peck! Peck! Peck…!*"

There's something wrong with Timothy's eyes, something Garrett can't recognize. He's not very good at reading people, but he sees *something*, a darkness that shouldn't be there. Why is Timothy being so mean to him? So much like the other kids in town?

Because this isn't his friend. It can't be. Garrett doesn't know this boy. Something has gotten inside Timothy, something that is making him be so nasty. Something like...

Something like the witch.

"*Peck! Peck! Peck....!*"

Timothy keeps poking his finger faster and harder into Garrett, prodding him everywhere, his eyes filled with that black malice that Garrett can't understand and wishes would just go away.

"*Peck! Peck! Peck....!*"

Garrett steps back, edging toward the precipice.

"They pecked at her guts..."

Timothy pokes a finger into Garrett's stomach below the ribs.

"They pecked at her tits..."

He jabs at Garrett's chest and Garrett winces at his friend's vulgarity.

"At her arms..."

A skinny finger stabs Garrett in the shoulder.

"At her eyes..."

The finger darts at Garrett's face and this time he smacks it away before it can make contact. But he does more than that. His fist flies out and slams right into that fearsome black mask on Timothy's T-shirt.

Timothy doesn't see it coming. Combined with the momentum of his lunge for Garrett's face, the blow to his chest is enough to put him off balance. His feet tangle beneath him. An ankle twists painfully and he stumbles sideways.

Right off the cliff.

The thirty-foot drop to the water below shouldn't kill him, not if he enters feet-first. Thrill-seeking teens have been jumping off Witch's Rock as a rite of passage for decades.

But Timothy doesn't get a running leap. He isn't expecting the plunge. He somersaults in the air on the way down and his head cracks against the rock with a wet and sickening *smack*. A bright splash of blood splatters the granite and Timothy hits the water in a tangle of limp limbs.

Garrett looks down in horror at the body of the boy floating face-down in the lake far below. The water around Timothy's head is turning a cloudy rust-color. Garrett's feet feel like they're melting into the solid rock beneath him, and his throat burns with bile. He's dimly aware that he should run and get help, but he's too afraid of what will happen to him if he does. He's already the town outcast; no one will believe what happened to Timothy was an accident.

Panic shoots through Garrett. He knows he has to find a way down to the shore quickly to see if Timothy is okay. He starts to climb down the cliff, using whatever handholds he can find. He's terrified of falling, but he knows he has to reach his friend before it's too late.

When he finally reaches the water's edge, he sees Timothy's body floating about twenty yards from shore. He still hasn't moved. Garrett's crying now, the tears coming like they never have in his life, his whole skinny body shuddering with his uncontrollable sobs. He wants to dive into the water and haul his friend back to the land, but he can't swim. He stares at the boy's lifeless body and waits and waits and waits. Timothy will wake up soon. He *has* to wake up soon…

But he doesn't. Not even after Garrett waits long minutes

for him there at the base of the enormous rock. Timothy's breathless lungs fill with water and his body sags lower in the lake until it sinks beneath the surface and vanishes from sight. Ripples crawl across the water toward Garrett's toes, and then they're gone too.

A few moments later, Timothy's comic book floats up the surface. Alone and grief-stricken, Garrett waits for the gentle breeze playing across the lake to coax it close enough to the shore for him to snap it up. He can't bear looking at it. His hands tremble as he carries it into the woods and buries it as deep as he can dig.

Garrett keeps going back to that spot by Witch's Rock every afternoon for the rest of the summer. He sits by the shore and talks to the friend who rests deep beneath the water's surface. As time goes by, he doesn't feel like he deserves to be anywhere else, that he doesn't deserve to be alive. He'll spend years going back into the woods to speak to his friend until one day, ten years later, he just doesn't go home.

And on a ferocious night in the dead of winter, Garrett's friend finally speaks back to him.

* * *

Officer Pittman found Thoreau convulsing on the floor during his ten o'clock cell count. A stream of light cut through the bars from the corridor, illuminating Thoreau's prone body shaking in the throes of a seizure. His limbs twisted and spasmed and his eyes fluttered beneath his half-closed eyelids.

Pittman fumbled with his keys and threw the door open. His heart raced with panic as he rushed to Thoreau's side.

"Hey! Hey, I need help in here!" he barked into his walkie-talkie. He called out to Thoreau, trying to get his attention, but the man was completely unresponsive, his eyes rolling back in his head.

As the minutes ticked by, Thoreau's seizure showed no signs of stopping. Sweat beaded on Pittman's forehead as he tried to keep the man from hurting himself, his training kicking in as he supported Thoreau's head and kept his airway clear.

It seemed to take an eternity, but eventually the medical team arrived and rushed Thoreau out of the cell block. He floated down a long corridor on his back, staring vacantly at the shadows gathered within the high ceiling. Ahead, a set of doors opened to a dark place.

Thoreau sailed through. The ceiling morphed into the night sky. A small flicker ignited in Thoreau's eyes at the vastness of the stars. It was a sight he thought was gone for good. There were a few hard, intentional jerks, and the stars shook as his collapsed gurney was heaved into the back of an ambulance.

Chapter 22

Sam's mood was dark as he paced the corridor of the Essex County Courthouse. He'd gotten the call shortly after midnight. They had transferred Thoreau to Elizabethtown Community Hospital after he suffered a seizure in his cell. The hospital was only ten minutes down Route 9 from the jail, and Thoreau had stabilized in the ambulance along the way, but the doctors were still keeping him overnight for observation.

Sam didn't buy it. Thoreau was up to something.

A gaggle of news crews, tripods, and cables lined the corridor on either side of the courtroom doors. Between the disappearance of Piper Flynn and the sensational story of the hermit who had spent three decades in the woods, the sleepy town of Balsam Lake was now the epicenter of nationwide media attention. Hordes of reporters had descended on the town from neighboring states, and hotels were fully booked all the way up to Plattsburgh. Some locals were even making a buck by renting out their places on home-share sites while they stayed with friends or relatives.

Sam recognized a junior reporter talking into a camera, doing a live hit for the local station, WPTZ. It was a CNN affiliate, so whatever he was saying was likely being beamed and streamed on screens across the country. What was the kid's name? Moore? Morgan? No, Meyer. Baby-faced and slender, his suit pants seemed to be too short around his ankles, exposing socks with bright, colorful stripes. Sam surmised it must be a new fashion he had no interest in adopting.

"In moments, a judge will rule on bail conditions for Garrett Singer," Meyer intoned with dramatic effect. "The strange and curious tale of this modern-day hermit has both fascinated and terrified the remote village of Balsam Lake for decades. Today, another chapter will be written…"

Meyer's eyes lit up when he glimpsed Sam drawing near. He motioned for his cameraman to swivel around. "Chief Hayden! Is Garrett Singer still a person of interest in the murder of Graham Danforth?"

Sam scowled at the mic Meyer shoved into his face. "That is still an active investigation. I won't be discussing the details."

"What about Singer's hospitalization?"

"Mr. Singer's medical file is private and confidential."

"C'mon, chief. You gotta give us more than that."

"No. I don't."

"What about the charges Singer faces today? Is it true all you've got on him is a single offense? The break-in at Camp Whippoorwill where he was arrested? Isn't that barely enough to keep him in jail before his trial?"

"Our investigation is still ongoing. We're prepared to bring additional charges when appropriate."

"Anything else you can tell us?"

"Yeah. Next time, don't put your pants in the dryer."

Meyer's follow-ups faded out of earshot as Sam brushed past him and entered the courtroom. It was a small hall that always reminded him of the set of *To Kill a Mockingbird*. Two rows of wooden benches marched away from the double doors on either side of the central aisle. They were nondescript and looked like they could be found in any park. There were more of the same benches in the mezzanine above. A rail of thick spindles separated the spectator gallery from the tables where the lawyers and defendants faced the judge. The coffered ceiling soared high above a red carpet covering the floor, and tall windows spilled light into the room. The walls were painted pale yellow and were hung with an assortment of oil portraits of men no one recognized. Flagstands flanked both sides of the judge's bench. Fixed above the white door that separated the bench from the judge's chambers were the words IN GOD WE TRUST.

The courtroom was already brimming with reporters and curious spectators. Their anticipation and excitement crackled in the air as they waited to get their first look at the infamous *Spooky*, the hermit of Balsam Lake. At Sam's request, a bailiff had reserved a spot for him in the last row of the gallery. He slid onto the bench and folded his arms across his chest.

Alanna Whittaker was already seated at her table, her head bowed over a notepad and a pile of files. At the table opposite her was the county district attorney, Harriet Fellman. She was an experienced prosecutor who had made this courtroom her second home since the days when Sam's dad had been the chief of police.

A sudden hush swept through the spectators, as if the air had suddenly been sucked from the room, leaving them breathless. A bailiff and state trooper had entered through a side door. Thoreau shuffled between them.

Even from across the room, Sam could see he looked like hell. His skin was ashen and his eye sockets were deep wells of sleeplessness. He seemed to have lost weight overnight, his orange jumpsuit now hanging from his lanky frame as if he were a coatrack.

Murmurs bubbled to the surface of the crowd and rippled across the room as Thoreau eased into his chair at the table next to Whittaker. She leaned over and said something in his ear. Thoreau swiveled in his seat and Sam followed his gaze to where Margaret Singer sat in the front row.

The judge's door swung open, and the bailiff ordered them to rise for Judge John Vanharlingen. He was a heavy, red-faced man in his early-fifties, with thinning, snow-white hair that he kept slicked back over his balding pate. A pair of old-fashioned, wire-rimmed spectacles balanced on the bridge of his upturned nose. Vanharlingen gaveled the court into session and didn't waste any time before reading the charges against Thoreau.

Thoreau kept his head bowed the whole time, his eyes fixed on the red carpet between his feet while Whittaker entered his plea of not guilty.

Sam leaned forward on his bench when they got to the topic of bail. This was what he had come here for. The D.A. argued that, given Thoreau had already disappeared from society once, he was at an increased risk of flight and should be remanded without bail.

Whittaker countered that Thoreau didn't own a passport with which to flee the country. He had never been convicted of a crime, and the one he stood accused of now was non-violent in nature. Finally, she produced the doctor's report from Elizabethtown Community detailing his preliminary assessment of Thoreau's health. With no known history of epilepsy, and no unusual brain activity, Thoreau had likely suffered what was known as a psychogenic non-epileptic seizure. Overwhelmed by the intense emotional stress of being thrust into such a new and hostile environment after decades of solitude, his body simply shut down as a defense mechanism. In the doctor's opinion, the episode was likely to repeat itself if they returned Thoreau to the county jail.

Vanharlingen took off his glasses and pinched the bridge of his nose as he addressed Thoreau. "Mr. Singer, never before have I had to rule on a case as unique as your own. On one hand, you have proven particularly adept at disappearing from society and eluding capture. Indeed, under any other circumstances, you would be considered a flight risk of the highest order and bail would be out of the question. On the other hand, given your current medical state, there is a compelling argument to be made that you are in no physical condition to flee."

The judge paused. Thoreau kept his eyes averted, as if the events playing out around him had nothing to do with him.

"It is with this circumstance in mind—and in consideration of the fact that the crime for which you are accused is non-violent in nature—that I see no reason to continue your detainment at Essex County Jail. You are hereby released on the recognizance of your sister, Ms. Margaret Singer, until such time that you are required to return to court for trial. While on bail, you are forbidden from venturing from Ms. Singer's property for a duration of longer than three hours. And you are certainly prohibited from entering any forested or woodland areas. Violation of these terms will result in your immediate return to Essex County and forfeiture of the bond Ms. Singer has posted on your behalf." Vanharlingen fixed his gaze on Thoreau. "Do you understand these conditions as I have explained them to you?"

Thoreau nodded but didn't look up.

"Do you wish to say anything?"

Thoreau shook his head.

WHAM!

Vanharlingen pounded his gavel and adjourned the hearing.

Sam didn't move, even as the other spectators rose to their feet and broke into chatter around him. He kept his narrowed eyes on Thoreau as the bailiff escorted him from the courtroom. This was exactly what Sam had been afraid of. No one could call Vanharlingen a bleeding heart, but he was still bound to follow legal precedent. Now, after eluding capture for over thirty years, Garrett Singer would be free again within the hour.

* * *

Megan couldn't shake the feeling of unease that had settled over her as she drove down the narrow, winding lane that led

200

to the old Singer homestead. The trees on either side of the road were tall and imposing, casting dark shadows over the muddy ruts.

Confronting Thoreau had seemed like a good idea when Megan heard they had released him on bail. But out here, with no one around but the news vans crowding the shoulder of Route 9 back at the mouth of the Singers' private lane, she couldn't help feeling apprehensive about what she might encounter ahead. There was no one around for miles, no one to hear her cries if things went wrong and Thoreau turned on her. But Megan had to believe he wouldn't. He was a wounded animal, not a predator.

As the forest thinned around her and the weatherbeaten farmhouse came into view, Megan could see the property was in a state of disrepair. The fences were falling down; the fields were overgrown, and the dilapidated barn slumped like an old dog with a bad back.

Despite the tension mounting in her gut, Megan parked her pickup and got out. She had come for answers, and she was determined to get them.

Heavy gray clouds hung in the afternoon sky, and a bitter breeze fluttered Megan's hair as she surveyed her bleak surroundings. The farmhouse was just as decrepit as the rest of the property. Its windows were dingy with grime, and the roof was missing several shingles.

A loud creak gave Megan a start. She turned to see the screen door of the farmhouse slowly opening. Her heart fired up, but the flimsy door had just been caught by the wind. It clattered and banged against its frame repeatedly with a lonesome rhythm.

Her heart pounding, Megan approached the house. The windows were darkened, and it didn't appear there was anyone inside. Still, even with her pistol holstered against her hip, Megan felt exposed and vulnerable.

Another sound made her pause before she reached the porch steps. It was coming from the crumbling barn, a slow and steady scraping like the sound of someone sanding wood.

Megan's eyes darted around the property as she rounded the house toward the barn and peeked inside. The space was dark and musty. Cobwebs hung from the ceiling, and accumulated heaps of mechanical detritus were heaped around Margaret Singer's Dodge and the picked-over carcass of her Jeep. Megan was sure she could hear mice scurrying against the walls.

Thoreau was sanding the floorboards of the barn's loft, chipping gray splinters off the timber planks one tiny fraction of an inch at a time. It would take him years to finish. He was too engrossed in his work to notice Megan's presence.

"Thoreau…" Megan said.

Thoreau stopped sanding abruptly and looked down. His expression didn't change at the sight of her standing below. "Why are you here?"

"I need answers. What happened that day by the lake? Did I really kill my father?"

"Leave me alone."

"You know where Piper Flynn is, don't you?" Megan pressed. "But you can't tell us because it might mean giving away your camp."

Thoreau blinked at her and ran a hand over his gray beard.

"Is that it? Is that why you won't tell me what you know?

Or is it something else that frightens you?"

Thoreau turned his back on her and walked out of eyesight.

"You weren't alone out there, were you?" Megan shouted after him. "What are you afraid of, Thoreau? There's something out there in those woods, isn't there? Something evil. I've felt it too. Tell me what it is. Help me save that little girl's life."

The harsh sound of sanding resumed.

"Thoreau!" Megan moved to the ladder to the loft and started to climb.

CLICK CLACK!

A chill prickled Megan's skin at the unmistakable sound of a round being chambered into a rifle. She dropped down to her feet from the ladder and spun around.

Margaret Singer was there with a loaded rifle. "Anything you wanna ask him, you can go ahead and ask his lawyer, Danforth. Unless you got a warrant to be here, get off my property before ya can't."

Megan's green eyes blazed with fury as she stood glaring at the wiry woman. Margaret was right; she had no justification for being there. Sure, she was a sworn law enforcement officer, but unless she had a reasonable suspicion that a crime against the environment was being committed on the Singer property, Alanna Whittaker could file a formal complaint against her for trespassing and harassment. Megan had no doubt the zealous lawyer would do it, too.

Her jaw muscles bunched beneath her skin as she clenched her teeth together and stalked past Margaret toward her pickup.

The crowd of reporters swarmed her truck as she rumbled

from the wooded lane to the intersection of Route 9. Megan slowed to a crawl but didn't stop, waving them aside irritably until her wheels met the solid blacktop and she screeched away. She threw something loud and angry on the stereo and let it blast the entire way home, trying unsuccessfully to find some catharsis in the raging aggression. Her skin itched for a drink, but Russ still hadn't re-opened the Beer n' Bait, and there was no way Megan was going back to the Trail's End so soon after her embarrassing incident there. Eventually, she'd go back and smooth things over with Danny, but not today. She knew she could always grab some beer at the gas station, but anything less than a whole case would only do half the job, and it just didn't seem worth the effort.

The late afternoon wind sweeping across the lake smelled like snow when Megan rumbled to a stop outside her cabin. Her ears were still ringing from the music as she stormed inside. She brewed a pot of coffee and took her steaming mug outside to the porch. It wasn't whiskey, but having something in her hands still gave her some comfort as she stared at the lake and tried to clear her mind.

Tiny windblown whitecaps churned across the steel-gray water. Tendrils of white twirled from the black coffee as Megan sipped and hugged the mug close to her chest, trying to warm herself against the chill in the air. She could have gone inside and lit a fire, but part of her craved the invigoration of the frigid wind.

Megan fished in her pocket for her phone and brought up the voice memos she had made during her talks with Thoreau. She picked one at random and hit *Play*.

"Can you tell me about your home?" Megan's own voice

came through the phone's small speaker.

"I watched a mushroom grow on the trunk of an oak for years. It's one of the more humbling things I've seen."

"You've probably seen a lot of things the rest of us haven't."

"Probably."

CLICK.

Megan cut the clip short and started another one.

"Why didn't you light a fire?"

"Couldn't give away my camp. I'd worked too hard to disappear."

"Mr. Thoreau, why were you out there?"

"I know there's something wrong with me. There always was. My father thought he could cure me…"

CLICK. Megan scrubbed further through the clip.

"Thoreau's masterpiece encompasses the entirety of human resilience and absurdity. There exists no purer account of the roots of human suffering."

CLICK.

Megan paused a moment, brooding. She had listened to these recordings dozens of times; there was nothing new to be gained from them.

From the corner of her eye, Megan's gaze fell on Thoreau's well-worn copy of *Walden*, still sitting on the apple crate where she had left it the night before. She crossed the porch to her chair and cracked the book open. Her attention lingered on the inscription her dad had written for her mother inside the cover.

Megan had very little memories of her father from before the night of the accident that had killed her mom. She thought of the photo of him she kept in her office. What kind of man had he been before tragedy sent his life into the endless spiral of destruction that engulfed Megan and dragged her down with it?

Megan moved on. The pages of the book were covered with underlined passages and notes Thoreau had made in the margins. His small handwriting was remarkably neat and meticulous, the letters perfectly formed and of an obsessively consistent size. Many of the entries were musings that had nothing to do with the content of the pages, as if Thoreau had simply been using the blank spaces on the paper to record his own thoughts. Megan noticed many pages with a number written in the empty space between the bottom of the page and the last paragraph: 262.

Megan stared at the number, pondering its significance. There didn't seem to be any pattern to it. Sometimes it appeared on a few pages in a row before it disappeared, only to resurface later. What did it mean? Maybe nothing?

Megan's gaze was drawn to something else—something strange. The page numbers were circled on each of the pages that bore the number 262. Megan skimmed through the book. The pattern never wavered, except that a few of the page numbers had been circled twice with concentric rings. It had to mean something, but what?

Megan stood and took the book inside. The heat of the cabin welcomed her as she went to her office and grabbed a pencil and a pad of paper. She flipped the book open and walked her fingers through the pages, jotting down the circled page numbers in the order in which they appeared. There were fifteen in all. The first was page three; the last was page ninety-six. There were no more after that, even though the book was over three hundred pages long. Intrigued, Megan studied the sequence of page numbers more closely:

3-4-5-6-7-8-9-10-11-17-20-24-80–90-96

Megan flipped through the book, her eyes scanning the pages for clues. Only the numbers three, seven, and nine were circled twice. Her mind raced with excitement as she looked for a pattern. Other than the mysterious number 262 written at the bottom of each page, the circled numbers didn't seem to have anything in common. Some pages were filled with Thoreau's notes and reflections; others had nothing at all.

Megan let the book tumble from her hands to the desktop with a thunk, frustrated at her inability to decipher the significance of the page numbers. Any insight she could glean into the workings of Thoreau's mind might be useful in finding his camp. She had the nagging sense she was onto something, but she was still no closer to unlocking the meaning behind the cryptic sequence of numbers.

Her face lit up when it suddenly came to her.

No. It can't be...

Megan snatched up the pencil again and began re-writing the page numbers, rearranging them and combining them into sets of three. Her heart raced with anticipation and dread as she worked her way through the list, re-using the numbers that had been circled twice. As she wrote the final combination, an icy chill ran down her spine: 7-4-10.

The numbers matched a date that was tattooed on her memory like the ink in her arms.

July 4, 2010.

The day her father disappeared.

Megan's hands started to shake as she stared at the groupings of numbers she had written. They all corresponded with the dates people had gone missing in the woods. Megan couldn't believe what she was seeing. It couldn't be a coincidence. Thoreau had hidden a secret code in the pages of his copy of *Walden*, and it was clear he was using it to record information about the mysterious disappearances.

All at once, Megan understood.

She grabbed the book again and flipped to page 262. A single passage was underlined. The book trembled in Megan's grip as she read, her eyes riveted by the words. A sickening horror washed over her at what she found.

"Son of a bitch…" she breathed aloud.

Her gaze wandered back to the first date on her list: July 8, 1980. It was the day Timothy Wright set off from his family's Great Camp and never returned. Wright and Thoreau had been boyhood friends. Megan thought of what Ol' Rory had said about finding the boy's bones washed ashore near Witch's Rock. The giant cliff wasn't too far away from where she had found the wolf traps.

The traps…

Thunderstruck by a sudden realization, Megan dropped the book and spun for the office door. She marched through the house to the foyer where she had left her heavy expedition pack. She rummaged through one of its many pockets, pulled out a topographical map, and spread it across the living room coffee table. Her eyes skimmed around the map, searching, searching…

She stopped and stood straight. Her finger located a spot

on the southeast edge of the long body of water that was Balsam Lake. A small gasp escaped her lips, and she raised a hand to her mouth.

"Oh God…"

Megan rushed back to her backpack and stuffed it with some warm clothes, fresh water, and batteries for her headlamp. The wind whipped across the lake and the porch steps trembled beneath her tread as she dashed to her truck. She tossed the backpack into the back and marched to the shed where she stored her canoe.

* * *

Sam made the mistake of looking up Piper Flynn on social media. He was at his desk in his office at the station. Beyond his closed door, he could hear Noah fielding the relentless calls from journalists asking for comment on the release of Garrett Singer. The damn phone had been ringing all day. What did they expect him to say? The media seemed intent on painting Singer as some kind of goddamn martyr, the misunderstood victim of a society without a soul.

Sam had been curious about how Margaret Singer had been able to post bail for her brother's release. From the state of her homestead, it didn't look like she had that kind of money to spare. Sam had made a few calls. It turned out that Margaret had inherited the settlement money the paper company had paid her mother as compensation for the mesothelioma she'd contracted due to asbestos exposure.

Sam heaved a sigh as he logged in to the department's social media accounts. He skimmed the posts about Garrett

Singer. A local guy named Zed Williams had offered to let Singer stay on his acreage rent-free if he was acquitted. Judy Langlois had started a crowdfunding campaign to get him enough cash for legal fees and a few years' worth of groceries to go back into the woods.

Sam ground his teeth together and moved on to the thread about Piper Flynn. He skimmed the posts. There weren't any new leads, but someone had started a dedicated "Find Piper" page. Sam clicked on it.

There were hundreds of messages offering thoughts and prayers for Piper's safe return. Piper's mom, Becky Flynn, reacted to every comment. But as Sam scrolled through the feed, he felt his stomach turn. Lurking among the well-wishers were hateful, inflammatory posts, people spewing venom about what terrible parents the Flynns were to have not taken better care of their daughter. A sense of disgust washed over Sam as he read one particularly nasty comment, full of cruel insults and personal attacks on Becky herself: *mom who lets he kid wander off in the middle of the nite isnt fit 2 b a mom if her girl dead then it her own fault…*

Sam's chest tightened, and he sat back in his chair. He couldn't believe people could be so heartless, so lacking in empathy and understanding. Is this really what the world had come to? He couldn't fathom how helpless Becky Flynn felt, how soul-destroying it was for her to know her little girl was out there somewhere, lost and alone and terrified, wanting nothing more than the safety of her mother's loving arms. He imagined Becky reading this comment and felt a surge of anger rise up within him. Who were these assholes to be passing judgement on her and adding to her agony in her time of suffering? These churlish parasites feasting like maggots on the rot of other people's pain?

Sam started typing to fire off a response, to let this jerk know exactly what he thought of them. He knew it wouldn't do any good. He had seen how these things went, how quickly they escalated, and how toxic they could become. Sam didn't want to sink to that level, to stoop to the same kind of behavior he was disgusted by. But he just couldn't let this go. Someone needed to stand up for Becky. If these things weren't just happening online—if he witnessed someone actually saying these things to her in person on the street or in Brenda's diner—Sam would knock the prick's teeth down his throat.

His phone interrupted him before he could post his reply. He glanced at the number and picked up. "Megan—"

"It's his journal, Sam!"

"What? Slow down. What are you—"

"Singer's copy of *Walden*. He was using it as a journal, written in code. He probably kept it with him at all times. That's why he had it with him when you arrested him." Megan explained the significance of the circled page numbers and the dates they represented. "There's another number written at the bottom of every one of those pages: two-six-two."

"What does that mean?" Sam asked. "Another code?"

"Another page number. Singer made notes and underlined passages all over the book, but there's only one sentence underlined on page 262." She repeated what she had read out loud for him. "*I do not wish to kill nor to be killed, but I can foresee circumstances in which both these things would be by me unavoidable.*"

The meaning of the words hit Sam like a bolt as he followed her thinking. "Kill or be killed? It's a confession, isn't it? All those dates…"

"You were right about him, Sam. He killed them. He killed them all. Except he didn't want to record what he'd done, so he referred to this passage instead. The real Thoreau wrote it in defense of a nineteenth-century abolitionist who led a deadly revolt to free slaves."

"And Singer believed the murders were the only way he could keep himself free in the wild."

"You got it," Megan said. "He used me, Sam. He was there that day at the lake. He saw how my father treated me—and when he saw me again at the station all these years later, he shared his own story of abuse to gain my sympathy and trust. That's why he would only talk to me."

"Wait. What abuse?" Sam asked.

"Singer's father used to keep him locked in the crawl space beneath the house when he was a kid. He said it's what drove him out into the woods."

"But that's not possible," Sam said. "Margaret Singer said their dad was diagnosed with Lou Gehrig's when Singer was little. State records confirmed it. Singer's old man collected disability pay for most of his adult life. There's no way he could have done those things to his boy."

"Son of a bitch!" The sound of Megan slamming her palm onto her steering wheel barked through the phone. "He lied to me, Sam. He lied about everything."

"It doesn't matter now. He's still going to jail."

"No, he didn't spend thirty years out there without a plan

for the day he got caught. Everything we know about Singer was a lie, part of a story he made up for one specific purpose."

Sam caught on. "To get himself released."

"He's going to disappear again. And this time, he'll make damn sure no one ever finds him. But I know where his camp is, Sam. I was right there!"

"What? Where?"

"A spot off the White Lily Pond trail, between the old Wright camp and Witch's Rock. The wolf traps I found there were over thirty years old."

"So?"

"The wolves only started reappearing in the park a few years ago. Those traps weren't intended for predators, Sam. Thoreau set them to protect his camp from *people*."

"Holy shit." Sam's mind reeled as the revelations slammed into each other like a highway pile-up. He got up, grabbed his jacket, and marched through the station to the parking lot. "Where are you now?"

"It's a three-hour hike from the trailhead to Witch's Rock, but I can be there in half the time if I paddle across from Black Point. I'm almost there now."

"No! Wait and we'll send the state boys in with you."

"Can't wait, Sam. Temperature's dipping below freezing tonight and Piper Flynn's already spent four nights out there in the cold. We can't risk another minute. I gotta get to her before it's too late."

"Megan—"

"Gonna lose reception any second. Keep an eye on Thoreau. Don't let him get away again. I'll get back to you when I can."

"No, don't go alone! If you—"

The call dropped. Megan had driven out of service range.

"Damn it!" Sam climbed into his SUV. His tires screeched and scorched the blacktop as he spun the truck around in a careening turn and floored it out of town toward the Singer homestead.

Chapter 23

The air was thick with a fine, gray mist that danced around the trees encompassing the old Singer house, as if trying to keep the secrets of the forest hidden from view. It was an eerie, otherworldly sight, one that filled Thoreau with a melancholy sense of longing. He stood by the porch rail and gazed at the endless expanse of wilderness. The incessant wind swirled around him, and his breath sent wisps of white out into the chilly air. His bulky duffel bag sat heaped next to his boots on the peeling floorboards.

Shrouded in white, there was a sense of stillness, of waiting, that hung over the trees. They called to Thoreau, beckoning him to return. His cool blue gaze drank in the misty landscape, and he let the haunting beauty of the silent woods transport him back...

* * *

July the Fourth, 2010. Thoreau grips the long handle of his timber axe as he creeps toward the edge of the cliff known as

Witch's Rock. A man's voice rises from somewhere near the lake below. He sounds agitated. Distraught.

Thoreau keeps low to avoid being seen as he draws to a halt at the cliff's edge.

He peers over the precipice...

Sees...

A young girl is on her hands and knees, vomiting into the reeds by the water's edge. She can't be more than eleven or twelve—thirteen at the most. The ground around her is littered with empty beer cans. A cheap fishing rod lies discarded nearby.

A lanky man hovers over her, making a feeble attempt to help. He nudges her. "Hey! Hey, are you okay?"

The girl's retching gives way to painful dry-heaves. Contortions wrack her girlish body as she spits up bile. Spent, she slumps and topples over onto her back.

"Hey..." the man gives her a shake. "Hey! Hey, wake up!"

There's no response. The girl's out cold.

Thoreau can't be sure, but the man doesn't look steady on his feet. He sways like a sapling in a strong wind. Is he drunk?

Suddenly, he glances up.

And glimpses Thoreau gazing down at him.

For a brief moment, their eyes meet across the distance before Thoreau can scuttle out of sight.

"Hey! I need some help here!" the man shouts. "My daughter's sick! I need some help!"

Thoreau's heart kicks against his breastbone and his overwrought breaths heave as he retreats through the woods. The man saw him! Thoreau is sure of it. He's been spotted less than a hundred yards from his camp.

He can't leave here…

A chilling voice whispers in Thoreau's ear and brings him to a skidding halt.

He knows you're here now. He'll bring others back here. When they come, they'll take you away from me…

The voice is low and sepulchral, like the rusty creak of a cemetery gate.

You can't let him leave here, Garrett…

Thoreau squeezes the axe handle tighter, his knuckles cracking around the solid wood.

Don't let them come and tear us apart…

There's a muted shuffling in the forest somewhere ahead. The man has entered the woods by the water's edge. His shouts bounce among the trees and echo through the forest as he searches for Thoreau, still pleading for help.

Do it, Garrett! Do it now, before it's too late!

Thoreau moves, picking his way silently from root to rock. His sweaty T-shirt clings to his lanky frame and his palms are slick on the axe handle. Nausea roils his gut. He loathes himself for what he's about to do, but he doesn't have a choice.

The forest thins around him. There's a hollow grove among the trees and boulders ahead. It's one Thoreau knows well. It sits at the mouth of the maze of boulders that guard his camp. There's only one real way into the hollow, a natural path through the woods that funnels Thoreau toward a fallen spruce. He clambers over, careful to avoid the wolf trap camouflaged in the underbrush on the other side.

The man's shouts swell in volume as Thoreau approaches the tree line at the lake's edge. He crouches behind the massive remains of an uprooted tree and waits, his blood thundering in his ears as he peers through the dense tangle of roots.

The man stands facing the woods with his back to the girl. He's got his hands cupped around his mouth, still shouting for help. "Hey, where'd you go? Didn't you hear me? I need some help!"

The man waits. When no response comes, he swivels around to the girl. Turning his back to the woods, he gets down on his knees by her side and shakes her shoulder to rouse her.

Thoreau bursts from the trees.

The man's head whips around. He sees Thoreau coming with his axe raised. Thoreau's eyes are wild and his bearded face is red and twisted. He lets out an anguished cry as he charges. A dumb look of incomprehension blooms on the man's face a split-second before it fills with terror. He has enough time to raise a hand in a laughable attempt at defense.

WHACK!

Thoreau brings the axe crashing down on his skull.

Blood spurts and sprays the air as the sharp blade sinks deep, nearly cleaving the man's head in two. It rains down on the unconscious girl, showering her face and body, covering her in crimson.

Thoreau's chest swells and deflates as he yanks the blade free. Blood and brains ooze from a jagged gash in the man's head and seep into the muddy ground beneath the reeds.

The icy voice breathes into Thoreau's ear as he stands over the stranger's mutilated corpse.

Good, Garrett… Good…

Thoreau can't leave the bloody corpse out here to be discovered, but he doesn't dare haul it back to his camp. Someone may come looking for this person. He drags the body to the canoe and heaves it into the hull, cramming it into the space between the benches. He risks a momentary pause, unable to resist getting a good look at the young girl's blood-spattered face before he slips the canoe into the water and paddles away.

Hours later, when darkness has fallen and the song of the night creatures assuages the horrors of the day, the booming echo of the fireworks rolling across the lake tells Thoreau it's the Fourth of July. He records the date, circling the page numbers in his worn copy of *Walden*. He doesn't know why he does it, but it feels like it should be done. Like marking a child's height on a door frame or keeping count of lost baby teeth.

Under the cover of darkness, Thoreau glides across the placid lake in the stolen canoe. He has stripped the intruder's body of his clothes and his naked corpse now lies wrapped in a green tarp at Thoreau's feet. He paddles silently toward the distant shore and lets the canoe glide to a halt in the middle of a lonesome cove. The corpse hits the water with a splash and rocks the canoe gently from side to side.

Thoreau watches the tarp-shrouded body sink, swallowed up by the black water.

* * *

The rusty creak of the screen door closing brought Thoreau back to himself. He glanced over his shoulder. Margaret was emerging from the house. She had a crocheted shawl wrapped around her shoulders as she joined her brother by the porch rail and followed his gaze toward the shadowy trees. They stood together in silence as twilight spilled like ink over the land and snowflakes began to flutter from the sky.

"The things I did out there… I did them because I had to," Thoreau said after a moment. "For *him*. You understand? I couldn't let them separate us. I couldn't leave him out there alone forever. Not after what I did to him."

Margaret shivered and clutched the corners of her shawl together over her chest with a bony hand. "You don't have to go back out there." Her voice was low and brittle. "He has the girl now."

Thoreau shook his head. "We're connected, he and I. We keep each other alive."

Thoreau turned from the misty forest to his sister. A dramatic change came over him as he dropped the character he'd been playing since his arrest. His eyes were now sharp and calculating. His voice became deep and articulate.

"The world's gotten worse since I've been gone. It's got more teeth and claws than I ever found out there." He motioned down the homestead's long and curving driveway toward where the news vans clustered like parasites at the far end.

Margaret placed a hand on his broad shoulder. "Go, Garrett," she said softly. "There's no life for you here. There never was."

Thoreau looked her in the face, conflicted. "They'll come for you if I leave."

"I'll be alright. What's the worst they can do to me? I never knew what to do with the money anyway. Ma would've wanted it this way." Margaret shivered and pulled her shawl tighter around her bony shoulders. "I should've stood up for you more when we was little. I know that now. I've known it for a very long time." She gestured toward the trees. "Go on. Go home."

Thoreau looked back at the forest, irresistibly drawn to its familiar silence. He couldn't resist its call.

As he descended the porch steps and made his way into the misty woods, he took a deep breath and filled his lungs with the crisp, clean air. He didn't look back at the house or his sister. The pull of the forest was too strong.

Snowflakes accumulated on the duffel slung over Thoreau's shoulder as he recited a murmured passage from Walden. "*I find it wholesome to be alone the greater part of the time. To be in company, even with the best, is soon wearisome and dissipating. I love to be alone. I never found the companion that was so companionable as solitude...*"

The falling snow covered Thoreau's footprints and erased them, as if he were never there at all.

Chapter 24

Megan's canoe glided across the glassy surface of the gloomy lake. The only sound was the gentle splash of her paddle. The water was still and inky-black, seeming to absorb all the light that touched its surface. It gave no indication of the frigid depths that lay beneath. The scent of pine lingered in the breeze, and the distant sound of rushing water echoed through the silence. Twilight was fading fast and thick shadows crept over the desolate landscape. Snowflakes had begun to fall, enveloping the lake in an eerie veil. They landed on Megan's eyelashes and dissolved into nothingness when they hit the surface of the water.

The damp air was thick with a breathless sense of foreboding as Megan cut through the gloom. Mist and heavy clouds shrouded the tall peaks surrounding the lake, giving them an otherworldly appearance. Megan felt like a lonesome ghost as she peered into the murk ahead, searching for the trees on the distant shore. There was nothing visible; no movement, no sign of life. No birds sang, and no animals stirred. It was as if the lake had been forgotten by the world, left to freeze and die in the icy embrace of the mountains.

Megan paddled faster, her strokes quickening as the excitement inside her grew. The water seemed to go on forever, stretching out into the misty horizon. And then she saw it. An immense shadow materialized from the gloom straight ahead. Its jagged rocks reached up from the water toward the sky like grasping fingers.

Megan's heart raced. This was it.

Witch's Rock.

Megan leaned into her strokes, her arms straining as she propelled herself through the deep, icy water. The towering cliff loomed over her like a dreadful sentinel as she glided beneath its base toward the trees crowding the shore. The bottom of the hull scraped against the bank and Megan leapt out onto the land, her footsteps echoing off the rocks. She hauled the canoe ashore, grabbed her big backpack, and looped it over her shoulders. She stole a look back over the water. It was like a black mirror reflecting the dim and starless sky above. Megan saw her own face, pale and drawn, staring back at her. She took a deep breath and entered the forest.

The trees stood still and were eerily silent around her. Megan's heart quickened as she picked her way through the cold and lifeless wilderness, the frosted terrain crunching beneath her boots. Clouds of breath billowed from her mouth. The shadows deepened between the trees and a fierce wind was now whipping the snow flurries into a frenzy.

Megan flicked her headlamp on. Snowflakes danced through the spectral beam as it cut through the gathering darkness. She stopped and scanned the woods with her light to get her bearings. All directions looked the same: nothing but endless trees. She checked her GPS for the coordinates of the spot where she'd found the wolf traps. It wasn't too far off.

The darkness was smothering now, and the cold was tightening its grip on her flesh. Megan unslung her pack and rummaged for a fleece beanie and a pair of gloves. She hugged her coat tighter around her, shivering as another gust of wind howled through the trees.

But it wasn't just the frosty air that prickled her skin.

There was something wrong about this place. She could feel it. These weren't the woods she knew; this was a place of death. Something dark and sinister lurked unseen in the shadows just beyond her light. Its malevolent presence sent currents of fear rippling through Megan's bones.

Her pace was slow and wary as she pressed on. The air grew even colder, and the trees seemed to close in around her; the branches reaching for her like bony fingers. They clawed at her clothes as if trying to grab her and pull her back into the darkness. Megan could almost feel eyes watching her from the gloom. The air was heavy with the scent of decay, and the rustling of leaves underfoot seemed to whisper secrets from the grave. She kept turning around, expecting to see a pair of glowing eyes staring back at her, but all she saw was the empty, shadowy forest.

Despite the frigid chill in the air, sweat beaded on Megan's forehead as she quickened her pace again. She tried to steady her breathing, but her heart was pounding in her chest, and she couldn't shake that terrible feeling that she was being watched. This was a mistake. Sam was right; she shouldn't have come here alone. But it was too late to turn back now. Piper Flynn was out here somewhere, and Megan wasn't going home without her.

Megan...

A voice crawled out of the darkness.

Megan froze, her blood turning to ice. She knew that voice. It was soft and faint, but there was no mistaking it.

It was her father.

"Dad?" Megan's shout echoed through the woods. Her breaths came in quick gasps as she spun around, trying to find the source of the sound. The voice seemed to have come from everywhere and nowhere at once. Snow swirled through her headlamp and made it difficult to see more than a few feet in front of her. The light bounced from tree to tree, but she saw nothing but snow and shadows. Maybe the whine of the wind was playing tricks on her nerves?

Megan hesitated, her hand shaking as she reached out to touch the gnarled trunk of a nearby tree. She knew she should turn back, that whatever was waiting for her in the darkness couldn't be good. But the voice sounded so real, so close... so much like *him*...

Megan...

There it was again. Even closer.

Megan jumped with fright. This time, she caught its location. She squinted into the gloom.

There was a figure standing in the shadows, a silent silhouette looming black-on-black in the darkened woods.

"Dad?" Megan whispered, her voice trembling.

The figure didn't answer, but remained very still and silent.

Megan took a step forward, then another, drawn in by the figure's mysterious presence. Her instincts screamed at her to turn around, but she was powerless against her own curiosity.

She had to know who—or what—was out there.

But it was already gone. The shadowy figure vanished so quickly before Megan's eyes, she questioned if she had seen it at all. She took a step back, one hand shaking as she reached for her pistol holster while the other hand fumbled in her pocket for her phone. She had to call for help; she had to get out of these woods. It was surely impossible to catch a signal out here, but she had to at least try. Maybe she would get lucky. Her hand closed around the device, but as she fumbled with it, she felt an icy breath on the back of her neck.

Megan let out a startled scream and ran through the darkness. Her headlamp danced madly and her boots pounded the frozen ground. As she crashed through the underbrush, her foot caught on a gnarled root and she hit the ground with a cry of alarm. She lay there for a moment, her eyes squeezed shut, waiting for whatever was out there to wrap its cold hands around her.

But as she opened her eyes, there was nothing but darkness and silence. The wind had died down, and the only sound was the pounding of her own heart. Breathless and shaking, Megan slowly rose to her feet. Her eyes darted around nervously as she tried to orient herself. She was in the same small hollow where she had found the wolf traps. Megan scanned her surroundings with her light. Deeper in the woods ahead, the forest seemed to end at what looked to be a solid wall of granite.

Megan knew it wasn't what it seemed.

She approached and brushed aside some overgrown vines to investigate the rock face carefully. There was a hidden fissure in the granite, just wide enough for a person to squeeze through. She pushed through the gap and navigated her way through a maze of immense boulders until she came to a sudden halt.

Megan's fear melted away at what she saw. She dropped her pack in awe, marveling at an intricate network of ropes and giant green tarps that formed a hut of four walls and a roof, nestled beneath an impenetrable canopy of evergreen boughs.

This was it. Thoreau's camp.

"Piper!" Megan shouted. Her voice bounded through the forest and was swallowed up by the darkness. Her pulse thumped in her ears as she waited for a response.

None came.

Megan scanned her surroundings, searching the site for any signs of life.

The place was deserted.

Megan felt a crushing sense of disappointment as she crept toward the makeshift hut. Her light swept over a boneyard of rusted propane tanks littering the perimeter of the site. She caught a glimpse of Thoreau's trash dump: a deep pit filled with thirty years of waste. Candy wrappers, chip bags, coffee, tin cans, bottles of alcohol, soda. Nearby was a weather-beaten toilet seat fastened to a crude wooden box built over a hole in the ground. There was also a water collection barrel: a spacious fiberglass tub now covered with a thin sheet of ice. Thoreau had manipulated the tree branches overhead to funnel moisture into the container.

Megan couldn't help admiring the hermit's resourceful ingenuity as she reached for the loose flap of a tarp that served as an entrance to the hut. She pulled it aside and peeked within.

Inside was a tidy and homelike refuge. Thoreau's Coleman stove was the centerpiece of the shelter; his life revolved around its warmth. An assortment of utensils, jugs, and tools dangled from ropes against one tarp wall. Another side of the shelter was stacked high with Tupperware bins and milk crates for storage. Assorted tin cans of winter provisions were organized neatly on makeshift wooden shelves supported by upturned logs. Other shelves were lined with dozens of books, like a personal library.

Pitched on the dirt floor, in the middle of the space, was a weathered canvas tent. Megan eyed it warily, scanning it for signs of life.

"Piper?" she whispered, her voice still sounding too loud in her ears.

There was no response. The tent sat still and lifeless in the silent darkness.

Megan crept deeper into the makeshift hut. The air was filled with the musty smell of old canvas, damp earth, and the lingering traces of cooking grease. She popped the lids off a few of the bins. Inside, she found spare clothes, tools, packs of batteries, and electronics that had gone obsolete decades ago. She moved to the bookshelves and scanned the spines with her light. There were old paperback thrillers and mysteries, but also books on law and medicine. One title stood out to Megan, a thick volume on autism spectrum disorder. She pulled it from the shelf and cracked it open to one of the most heavily dog-eared pages. It was the start of an entire chapter on Asperger's syndrome.

Megan swore under her breath. More lies. The bastard had spent decades piecing together everything he needed to get himself released if they ever caught him.

A sound broke the deep silence.

Megan's head snapped around to the tent, certain she had heard a faint rustling from within.

Someone was in there.

Megan's adrenaline surged. Her headlight beam cut through the darkness and she rested a hand on her pistol as she slowly, slowly approached the canvas tent. It was old and worn, with frayed edges and patches that had seen better days. The flaps were closed, but Megan knew what she had heard.

"Who's in there?" she demanded.

No response.

Megan hesitated, her feet suddenly rooted to the ground. She had a strong sense that something was off about this place, that there was danger lurking within the folds of the tent. What if this was all a trap? What if there was something terrible inside waiting for her?

But she had to know the truth. Megan knew she had to go in, but her instincts were telling her to turn and run. Her heart pounded, and she found herself holding her breath as she reached out a trembling hand and unzipped the tent flap. She pushed it aside just enough to peer within, revealing a dim and cramped interior.

And a motionless figure covered in a shroud of shadows.

Megan recoiled, her blood running cold until her headlamp lit up the pale face of a frightened young girl staring back at her.

"Piper!" Megan scrambled into the tent and knelt next to the girl among the heaped mass of wool blankets. "Are you okay? Why didn't you let me know you were in here?"

Piper stared at her with wide and fearful eyes. Her mouth opened and closed for a moment, as if too terrified to find a voice. "He… He doesn't want me to say anything. He doesn't want me to ever leave here."

"Who? The big man with the beard? Thoreau?"

Piper shook her head, and her voice dropped to a whisper. "No… the skeleton boy."

A chill ran down Megan's spine. "Piper, my name's Megan Danforth. I'm kind of like a forest ranger." There was an urgent edge in her voice. Every moment they spent here made her skin tingle with unease. She wrapped an arm around Piper's shoulders. "Come on. I'm taking you home."

She ushered Piper from the tent and threw back the hanging tarp of the shelter to the cold night air beyond.

A hulking shape stood in the snowy darkness at the mouth of the maze of boulders.

Piper let out a panicked cry and Megan skidded to a halt as her light glinted off the sharp blade of the hunting knife in Thoreau's hand.

Chapter 25

Sam crouched behind the cover of a big pine, his eyes fixed on the dilapidated farmhouse in the distance. He had left his truck about a quarter of a mile up the Singers' private lane and hiked the rest of the way on foot, not wanting to alert them to his presence. There was no legal reason to be trespassing on their property or spying on their whereabouts, but if Megan was right, Sam wasn't about to let Thoreau simply vanish into the forest again. He had too much to answer for.

Sam had radioed the state police for backup for Megan on the drive over, but the barracks in Ray Brook were nearly an hour from Pilot Point, and most of the troop were still out searching for Piper Flynn. The dispatch promised to divert troopers to Witch's Rock, but it would take some time for them to get there.

Now, the light had faded from the sky and snowflakes tumbled lazily through the air. Sam's muscles ached and his stomach growled with hunger, but he knew he couldn't afford to let his guard down. He had to stay alert, ready for anything.

As the minutes ticked by, Sam's thoughts wandered to what Megan had said about Thoreau. If he'd lied about being abused by his father to manipulate her into taking his side, what else had he made up? The psych test that had convinced Dr. Rose he was a man living with Asperger's? The seizure that had all but guaranteed his release on bail? Sam considered what they knew for certain about Thoreau, and the answer was *nothing*. Was it possible Thoreau had faked all of it? Was he really that cunning?

A slow feeling of apprehension came over Sam as night fell and the shadows thickened around him. Something about the old farmhouse felt off. It showed no signs of life. The windows were dark, and no one had come or gone since he arrived. What were they doing in there? Sitting around in the dark, catching up on the last thirty years? Sam wondered if he was too late. Maybe Thoreau was already gone. But just as he was about to stand up and stretch his cramped legs, he saw a flicker of movement in one of the darkened windows.

Sam's heart raced as he rested his palm on the butt of the pistol holstered on his hip. He couldn't actually see anyone, but he got the sense someone was in there, watching him from the darkness.

Suddenly, the back door to the farmhouse creaked open, and a figure stepped out onto the porch. It remained there a moment before descending the steps and coming Sam's way, shuffling through the dusting of snow that had settled on the overgrown yard. Sam's finger tightened on the trigger, ready to fire if the figure made any sudden moves.

But as the person drew closer, Sam realized it was a

woman, not Thoreau. Margaret Singer looked scared and disheveled, as if she had just survived a struggle.

Sam lowered his gun and approached her cautiously. "Are you okay?" he asked, his voice low and reassuring.

Margaret nodded, tears streaming over the deep creases of her face. "He's going to kill me," she whispered, her voice shaking. "My brother. He's... He's... Oh, God, please help me..." She sobbed and covered her face with her hands.

Sam's pulse pounded in his ears as he turned and sprinted towards the farmhouse, his gun drawn and ready. He knew it was going to be a tense and dangerous confrontation, but he was bringing in Thoreau for good this time, no matter what it took. Sweat dripped down his forehead as he stormed through the back door into the kitchen. He scanned the room quickly, taking in the dim interior. The air was thick with the smell of burnt toast and rancid bacon grease.

"Come out here, Singer!" Sam shouted.

The farmhouse remained silent. The only sound was Sam's heavy breathing and the drumming of his pulse in his ears. He crept from the kitchen, his eyes darting from side to side as he searched for any sign of movement. The floorboards creaked beneath his feet, and every shadow seemed to shift and stare back at him.

As he entered the living room, a gust of wind blew through an open window, causing the thin curtains to billow out. Sam spun around, his heart racing. But there was nothing there. Just the shabby old furniture, overflowing ashtrays, and Margaret's collection of soda cans that seemed to cover every inch of the room.

Sam continued his search, making his way down the

hallway, the once bright walls now dull and peeling. He could feel his pulse quickening as he approached the last room in the back of the house, knowing Thoreau could be hiding anywhere.

He pushed the door open, gun at the ready, and stepped inside. The room was dark and musty, the only light coming from a window high on the wall. As his eyes adjusted to the darkness, Sam saw a figure standing in the corner. He aimed his gun and took a step closer, his heart pounding in his chest.

"Come out where I can see you," he growled.

But the figure didn't move. It just stood there, silent and still. Sam took another step closer, his finger hovering over the trigger.

As he reached out to grab the man, he realized with a shock that it was just a heavy winter coat hanging on a rack in the room's corner.

Sam let out a sigh of relief and lowered his gun, but he knew Thoreau was still somewhere in the house, watching and waiting for the perfect moment to strike. Despite his years as a cop, Sam couldn't help but feel a sense of foreboding as he continued his search. He was looking for a killer—a man who had eluded capture for thirty years and who had possibly murdered over half a dozen people. Sam had always questioned why Thoreau had just given himself up the night of his arrest instead of using his knife to get away from Hank Morrison. After his conversation with Megan, it finally clicked. An attempted murder charge would have ruined Thoreau's plan to get himself released. But now that Thoreau was almost certainly going to prison, he had nothing to lose. What would he do to avoid capture this time?

As he made his way up the creaky staircase, Sam couldn't shake the feeling that someone was following him. He turned around, but again, there was nothing there. Sam ground his teeth together. He knew he was on edge, but he couldn't help it. Something about this place just didn't feel right.

Finally, he reached the top of the stairs and turned down a darkened hallway, his gun held out in front of him. He found himself growing more and more uneasy as he searched room after room on the second floor with no sign of Thoreau. All were empty and looked like they hadn't been entered in years. Cobwebs clung to the corners, layers of grime covered the walls, and the beds were stripped to the mattresses. Sam could barely make out the shapes of the furniture in the gloom.

Except for one room.

A faint light filtered from underneath the door to the corner room at the end of the hall.

Sam aimed his gun and hesitated. Was Thoreau in there, waiting for him on the other side of the door? He steadied his hand as he reached for the handle and eased the door open, his pulse thrumming in his throat. In the dim yellow light of a bedside lamp, he saw the dresser had been dusted, an old TV had been placed on a low table, and clean sheets had been laid on the bed.

This was supposed to be Thoreau's room.

Sam noticed the rumpled spot where someone had recently sat on the edge of the bed. The room was empty, but something about the way the dust hung in the air made it feel like there were unseen eyes watching his every move. A sinking feeling wormed its way down into his gut.

Thoreau was gone.

And Margaret had lied to him.

Only then did a distressing thought come to him: where had she gone?

A floorboard creaked behind him. Sam's heart lurched, and he spun around.

Right into the barrel of the rifle pointed at his face.

Chapter 26

Megan didn't hesitate. She reached for the pistol holstered against her hip. Her fingers closed around the cold metal as she yanked it free and aimed it at Thoreau's chest.

"Don't come any closer, Thoreau…" she warned, wishing she sounded more confident, that her voice didn't tremble when she said his name. She kept Piper shielded behind her as she circled around Thoreau warily, trying to keep a safe distance between them as she searched for an opening. She had always been a decent shot, but never fired at a living man.

Thoreau watched her with a predatory gaze, the knife held loosely in his hand.

"She's leaving here with me," Megan hissed. Her grip on the pistol tightened as she cocked the hammer. "You're not going to hurt anyone else. I won't let you."

Thoreau didn't answer. He simply stared at her, his eyes icy and calculating. And in that moment, Megan realized the terrible truth. Thoreau had come home, and like any creature that lives in the wild, he would kill to protect his territory.

He lunged at her without warning.

Megan dodged to the right, narrowly avoiding the blade as it swiped through the air where she had been standing just a moment before. She squeezed off a shot and missed, too off-balance to hit her moving target. The roaring blast of the gun blew shockwaves through the black and silent forest.

Thoreau snarled and swung the knife again, this time aiming for Megan's stomach. She skipped back and whipped the gun around. But he was too close and quick. He came at her with his teeth bared, the knife flashing through her light as he slashed at her. A searing pain ignited in Megan's arm as the blade sliced through her flesh, and she cried out in agony. Thoreau followed-up with a vicious punch to her jaw that spun her around on her feet and sent her crashing to the ground. The pistol flew from her grip and went skittering away into the darkness.

Blood poured from Megan's mouth and her tongue flicked to her teeth to make sure they were all there. Her vision shifted in and out of focus and her breaths came quick and shallow as she lay there, sprawled on her stomach among the dirt and pine needles. In her daze, she was dimly aware of Thoreau stepping over her to get to Piper.

Megan refused to let the pain defeat her. She was no stranger to being hit, and this wasn't the first time she'd been knocked flat. She had learned two things from her father: how to drink, and how to get up from a beating. For years, she had been the nail he liked to hit.

Until she'd grown up to be a hammer.

Megan dragged herself to her feet. Blood still streamed from her lips and dripped from her chin as she rocked on her heels. With a fierce determination, she faced Thoreau, ready to take him down once and for all. He took a step back, too stunned by her resilience to remember the knife in his grip. A look of shocked disbelief sparked in his icy stare a split-second before her fist collided with his bearded cheek. His head whipped around on his neck. Megan didn't give him a chance to recover before she hammered him with another powerful blow to the temple.

Thoreau staggered under Megan's assault, but he didn't go down. He continued to slash and thrust with the knife, determined to end her resistance. Megan darted and dodged, narrowly avoiding the blade each time, and landing devastating blows to vulnerable points in his ribcage and head. The sounds of their grunts rang through the snowy grove as they struggled, locked in a primal dance of determination and will.

Savage rage had replaced the wicked glint in Thoreau's eyes as he swung at Megan madly, forcing her to duck and roll to the side. She was back in the ring now, and she had to keep moving, to stay on the offensive if she wanted to survive. Her muscles strained and her knuckles were raw and bloody as she gathered all her strength and launched a final, desperate attack. The dull thud of her fists against Thoreau's flesh filled the air as she pummeled him mercilessly, beating him back until his knees buckled beneath him and he crumpled to the ground.

Megan wasted no time waiting to see if he would get up again. Breathless and battered, she grabbed Piper and dragged her into the maze of boulders. Megan's heart pounded in her chest as they fled, her feet pounding the ground. Behind her, she could hear Thoreau's heavy footsteps, getting closer and closer. She darted left and right, hauling Piper along with her, trying to throw him off her trail. But no matter how fast they ran, they couldn't shake him. He'd had thirty years to explore this granite labyrinth. He alone knew its secrets. He knew every exit... and every dead-end.

Megan darted around a corner, her breath coming in ragged gasps. She knew she couldn't keep this up for much longer. She spotted a crevice between two boulders and shoved Piper in before she squeezed through herself, hoping Thoreau wouldn't be able to follow. They emerged on the other side and kept running, Megan's eyes scanning the darkness for any sign of an escape route.

Suddenly, she heard a loud crash and the sound of rock crumbling. She turned to see Thoreau had followed her through the crevice, his knife glinting in the beam of her light. Megan let out an exhausted gasp, and they took off again, their legs pumping as fast as they could. She could feel Thoreau's breath on her neck, could hear his ragged panting.

Megan spotted an opening in the boulders up ahead and they darted for it, her heart pounding in her ears. They burst through the opening and into the open air of the forest. Megan's lungs burned as she ran. She risked a glance over her shoulder, her whole body shaking with adrenaline.

Thoreau was nowhere to be seen.

An icy chill rippled Megan's flesh. This wasn't right. Where had he gone? What was he doing?

Piper's shrill scream shattered the dreadful silence.

Megan whirled and there was Thoreau in their path. Somehow, he had skirted around them to cut them off.

Megan's heart plummeted. There was no escaping him out here. These were *his* woods.

Thoreau stalked toward them, his breath forming frosty plumes in the cold air. His knife gleamed in Megan's light as he moved slowly, warily, remembering what she was capable of. She had surprised him once; he wouldn't underestimate her again. Megan pushed Piper behind her and faced him as she advanced through the swirling snow. She was determined to protect the girl at all costs.

A low growl rolled out from the darkness.

Megan felt the hairs rise on the back of her neck. There, in the shadows between the trees, she saw a pair of glowing yellow eyes and the glint of teeth.

Thoreau saw it too. He froze in his tracks and swiveled around slowly as a massive gray wolf emerged from the underbrush, fangs bared and saliva dripping from its jaws. The beast's lips were pulled back to reveal a set of razor-sharp teeth, and its fur was standing on end. Deep and menacing snarls rumbled in its chest as it stalked toward Thoreau, low to the ground, its yellow eyes fixed on him with a murderous glint.

Megan had never witnessed such unprovoked ferocity in a wolf. This wasn't the animal's normal predatory behavior. Something was terribly wrong. Something had scared this beast to the point of lashing out for self-preservation. Megan thought of the overwhelming sense of malevolence and danger she had experienced in these woods. Did this wolf feel it too? Had its terrified instincts now driven it to kill or be killed?

The shadows rustled around them. Three more pairs of eyes

burned in the darkness. The entire pack had them surrounded.

The alpha wolf's eyes narrowed to yellow slits as it glared at Thoreau. Its body tensed as it prepared to attack. Megan clutched at Piper and hugged her close against her hip.

The wolf snarled and lunged with lightning quickness.

Thoreau barely had time to react before it was upon him, throwing him to the ground with staggering force. A strangled scream of pain burst from his lips as the wolf's jaws clamped down on his shoulder, its fangs sinking deep into his flesh. With a frantic burst of adrenaline, he flailed with his knife, slicing a gash along the wolf's shaggy side. But the wound only seemed to flame the heat of the beast's bloody rage. It clawed and bit at Thoreau's face and neck as he battered it wildly with his fists. Its fangs found his right ear and bit down hard, tearing it off. Thoreau shrieked in agony, blood spurting from the gaping wound in the side of his head.

The other wolves burst from the woods, snarling and ready to kill. Megan hid Piper's face in her jacket and watched in rapt horror as they descended on Thoreau while he lay fighting desperately for his life.

But just as they were about to tear him to pieces, an eerie blue light spilled over them. The alpha male's teeth were inches from Thoreau's throat when it let out an agonized yelp that froze the others in their tracks. The wolf was suddenly yanked off its intended victim, flying through the air as if some powerful, unseen hand had grabbed it. It remained hanging suspended a few feet above the ground, its eyes wild and terrified as it snarled and snapped as if fending off some invisible attacker.

"Oh God, it's him!" Piper whimpered. "It's him, it's him, it's him…"

A soul-freezing chill shot down Megan's spine when she saw the skeletal figure hovering in the shadows behind Thoreau. It was small, the size of a young boy, and its translucent bones glowed a ghostly blue in the darkness. A spark of something like an ethereal flame burned within its ribcage where its heart should be. Clumps of dead leaves and moss clung to the skeleton as if it had just been raised from the earth. Wisps of bluish mist streamed from the ghastly apparition and small, otherworldly orbs of blue and white shimmered like electricity in the empty spaces within its bones and skull.

The ghostly boy focused the awful hollow holes of its sightless eyes on the wolf as the scared animal snarled and thrashed in the air. Impelled by the boy's unearthly power, the beast's big head turned against its will, twisting further and further around on its neck until it faced a grotesque and impossible angle. A sickening *CRACK!* shot through the forest as the vertebrae of its spine fractured and snapped one by one. All at once, the wolf let out an agonized whimper and crashed to the ground, its body convulsing as it took its last breath.

A brilliant flash of blue lightning blasted through the forest as the skeletal boy flickered into nothingness, leaving behind only a lingering aura of otherworldly energy. Darkness surged through the woods, reclaiming its territory.

Thoreau wobbled to his feet. Blood oozed from the deep puncture wounds in his shoulder and poured down his neck from the hole where his ear had been. But to Megan's horror, despite the damage the wolf had inflicted, his shoulders actually shuddered with a raspy chuckle. Whatever that ghastly apparition had been, it had saved him from being torn to pieces. His body trembled with shock and his clothes were torn, but he still clutched the knife. The danger wasn't over, and Megan didn't waste another instant before grabbing Piper and dashing deeper into the black reaches of the woods.

Chapter 27

The harsh wind sweeping over the dark and desolate acres greeted Sam as Margaret marched him from the back door at gunpoint, his heart pounding in his chest. He could feel the barrel of her rifle pressed against his lower back, urging him forward toward the barn with a sense of urgency. Snowflakes swirled in the night air and the ground was hard beneath his feet, the only sounds coming from the crunching of his boots against the gravel and the raspy breaths of the woman holding him captive.

Sam's mind raced with possibilities as they approached the barn. Was he being taken to be executed? Held captive until Thoreau's return? Or was Margaret Singer just as cold-blooded as her brother? Sam had no way of knowing, but he knew he needed to stay calm and find a way out of this situation. The cop in him was screaming to make a move, to try to disarm his assailant, but the years of training had also taught him when to pick his battles.

The barn loomed ahead, an ominous structure that seemed to swallow the light that spilled out of the house. Sam could hear his own breathing, harsh and ragged in his ears. He knew he was walking into a trap, but he had no choice.

They reached the barn and Margaret shoved him through the door. He stumbled and nearly fell to the ground before catching himself. His eyes struggled to adjust to the inky blackness, and for a moment, he was disoriented. The smell of dirt and oil filling his nose was even more powerful in the dark. The old wooden walls creaked and moaned as if they were alive. Outside, the wind howled across through the nearby forest, adding to the sense of desperation and danger.

Sam willed his gaze to be cold and calculating as he faced the woman. She remained standing in the wide-open door, silhouetted against the pale light of the moon glowing through the heavy clouds.

"What do you want from me?" he asked, his voice steady despite the fear that gripped him.

Margaret sneered, her rifle still trained on him. "I want you to leave my brother some goddamn peace. But you just can't do that, can you, Hayden?"

Sam's feet were rooted to the ground as he tried to come up with a plan. But the cold metal barrel staring him in the face made it hard to think. Margaret had taken his pistol when she'd ambushed him up in Thoreau's bedroom. She now carried it tucked into the belt of her thin coat. He couldn't risk any sudden movements while she still had the rifle aimed, but maybe he could talk his way out of this.

"How exactly do you think this is going to end, Margaret?" Sam swallowed hard, trying to keep his voice even and calm. "Almost a dozen news crews saw me turn in here and my truck's still parked up by the road. Their speculation alone is enough to make headlines. If anything happens to me out here, they'll know it was you. But you can still walk away from this. Lower the gun and let me go."

Margaret's shrewd eyes glittered behind her thick glasses, but it was the cold chuckle she let out that chilled Sam's blood.

"Oh, I don't know, Hayden," she said. "See, the way I'm gonna remember what happens next is that Garrett and me got into a nasty scrape after he came home. He was threatening me with a knife, hollering about how he's going to kill me, when I chased him into the woods with this here rifle. Except I didn't think he was really gone, so I sat up waiting for him to come back to make good on his word. And he did! I saw him skulking around out there in the dark! And I took a shot at him to scare him off. Only it wasn't him. It was the local police chief, who, for God-knows what reason, took it upon himself to trespass on private property without a warrant. How was I supposed to know he was out there?" Margaret's tongue clucked against her teeth. "Damn shame, tragic accident like that."

Sam's stomach dropped. She was right. He was stupid and reckless to have come here by himself, with no way of calling for backup. He felt the tension in the air, thick and heavy like a fog. The stale scent of the barn choked his lungs. A desperate urge to survive took over, and he scanned the dim interior for any potential weapons or escape routes, but there was nothing. Margaret guarded the only exit, and anything that could be used to defend himself was too far out of reach.

That's when he noticed Margaret's glasses. They had fogged up in the frosty night air and she could no longer see him clearly. She took a hand off the rifle to wipe the lenses.

Sam wouldn't get another chance. He made his move and darted deeper into the barn, throwing himself behind the chassis of Margaret's old Jeep as rifle shots rang out—two quick ones in rapid succession. Brilliant blasts of light filled the barn from the muzzle flash. Sam heard the high-calibre bullets puncturing the rusted Jeep and ricocheting around inside, sending shards of sharp metal flying as they punched their way through the other side. He ducked and covered his head with his hands, his heart in his throat. He couldn't stay here for long without a weapon. It was only a matter of time before Margaret rounded the Jeep and picked him off at point-blank range.

Sweat trickled between Sam's shoulder blades as he fought to catch his breath. He peeked out from behind the vehicle, trying to get a glimpse of Margaret. But she was nowhere to be seen. *Where has she gone?* The metallic clink and thunk of rounds being chambered rang through the silence. *Damn!* She was reloading. He ducked back behind the Jeep before he gave himself away, but a glimpse of something in the back of the vehicle gave him an idea. There were two old road flares in the empty compartment behind where the seats had been. They were his only chance.

Sam's pulse thundered in his ears as he stretched a shaking hand up over his head, fumbling around blindly in the compartment. He could hear Margaret moving again now, drawing closer and closer through the gloom. Her footsteps were barely audible on the dirt floor. She was in no hurry; she had him trapped, and she wasn't about to risk being ambushed in the dark. Where were the damn flares? At last,

Sam's fingers grazed one, and he grabbed it before darting back. He heard Margaret's approaching footfalls hesitate at the noise he made.

Sam's palms were slick as he struggled with the flare, trying to get it lit. It was decades old and there was a good chance it would either misfire or simply fizzle in his hand. He swore under his breath. *Come on, come on!* Finally, with a burst of sparks, the flare ignited.

Sam stood up and lobbed the flare through the barn toward where he thought Margaret was. It arced through the air, trailing sparks behind it, and landed with a thud a few yards away from her feet, lighting her up in a hellish glow.

Margaret whirled toward the sudden movement and scampered away from the brilliant jet of flame, distracted for a split second.

It was all the opportunity Sam needed. He bolted from behind the Jeep and lunged for her.

A searing flame tore across Sam's upper arm in the same instant the boom of the rifle blasted through the barn. He slammed into Margaret and they both went tumbling over into the dirt. He tried to pin her down, but she let out a bloodcurdling shriek and lashed out at him like a rabid animal, raking his face with the nails of one hand while battering him with the butt of the rifle. Her face was a savage snarl in the lurid light of the flare as she thrashed and kicked. The rifle struck him with a vicious shot to the temple and the world snapped out of focus. He felt the stale reek of Margaret's hot breath as he reeled back and staggered off her —but not before stripping her of the pistol tucked in her waistband.

Sam's knees wobbled beneath him, and he clamped a hand on the blood oozing from where the bullet had grazed his arm as he scrambled out into the snowy night. He didn't look back as he fled, firing blindly through the open barn door. He heard his shots pinging off metal until Margaret let out an anguished scream. He hoped to hell it would be her last as he raced across the open field, his feet trampling the snow with each step.

The dark forest loomed ahead, a mass of shadows and twisted branches, the trees seeming to stretch up into the night sky forever. It was his only hope of escape. The black hole of a path yawned like an open mouth on the horizon. If Sam could just make it there, he could take cover among the trees.

He heard the bullet whizzing past his head before he even registered the shot. Instinctively, he ducked and swerved aside. His heart pounded in his chest as he sprinted, the tall grass whipping at his legs. Margaret's bullets continued to rain down around him, sending up puffs of dirt and snow with each impact.

Sam could feel the heat of the barrel on the back of his neck, could practically taste the metal of the bullet as it raced toward him. With a burst of adrenaline, he pumped his legs harder than he ever had, sprinting the final yards toward the cover of the trees. He was almost there. Just a few more steps. The shadows of the trees reached out for him like long fingers.

Just as he crashed into the underbrush, Sam heard the loud crack of the rifle and felt the heat of the lead as it whizzed by his skull, missing him by inches. He stumbled and fell to the ground, gasping for air.

More shots rang out behind him, the bullets tearing through the branches and leaves. As he lay there among the snowy leaves, struggling to catch his breath and shaking with adrenaline, Sam knew Margaret was firing blindly. He had made it to safety. He clutched his pistol and dragged himself to his feet. As he carried on, the path seemed to stretch on forever, with no end in sight. Darkness enveloped him as he pushed his way deeper into the forest, clinging to the hope that he would somehow catch up to Thoreau before he found Megan.

Chapter 28

A fragile layer of snow covered the forest like a veil as Megan and Piper stumbled through the underbrush, their breaths coming in short, panicked gasps. They had been fleeing for what seemed like hours. Megan's compass and GPS were both still in her pack where she'd dropped it at Thoreau's camp, and her sense of direction was now completely muddled by the twists and turns they had taken in their desperate search for a trail that might deliver them from these cursed woods. The air was heavy with the scent of cold pine and the distant howl of wolves in mourning. Megan's headlamp provided the only source of light, casting eerie shadows on the gnarled trees and snowy underbrush.

The memory of the skeletal boy and the gruesome death of the wolf still haunted Megan. She could feel the eyes of the ghastly child upon her, his presence palpable in the stillness of the woods. She clutched her jacket around her, trying to ward off the chill that seeped into her bones.

"Wait. I can't..." Piper panted and trudged to a halt. "I need to catch my breath."

Megan's heart pounded in her chest while she waited. Every sound made her jump, her nerves frayed to the breaking point. She knew they had to keep moving, but she was also so tired, so battered and bruised from her deadly fight with Thoreau. And no matter how fast they ran, she couldn't shake the feeling that he was still on their trail, his presence looming over them like a shadow. When the wind lulled, she swore she could hear the snapping of twigs and the rustling of leaves behind them, growing louder and closer with each passing moment.

"We have to keep going." Megan grabbed Piper's hand and pulled her along. Her gaze followed the bouncing beam of the headlamp as she searched the darkness of the forest, looking for a place to hide. But with the trees so densely packed and the snow making it hard to see, there seemed to be nowhere to go. As they stumbled along, Megan's mind raced, trying to come up with a plan. They had no weapons, no means of communication, and no idea where they were. All they could do was keep running. Their only hope was the abandoned Wright Great Camp. If they could make it there, they'd have shelter from the cold and a place to hide until morning. But first, they had to find it.

The snow came down in fat, fluffy flakes as they pressed on through the overgrown brush. The crunch of their footsteps on the frozen underbrush seemed unnaturally loud in the forest's stillness. Megan's headlamp beam flickered and danced as they made their way down the overgrown path, the dense foliage pressing in on all sides. The chilling possibility that they were lost out here started planting the seeds of despair in her mind when she detected the sound of rushing water ahead. She hauled on Piper, urging her onward.

Soon, they arrived on the bank of an icy stream rushing down from the mountains. Megan took hope at the sight of it. The only stream of this size that flowed through these woods was Calamity Brook. About five miles upstream was Stag Rock Falls, where Piper had wandered away from her parents' camp. And somewhere in the woods on the other side stood the old Wright camp.

Megan shined her light up and down the water, but there didn't seem to be any way of fording the deep, rushing water. She led Piper downstream, searching for rocks large enough to be used as a footbridge, until they came upon the rotting wreckage of the timber bridge that had been swept away in the flooding of Hurricane Irene. All that remained were a few broken planks jammed between the rocks, and a single massive beam wedged sideways across the stream where the banks pinched together. The thick, square length of timber now sat a few feet above the water, but it would no doubt be submerged like a dam during the swollen rush of the spring thaw.

The icy water rushed past them, cold and unforgiving. Megan stood at the edge of the stream, her heart racing as she gazed at the narrow, slippery beam that stretched across the water. It seemed impossibly far, a thin and precarious bridge over the frigid water. She knew they had to cross, but the thought of setting foot on that log filled her with fear. The icy water below seemed to call to her, tempting her to give in to her misgivings and stay on the safe side of the stream.

Piper clung to her side, her eyes wide with terror. "No. We can't cross that," she whimpered.

Megan wrapped an arm around her, trying to give her some comfort. "We have to. It's the only way across."

Piper shook her head, tears welling up in her eyes. "I can't. It's too scary."

Megan's heart ached at the sight of the young girl's fear. She wanted nothing more than to turn around and find another way, but she knew that was impossible. Thoreau was back there, and they had to get to the other side, no matter what.

"Piper, listen to me," she said, trying to keep her voice steady. "I know this is scary, but we can do it together. I'll be right by your side the whole time. We'll take it one step at a time, okay?"

Piper looked up at her, her eyes filled with doubt. But then she took a deep breath and nodded. "Okay."

Megan squeezed Piper's hand, her own fear giving way to determination. They could do this. Together, they stepped onto the log. Megan held onto Piper tightly, trying to keep them both steady as they inched their way across the slippery length of timber. The water was up to their thighs below, and Megan could feel the icy fingers of fear creeping up her spine. Every step was a struggle, and the icy water seemed to mock them with its relentless rush beneath their feet. Megan's boots slipped and slid on the icy surface, and she had to use all of her strength to keep them both upright. She could feel Piper's small body trembling in her arms, and she knew they had to keep moving.

But the beam was treacherous, and every movement was a risk. Megan's heart thundered in her chest as she tried to gauge the strength of the wood beneath them. How much had it cracked and weakened while being battered by the devastating flood of the hurricane? One wrong move, and they could both plunge into the icy water.

At last, they were just a few feet away from the other side. Megan let out a sigh of relief and redoubled her efforts, determined to make it to safety.

But as they took the final steps, the beam groaned and flexed dangerously beneath them. Megan had enough time to fling Piper across to safety before the rotted wood snapped in half beneath her. She tumbled off, the icy water taking her breath away as she submerged up to her thighs.

The current was strong, and it was all Megan could do to keep herself upright. She could feel her energy draining away, but she refused to give up. She had to make it out of this alive. With a burst of strength, she lunged for the shore. She fell short, but Piper was there with an outstretched hand. The girl hauled with all her might, and with her help, Megan was able to scrabble out of the frigid water. She collapsed on the snowy ground, but there wasn't time to waste resting.

Icy pins and needles pricked at Megan's numb feet as they scrambled up an embankment from the stream and broke through the trees into a clearing. There it was. The massive timber buildings and stone chimneys of the old Wright Great Camp loomed ahead, nestled deep in the woods, its windows dark and empty.

Like many of the magnificent great camps established as mountain retreats by wealthy industrialists in the early 20th century, the Wright camp was a sprawling compound of guest houses and outbuildings all clustered around an enormous grand lodge. Vines and weeds had now overtaken the once-pristine grounds, and they lay shrouded in beneath a dusting of white.

Something about the fallen grandeur of those silent buildings looming in the snowy darkness conjured images of gothic ruins that made Megan's skin crawl. Rumors about the old camp swirled among the locals in town. They said it was haunted, and spoke of strange noises and ghostly apparitions, but Megan had never believed in such things—until tonight.

"Where do we go?" Piper whispered. Her voice shook with fear.

"We'll find somewhere to hide," Megan replied, trying to sound more confident than she felt.

She led the way as they moved cautiously through the abandoned compound, her headlamp beam flickering over the decrepit outbuildings. Windows were broken and roofs were caved in, giving the impression of crumbling mausoleums, not a luxurious haven of the Gilded Age. Megan peered into each of the guest cabins as they passed, searching for anything to defend herself with. They were all empty and silent, their furnishings covered in dust and cobwebs.

The crunching of leaves and twigs under their feet echoed through the endless silence as they made their way deeper into the camp. The air was still and heavy, as if the very trees were holding their breath in anticipation. Megan glanced back at the trail of footprints they were leaving in the newly fallen snow. If Thoreau had managed to follow them this far, their fresh tracks would lead him right to them. Their only hope was for the wind to scour the footprints away before he arrived. Megan tried to fight off the creeping sense of dread that seemed to wrap around her like a cloak, but it was no use.

The two-story main lodge loomed ahead of them now. The sight of it sent a shiver down Megan's spine. Was it a refuge from their pursuer or a trap? The building's timber walls and roof were barely standing, covered in withered vines and moss. Many of the shattered windows were boarded up, and the door hung open a crack on rusted hinges, inviting them inside.

Megan's wet feet were still numb and heavy as she climbed the porch steps to the front door, taking care to avoid the rotted boards and broken glass. She hesitated for a moment, listening for any sign of movement within. All was still and silent. She pushed open the creaky door, the sound echoing through the empty halls. Piper kept close behind her, the floorboards groaning under their weight as they stepped inside. The air was heavy and still, and every creak of the planks made Megan jump. She told herself it was just the old wooden walls contracting with the cold, but deep down, she sensed it was more than that.

The headlamp beam cut through the gloom, illuminating the dark corners of the lodge's great room and revealing the wreckage of what must have once been a grand retreat. A thick layer of dust covered the furniture, and cobwebs hung from the ceiling. A massive fieldstone fireplace dominated the space, its soot-blackened firebox so big Piper could almost stand inside it without stooping.

The wind whistled and howled through the cracks in the shuttered windows as they crept their way through the spacious room, peering into the various rooms and hallways that led off of it.

Suddenly, a loud crash echoed from behind them. Megan spun around, heart racing. There was nothing there, but the front door had slammed shut with the wind.

Megan shuddered, her skin crawling with the sense that they were not alone. If they were going to shelter here for the night, she needed to be sure there was no one else here. "Let's check upstairs," she whispered.

As they made their way up the loose boards of what had once been an elegant staircase, Megan felt a growing sense of apprehension. The air was colder up here, and she thought she heard strange noises coming from the shadows. She quickened her pace, her heart pounding in her chest. The beam of her headlamp danced over the dusty interiors of the empty bedrooms. Some of the shattered windows weren't boarded up here. Snow was accumulating on the windowsills and spilling over into the rooms.

Megan couldn't shake the feeling that they were being watched as they searched the rooms. More than once, she heard the creak of footsteps on the floorboards behind her. But when she turned to see who was there, the hallway was empty.

When she was satisfied that the second floor was deserted, Megan paused and crouched in front of Piper. She angled her headlamp upward so that its light bounced off the ceiling and didn't shine in the girl's face while they spoke.

"Piper, what was that back there in the woods?" she asked. "That thing that killed the wolf, the one you called the skeleton boy?"

Piper's lip quivered, as if afraid to even speak of it. "I... I don't really know who he is. Like… I don't know. Maybe a ghost?"

"Have you seen him before tonight?"

Piper nodded. "Every night, just for a little bit. Thoreau talked to him, but I never heard what the boy said. It was like listening to Thoreau talking to someone on the phone, or to himself, you know? As if he could hear the boy's voice in his head. The night after Thoreau didn't come back. I was all alone, but I could feel the skeleton boy out there in the forest. And then he came to me while I slept. He was in there with me in the tent and I felt all cold and sick inside, all the way to my heart. He didn't say anything, but the way he looked at me, it was like a warning, you know? Like he was telling me he'd find me if I tried to leave. And then he was gone. It's like appearing like that—like being able to really be *seen*—drains him and he needs time to get his energy back."

"How long? How long until he comes back?"

Piper shrugged and shook her head. "I don't know. What he did to that wolf… I didn't know… I've never seen him do anything like that."

"Did Thoreau ever try to hurt you?" Megan asked.

"No, but I know he wanted to. He was scared people would come looking for me and take him away. But I think the skeleton boy stopped him. I think he wanted Thoreau to keep me safe."

Megan chewed her cheek. A chilling sense of dread crawled over her flesh as she came to suspect the baleful skeleton boy was the ghost of Thoreau's childhood friend, Timothy Wright. She cast another uneasy glance around the second floor.

"Let's get back downstairs," she said. "It's not safe up here."

The ground floor lay in still and quiet darkness below. As they moved through the silence of the kitchen, Megan noticed an open door leading down into the pooling blackness of the cellar. She hesitated a moment, trying to convince herself there was no one down there, that there was no reason to investigate that foreboding black portal into nothingness. But that terrible feeling of not being alone kept scratching at her senses. It was as if she could feel the eyes of the ghosts that lingered here, watching her every move. She knew she couldn't leave any part of this place unexplored.

Piper didn't move when Megan started for the door. She shook her head and stared at Megan, blue eyes wide with fright. Only when Megan reached out and took her palm did the girl finally muster the courage to follow. She kept huddled close to Megan as they descended the rickety stairs.

It was pitch black, and Megan focused her headlamp on the wooden steps ahead of them, her heart pounding in her chest. The air was even colder and damper than it had been upstairs, and it was permeated by the foul scents of mildew and decay.

When they reached the dirt floor at the bottom of the stairs, Megan shone her light around the cavernous space, taking in the old and rusted equipment that lay scattered about. Mildewed boxes and worm-eaten crates slumped like drunks against the stone walls. Anything useful had been removed or picked-over by looters decades ago. The moldy smell was even stronger now, and Megan could hear dripping water coming from somewhere in the shadows.

"Do you feel that?" Piper's whisper trembled in the silence.

"Yeah," Megan replied grimly. There was something malevolent lurking in the shadows, and the air was heavy with an otherworldly energy. Megan took a deep breath and steeled herself for whatever they might find hiding in the darkness.

They cautiously made their way deeper into the cellar, Megan's light cutting through the blackness like a knife. Suddenly, the beam caught something that made Megan gasp in shock.

There, heaped on the dirt floor, was a pile of old bones.

"Oh God, is that... Is that..." Piper whimpered and covered her mouth with her palm.

Megan's hands shook as she approached the pile, her heart racing with fear. She knelt down to get a closer look. It was the skeleton of a boy about Piper's own age.

A shiver raced down Megan's spine when she realized what she was seeing. These were the bones Ol' Rory had seen washed ashore beneath Witch's Rock, the ones he believed were the remains of Timothy Wright. Megan's stomach went cold with horror as she pieced together what had happened. Thoreau must have collected the bones and brought them here.

He'd brought his friend home.

Megan jumped as another teeth-rattling crash reverberated from the floor above them. The wind has slammed the front door shut again.

Except this time, the jarring sound was followed by the heavy thump of a boot.

And then another.

And another.
Someone was in the lodge.
Thoreau had found them.

Chapter 29

Megan tried to stay calm, but she could feel Piper shaking beside her. Her heart hammered at her ribcage as her gaze raked across the cellar, frantically searching for a way out. The stone walls were windowless, and the staircase was the only way up or down. Thoreau's footsteps grew louder, the sound echoing off the walls of the empty rooms above. If he caught them down here, they'd be trapped, with no hope of escape. They had to get out now, while they still had a chance.

Megan killed her headlamp and yanked Piper up the steps. "Come on!"

Together, they crept their way up the staircase through the suffocating blackness and inched through the open door into the kitchen. They darted around an island and paused with their backs against the wood. Megan pricked her ears, listening intently for the location of Thoreau's footsteps. They were quieter now, more muffled. Had he moved into some distant part of the lodge?

Ghostly rays of moonlight filtered through cracks in the old window boards. Snow whisked by, casting shadows on the kitchen floor as Megan and Piper huddled in the darkness, trying to make themselves as small as possible.

Megan's mind raced. She couldn't let Thoreau find them, not after everything they had been through. She had to think of a plan for this little girl's sake, but her thoughts were scattered and panicked. They couldn't stay hidden here forever, but she didn't know where else to go.

Thoreau's heavy thumps grew louder again. He was coming back their way, but it wasn't clear from which direction. They were running out of time. Whatever Megan planned to do, she had to do it now.

She grabbed Piper's hand and pulled her to her feet, leading her from the kitchen. If they could reach the great room, they could flee the lodge and take their chances escaping through the forest while Thoreau was distracted. As they crept down the narrow hallway, Megan swore she heard strange noises all around her. It was as if the walls were alive, the wood groaning and creaking as if in pain. She quickened her pace, her pulse racing. They moved lightly on the balls of their feet, heading for the great room, when she heard footsteps around a corner straight ahead.

Megan's heart skipped a beat, and she pulled Piper towards the nearest door. They stumbled into a small powder room. There wasn't time to close or lock the door. All they could do was huddle in a dark corner, listening as the footsteps drew closer and closer. Thoreau's shadow fell across the doorway and Megan held Piper close, trying to still the trembling that threatened to give them away. She could hear Thoreau's heavy breathing outside the open door, and she prayed he had already searched this room and wouldn't bother to stop again.

Just when she thought they were about to be discovered, the footsteps continued on, and Megan let out a sigh of relief. She waited for Thoreau to move further down the hallway, his footfalls receding into another distant wing of the lodge. Together, she and Piper fled the room and scurried down the hallway. Megan could only hope Thoreau wouldn't hear their footfalls now that he was missing one ear.

The front door stood shut on the far side of the vast space of the great room. Megan led the way as they dashed across the open floor and yanked on the handle.

The door wouldn't move.

Megan jerked it again, harder this time.

Nothing.

Thoreau had either locked it, or the wind had slammed it too hard in its crooked frame for it to budge.

Megan spun from the door and gathered Piper to her side in the gloom of the musty old great room. Their breaths came out in ragged gasps as they listened to Thoreau's footsteps echoing down the hallways, growing louder and closer as he returned. His heavy breathing echoing through the empty rooms sent shivers down Megan's spine. Tears welled in Piper's terrified eyes as she stared at Megan, silently imploring her to find some way of saving them both. Megan clutched her tightly as if the girl was her own daughter, trying to calm her trembling body.

"It's going to be okay, sweetie," she whispered, even though she knew it was a lie. All the windows were boarded shut and there was nowhere to go, no escape from Thoreau's relentless pursuit. They were trapped between a locked door and a killer, with no hope of rescue.

Megan could hear Thoreau stalking down the hallway toward them when she had an idea. But she had to act fast. She grabbed Piper's hand and hustled her to the fireplace. Cold air swept down the chimney as Megan pushed the girl into the giant firebox and motioned for her to climb up into the darkness above. Piper hesitated, but the swelling volume of Thoreau's approach propelled her into action. Megan boosted her up and craned her neck to peer up the chimney after her as she climbed. It was a snug fit, but Piper was soon able to wedge herself between the giant fieldstones. Concealed in the darkness, she seemed safe enough, at least for now.

Soot and dust rained down at Megan as she watched Piper's shape nearly vanish into the darkness. She blinked and turned from the fireplace just as Thoreau's footsteps came stomping down the last stretch of the hallway. Her eyes darted to a dust-covered couch, but there wasn't time to reach it and hide. She had nowhere to run, no weapon to defend herself with. All she had was the only gift her father had ever given her: the strength of her own two hands. She clenched her palms into tight fists, summoning all the courage she had left.

Thoreau burst into the great room. He was little more than a shadowy figure in the darkness, but Megan could almost sense the twisted grin on his bearded face. Something heavy weighed his arms down below his waist. Megan's blood ran cold when she realized he'd brought something with him from his camp.

He now clutched a heavy timber axe.

Megan swallowed hard as she faced him. She had survived a lifetime of abuse and betrayal, and she wasn't about to let this killer take her down without a fight. But she knew she only had one chance at survival. She had to take him by surprise, do something he'd never expect.

Megan ran at him without warning and flicked her headlamp on at the last moment. The brilliant beam lit up his face as she stormed across the room, and his blinded eyes squinted shut reflexively.

It was just the opening Megan needed. She wound up her right fist and slammed a roundhouse blow into his jaw.

Thoreau let out a grunt and stumbled back, the axe clattering to the floor. Megan lunged for it, but Thoreau caught her with a punch to the ribs that sent her skidding sideways. She grimaced in pain and swung around, driving her fist into Thoreau's gut with all her might. A hoarse wheeze escaped his lips, and Megan seized the opportunity to land another punch, then another, trying to wear him down.

Thoreau staggered and reeled under her assault, backpedaling across the floor. Megan redoubled her efforts, knowing this was her last chance. She launched herself at the killer, fists flying, and finally, after what felt like an eternity, he went down on one knee… right next to the axe.

A wicked grin spread across Thoreau's face. He let out a guttural roar as he clutched the axe handle and swung it hard through the air. Megan darted to the side, narrowly avoiding the blade as it came crashing down. She threw a punch at Thoreau's exposed ribs, but he was too fast, dancing out of reach and swinging the axe at her again. Megan fought with all her might, dodging and weaving the deadly blade as she tried to get in a hit. But Thoreau was relentless, his blows coming faster and harder with each passing moment. Megan could feel her energy flagging, her blows growing weaker and slower. She staggered back across the room and tripped over a side table. Her headlamp beam shot straight up toward the ceiling as she hit the floor and lay sprawled on her back.

As Megan watched in horror, Thoreau stood over her and raised his axe over his head to strike the final blow.

But just as he was about to hack her to pieces, something strange happened. The timber walls shook and the floorboards beneath them creaked and groaned.

Thoreau stumbled back as a bright light filled the room. A shimmering figure materialized behind him, its translucent form glowing with an otherworldly light.

Megan rolled to her side and shielded her eyes in terror. But not before glimpsing something that made her gasp as it sucked the air from her lungs.

The spectral figure wore her father's face. Megan saw it clearly, shimmering with an ethereal luminescence, his eyes burning with blue flames.

Thoreau sensed something behind him, but it was too late. The ghost of Megan's father reached out with claw-like hands, his touch freezing Thoreau's flesh right down to his spine.

Thoreau let out a cry of terror and fell to the ground, writhing in agony as the ghost's power flowed through him. Megan watched in horrified amazement as her father's ghost lifted the maniac off the ground, his grip tight as he held the struggling figure aloft.

Graham's spirit looked at his daughter. His flickering eyes

were dreadful to behold, but Megan couldn't turn away. She heard his familiar voice flow into her head, filled with a love and sorrow she had never thought him capable of. This was the voice of the man her mother had fallen in love with.

I should have protected you when I was alive...

Thoreau screamed and crashed to the floor, clawing at his flesh as if he was in agony. Tears streamed down Megan's cheeks and her jaw quivered as the ghostly form of her father hovered over Thoreau's tortured body.

A bone-numbing chill suddenly filled the room, and a crushing sense of malevolence writhed through the air. Megan's skin prickled with the otherworldly energy and the hairs stood up on the back of her neck.

Timothy Wright was returning.

Images of what the skeleton boy had done to the wolf flashed through Megan's mind. Thoreau was hurt, but the boy's spirit wouldn't let anyone take away the only companion he had in his eternal solitude.

With a blast of unearthly light, the boy's ghastly figure exploded into the room.

Graham's spirit swung around, otherworldly vapors streaming from his shimmering form as he moved. For a moment, the two ghostly figures stood facing each other from opposite sides of the room, their glaring eyes burning with otherworldly fire. Then they shot at each other like crackling bolts of electricity.

Dazzling shards of light sprayed the air as they collided. Locked in a fierce battle, their ghostly forms flickered and pulsed with energy. They fought with a ferocity that was both terrifying and mesmerizing, their otherworldly figures passing through the furniture as if they weren't even there as they flung each other across the room. The dreadful sound of their clash echoed through the empty halls. Blasts of energy illuminated the giant room with an otherworldly light as they clawed and tore at each other. The floor quaked, and the walls shook with the deafening ferocity of their screams.

As the battle raged, Graham's glowing form began to dim. His flowing movements seemed to slow and weaken. The boy's ghost was older and much too powerful to overcome. With a final burst of energy, he let out a blood-curdling shriek and unleashed a powerful blast of energy that sent Graham's spirit hurtling backwards through the air.

Megan staggered to her knees and snatched up the axe from where it had fallen. With Thoreau still weakened, escape was her only chance. If her father's ghost lost this fight, she had to draw the killer away from where Piper remained hidden away in the chimney.

She darted to the nearest window and brought the axe blade crashing through the board. The plywood was thin and soft and smashed easily. She cleared away the jagged shards of the broken window with the axe and tumbled out into the snowy night just as the room behind her erupted with spectral light.

Chapter 30

Megan scrambled through the snow, racing from the lodge toward the shadowy maze of dilapidated cabins and overgrown paths. From the corner of her eye, she saw Thoreau's hulking form crashing through the shattered window, silhouetted against the unearthly light spilling from within the great room. He was about fifty yards away now, but Megan imagined she could almost hear his footsteps crunching through the snow behind her, getting closer and closer with each passing moment. She still carried the axe. But what good would it do against Thoreau's malevolent guardian? She needed a place to hide, but where? The cabins were crumbling with disrepair and the icehouse was too exposed for all to see. She needed somewhere secluded, somewhere Thoreau wouldn't think to look.

An idea came to her. The old boathouse! The Wright camp sat between Calamity Brook and the wealthy family's own private lake. It was small and hidden, nestled deep in the woods. If she could make it there, she might find some way of fleeing out to open water where she could wait for dawn.

Snowflakes lashed at Megan's eyes as she pushed herself harder, her tired legs aching as she dashed through the underbrush. The trees whipped past her in a blur and the branches scratched at her face. She could sense Thoreau's presence behind her, his heavy footsteps echoing through the forest. He was getting closer, and Megan could feel her energy withering. But she had to keep moving, no matter what.

Just when she thought she was hopelessly lost, she saw it—the old boathouse. Its weathered boards and rusted roof rose out of the darkness on the shore of the black void of the lake. Megan's burning lungs screamed in agony as she raced toward her only hope of escape. She could hear Thoreau's footsteps getting louder, and she knew she had only minutes to spare.

Megan burst through the door, her chest heaving as she gasped for air. The boathouse reeked of rot as if something had recently died within its walls. Megan's hands scrabbled against the rough wood as she fumbled around in the darkness. At last, she came upon what felt like the curved hull of a canoe hanging from the rafters. The looters that had ransacked the camp weren't likely to have missed it, but they must have been daunted by the task of lugging something that big on foot through miles of unforgiving forest.

A kindle of hope ignited within Megan. She quickly grabbed the canoe and lowered it to the ground, her fingers shaking as she fumbled with the ropes. The axe clattered against the bottom of the hull as she tossed it in next to the paddle. She dragged the boat from the boathouse, cringing as the hull scraped noisily over the rocks at the lake's edge. The boat hit the black water with a loud splash. Megan had no way of knowing if it would stay afloat, and she didn't care. It was her only chance of survival. The frigid water was choppy with windblown waves and the canoe rocked madly beneath her as she climbed in and grabbed the paddle.

But Thoreau was right behind her.

His hand seized a fistful of her hair and yanked. Megan screamed as he dragged her from the canoe. She landed hard on her back on the rocky shore of the lake. A searing flame tore through her scalp and more screams burst from her lips as she kicked and flailed in Thoreau's powerful grip. But somehow she knew this was the end. Thoreau's gnarled hands wrapped around her throat and squeezed, choking the life out of her. Megan summoned everything she had left and clawed at his wrists, trying desperately to pry his fingers loose, but it was no use. Thoreau was too strong, and Megan was too exhausted to fight back any longer. The snow falling in her eyes became exploding stars that extinguished one after another as a fathomless darkness descended upon her.

The roar of a gunshot shattered the silence and echoed across the water.

Thoreau let out a gasp as the bullet hit its mark. He stumbled backward, a look of surprise on his face as he clutched at his upper chest.

But he didn't go down.

Megan gulped air down her bruised throat and curled on her side on the rocks. Sam was there at the forest's edge, his pistol drawn and aimed at Thoreau.

"Get down, Singer!" Sam thundered.

Thoreau didn't listen as he glared at Sam with baleful eyes. He was big and strong, and he was recovering from the initial shock of being shot.

Sam's finger pressed against the trigger and hesitated. If he killed Thoreau, all the man's secrets would die with him. Thoreau suddenly lunged for the axe in the canoe's bottom, but before Sam could get off another shot, a bone-chilling shriek unfurled from the darkness.

Sam whirled as a ghostly blue radiance flared to life behind him. The ghost of the dead Timothy Wright appeared without warning, materializing out of thin air. His translucent bones flickered and pulsed with otherworldly energy, and the hollow sockets of his eyes seemed to burn right through Sam's soul. His dreadful form hovered in the air, his skeletal jaw open wide in a silent wail.

Sam could not move or even scream as the boy's ghost floated toward him. His small arms were outstretched as if he meant to wrap Sam in a deadly embrace. He reached out with a bony hand, his icy fingers grasping for Sam's throat. Sam let out a bloodcurdling scream and collapsed to his knees in the snow-covered underbrush, his body contorting in agony. The gun tumbled from his nerveless fingers as the ghost's freezing grip left him paralyzed, a prisoner in his own body.

Megan rolled to her knees and groaned in sickening horror as Sam's hoarse cries became choked gurgles. She could feel the ghost's malevolent energy, could sense the hatred and anger that flowed from his spectral form like a black river. She scrambled over the rocks, lunging for the pistol where it lay in the snowy underbrush. Her palm closed over the cold steel just as she became aware of Thoreau lumbering toward her with the axe raised high, ready to hack her to pieces. Blood oozed from the wound in his chest, and his pale face was twisted with a grotesque snarl.

Megan fell to her side and fired, this time catching Thoreau in the shoulder. Blood spurted from the wound and the impact spun him around, but he still kept coming. He swung the axe down with both hands, as if he meant to split a timber log in two. Megan rolled aside and felt the wind of the blade kiss her cheek as it crunched into the rocks inches away from her face. She squeezed the trigger and fired another shot into Thoreau's thigh. He crumpled to the ground with a strangled cry, the axe falling from his grasp.

Megan didn't hesitate. She aimed for Thoreau's head and fired. The bullet tore through his left eye and blasted shards of his skull out across the frigid water.

Thoreau's lifeless body toppled over onto the rocks, blood pooling in a crimson halo beneath his shattered head. In the same instant, the skeletal spirit of Timothy Wright let out a hellish wail and released his deadly grip on Sam. He flew at Megan, bony fingers stretched into claws, wisps of ethereal smoke streaming from his skull. Megan screamed and fired the gun again and again, pulling the trigger until the hammer clicked and the chamber was empty. The bullets roared through empty air. Megan recoiled, eyes wide with terror. She felt the icy touch of the ghost's fingers against her flesh when Thoreau's last tortured breath escaped his lips.

All at once, the unearthly orbs shimmering beneath Timothy Wright's translucent bones exploded with light. Megan winced and stumbled backward, shielding her eyes against the otherworldly brilliance as Timothy's spirit soared into the air and burst into millions of tiny blue sparks. They swirled around her in the air like icy embers, filling the snowy night with a dazzling display of light that was almost too blinding to look at. And then they melted away one by one, dissolving into the snowy darkness, leaving behind nothing but faint wisps of smoke.

The stiff wind howled across the lake, whipping up a frenzy of snowflakes as Megan staggered to Sam's side and dropped to her knees beside him. Her hands shook and her chest heaved with shuddering gasps as she searched frantically for a pulse, her heart racing with fear.

Sam's dark eyes fluttered open, and he grasped at her hand with his palm. His body trembled with shock, and his other hand clutched at his wounded shoulder, blood seeping from between his frozen fingers. His face was pale and his breathing was shallow.

Megan saw the fear in his eyes and felt an icy tingle in her gut as she realized the gravity of the situation. "We have to get out of here," she said, trying to help him up. "Can you stand?"

Sam gave a weak nod and together, they struggled to their feet. Megan wrapped an arm around his waist, supporting him as they made their way into the snowy forest. She cast a quick glance over her shoulder, half-expecting to see Timothy's ghastly form floating after them. But the lakeshore was dark and empty. The only sound was her own ragged breaths in the undying silence of the mountains. The nightmare still wasn't over, and Megan wasn't sure Sam would survive the night. But with the forest closing in around them, she held on to hope, and to Sam's hand, as they left the blood and horror behind.

Epilogue

Sam sat alone in his office, completing the last of his seemingly endless pile of paperwork. It was almost eleven, and the station house was eerily quiet. The scratch of his pen on the pages and the occasional tap of his keyboard were the only sounds. He leaned back in his chair and rubbed his tired eyes, trying to focus on his task. He glanced at the clock on the wall and sighed. The day had been long, and he was feeling the fatigue.

A week had passed since that harrowing night in the woods. Sam had lost a lot of blood and was nearly hypothermic by the time Megan had guided him and Piper Flynn back to her canoe. It was during the long paddle across the snowy lake that Sam came to the chilling realization that he might not make it. But he was nothing if not stubborn. After receiving a blood transfusion and stitches for his gunshot wound, he'd insisted on being discharged less than twenty-four hours after they'd all staggered into the emergency room. He had spent his entire life hunting the infamous hermit of Balsam Lake. He'd be damned if he was going to just hand the case to the state troopers now that it was finally over.

Despite his injuries, Sam had been with the troopers when they followed a trail of blood to Margaret Singer's frozen body. It lay in the snowy field between her barn and the woods. Her skin was pale and waxy in the cold, and her face was twisted in a horrible grimace. There was frost on the lashes of her open eyes and icicles hung from her nose, but her outstretched hand still rested on the cold steel of her rifle. A pool of frozen blood surrounded a gunshot wound in her upper thigh. As Sam stood over her, he took some satisfaction in knowing he'd been the one who shot her.

That same day, the forensics team had begun the painstaking process of dismantling Thoreau's camp. They worked slowly and methodically, taking photos and collecting samples of fibers and other evidence. They still hadn't discovered any more bodies, but they had recovered more than a few personal items that had belonged to victims unfortunate enough to have crossed Thoreau's path. Sam had no doubt their bodies rested somewhere deep in the lake.

The Wright family had claimed Timothy's remains as soon as DNA confirmed the identity of the skeleton in the lodge's cellar. They had the remains removed to their hometown downstate. Two days ago, they had buried their boy's bones in the family plot with a private service. Sam hoped a proper burial would finally put the child's malevolent spirit to rest. But he wasn't certain of anything anymore.

Once the forensics team had documented and tagged every item in Thoreau's collection of storage crates, the question arose about what should be done with all the things he had stolen over the years. The village board voted they should be returned to their rightful owners, if possible. And so, a week after the discovery of Thoreau's camp, rows of tables and bins had lined the gymnasium of Balsam Lake Elementary, displaying the vast assortment of personal items that had been recovered.

That afternoon, residents had crammed into the gym. The mood was light and easy. Nostalgia swirled the air as they perused all of their old belongings, their faces lighting up as they came across things they had long forgotten. It was a thirty-year lost-and-found. For once, there wasn't a phone in sight. In a strange way, Thoreau had brought the community together in a way it hadn't been in years.

At the end of the evening, before returning to the paperwork awaiting him in his office, Sam had rummaged through one of the many bins of books Thoreau had stolen. There was poetry, cheap thrillers and crime fiction, first aid manuals, history, volumes on law and medicine, and a collection of old *Supernatural Thrillers* comics. Sam remembered his old man telling him about these classics when Sam was a kid, back when all he had been into was *The Punisher*. Had Thoreau stolen these from their home? Did they once belong to Sam's father?

Now, with the hour growing late and the excitement of the day wearing him down, Sam took a break from his forms. He gazed at the stack of comics piled on the chair across his desk from him. He still hadn't fully recovered from his ordeal in the woods. He'd hoped the mindless task of filling out the forms would help clear his thoughts, but his mind kept drifting back to the scene at the lake. The awful image of

Timothy Wright's ghostly skeleton was etched into his brain. He could still smell the metallic scent of his own blood, feel his own terror as the boy's spirit froze his flesh to the bone.

Sam shook his head, trying to clear the images from his mind. He worked through the final few documents on his desk until he came to the only folder remaining.

He had saved Piper Flynn's missing person's file for last. He remembered how his heart had raced that night at the hospital when he watched the girl run into her sobbing mother's arms. He remembered seeing Becky Flynn looking at him through her tears over her daughter's shoulder; the way her husband had been unable to express his relief and gratitude without breaking down with emotion. Sam didn't know what nightmares lay ahead for them after what they had all been through, but at least they had each other. If Piper could survive such terrors out there alone in the woods, she would survive the memory of those haunting nights as well.

Sam tore Piper's empty file in half and tossed it into the recycling bin. He sat back in his chair and exhaled a long breath, staring at his empty desk, trying to beat back the unwanted memories that clawed at his imagination. He willed his thoughts to the call he'd received from Mayor Hough that afternoon. There was already talk that the governor intended to award Sam the Medal of Honor along with the Purple Shield for being injured in the line of duty. He didn't know what to make of the recognition, but at least that prick Wade Ramsay would have a harder time shutting down his department.

The mayor had also reminded Sam he was entitled to a

leave of absence after being wounded on the job. Sam wasn't sure what he'd do with his time if he took it. Megan had invited him to a Thanksgiving dinner at her cabin, and he thought he'd take her up on the offer. After that, who knows? He hadn't seen the ocean in a very long time. Maybe it was time for an overdue road trip.

After a moment, Sam slid open his bottom drawer and grabbed the good bottle of Scotch and the glass tumbler he kept there. He pulled the cork and poured himself more than usual before he returned to the drawer for something else.

Sam savored the smoky burn of the whisky as he stared at the framed portrait of his father. Nothing they had discovered at Thoreau's camp had completely exonerated Roy Hayden from the terrible things he was accused of, but the townspeople could no longer call him a murderer. There was no doubt about it now. Garrett Singer had killed Graham Danforth by the lake that Fourth of July, not Sam's father. And if he was innocent of that crime, there was always the possibility he had been wrongly accused of raping that girl all those years ago as well.

Sam took another sip and returned the photo to its resting place at the bottom of his drawer. He'd never know the truth, and it would haunt him for the rest of his days. But at least now, nobody could say anything about Roy Hayden without remembering how the man's son helped rescue a little girl and brought an end to a killer's thirty-year reign of terror. And that was good enough for Sam.

* * *

Megan sat beneath a wool blanket on the couch in front of the crackling fireplace. The warm glow cast a golden light on the room as she strummed a soothing melody on her guitar. The notes flowed from her fingers, filling the cabin with a sense of peace and contentment.

Outside, the snow was falling softly, blanketing the ground in a downy, white layer. Megan watched through the picture window as the flakes danced and twirled in the night air, caught in the firelight's glow spilling through the windowpane.

She let out a contented sigh and continued to play, letting the melody wash over her and banishing all her trauma. Music and nature had always been her solace, and the peacefulness of the snowy landscape outside made her feel completely at ease, lost in the moment's beauty. She hadn't had a real drink since that night at the Trail's End, and she didn't know if she ever would again. It was too soon to say she had quit drinking for good—or if that was what she even wanted. But for the moment, she was content to enjoy the clear-minded vitality and focus that came with being sober.

And Russ did make a damn fine coffee.

Among the items they had found at Thoreau's camp was a stainless steel stovetop espresso maker. When no one else claimed it, Russ took it home as his own. After her first velvety cup, Megan wondered how she could ever go back to the bitter black tar she had brewed for the entirety of her adult life.

Now, Megan kept strumming and watched from her spot on the couch as Russ tended the embers and put another log on the fire. As she played, she let her mind wander, lost in the rhythm of the song.

Russ and Sam had been the only people with her that morning when they'd put her father's bones in the ground. Megan didn't know why she had invited them, only that she didn't want to do it alone. She had remained in stony silence, choosing not to say anything in memoriam. But before they started covering her father's remains with dirt, she had returned the fishing lure he had left her to let her know he was with her. She knew what it meant now, but she didn't want to keep it any longer. She didn't know if she would ever forgive her father for what he had done to her as a child, but she wanted to try. He had at least wanted to be a better man. And that was worth something.

As the fire crackled and the snow continued to fall, Megan now felt she was exactly where she was meant to be; safe and warm with nothing but the music, Russ, and the wild mountains outside to keep her company.

The song ended, and Megan set the guitar aside to sip her coffee. She lifted the blanket for Russ to join her beneath it as he returned to the couch. They sat in silence for a moment, letting the heat of the flames warm their skin. Russ was strangely quiet and brooding, and Megan suspected she knew what was on his mind. It was time to talk about something they had avoided since that dreadful night.

"What about the others?" Russ asked at last. "Those people whose bodies were never found. Do you think they're still out there somewhere? Haunting those woods?"

Megan remained quiet as she tried to put her thoughts into words. She had contemplated the same question often in the days that had passed. She thought of Timothy Wright's ghost, how he had vanished in the same instant as Thoreau's death, as if his old friend were the only thing keeping him tethered to the world of the living. Had Thoreau's guilt for what he had done somehow conjured the dead boy's spirit into existence during the long and lonely years he'd spent in solitude? Megan's thoughts drifted to her own father, how the discovery of his bones had awakened such strong emotions and painful memories for her. Is that what had brought him back to her? Was it her own burning need for him to be the father she never had?

At last, Megan shook her head and stared into the fire. "Places aren't haunted," she said. "The ghosts are already there inside our heads, just waiting for us to open the door and let them out."

Author's Note

Thank you, dear reader, for the generous gift of your time and attention. If you enjoyed this book and would like to see more, please consider taking a moment to leave a quick review on Amazon and/or Goodreads. A kind word from a reader like you is one of the best ways you can support independent authors and is very much appreciated.

Until next time, look under the bed, close the closet door, and whatever you do, don't turn around…

BOOKS BY MICHAEL PENNING

***Book of Shadows* Series**
Novels:
All Hallows Eve
The Suicide Lake
The Wolf Society
The Black Testament
The Hellfire House

Companion Stories:
The Damnation Chronicles

Other Novels
Solitude
Devil Music
Where All Light Dies

Michael Penning is a best-selling author and award-winning screenwriter of horror and dark fiction, crafting stories so chilling they could make a ghost shiver. As the macabre mind behind the *Book of Shadows* series, he has been weaving nightmares since before he could finish his own sack of trick-or-treat candy. When he's not conjuring new ways to make readers sleep with one eye open, he enjoys traveling, photography, and brewing beer. He lives in Montreal with his wife and daughter, who have yet to flee in terror. For updates and free giveaways, visit www.michaelpenning.com and follow Michael on social media @michaelpenningauthor.

www.ingramcontent.com/pod-product-compliance
Lightning Source LLC
Chambersburg PA
CBHW011132190726
48289CB00012B/3012